"WE COULD DO THIS ANOTHER TIME."

Mike nuzzled her hair, speaking tenderly.

"You would stop for me?" Caroline pulled back. "What about you? You could just turn away? You wouldn't—"

"Wouldn't what? Suffer untoward frustration and walk with a funny gait all day?" Mike rolled over, sitting up in bed. "My God, Caroline, male arousal isn't synonymous with raving lunacy."

"Mike—" she caressed his back "—I really don't want you to go."

"Caroline, *it's all right.*"

"Not for me...not now," she admitted. "You've revived a feeling that I need some help with...."

A smile crept over Mike's face. Turning, he lowered his lips to hers, already parting. Slowly his thumbs stroked her breasts. "Do you h___ any idea what you just did to my self-r___ male libido?"

"Bring it here and let me see. .

D1510590

ABOUT THE AUTHOR

Georgia Bockoven gave up a career as a free-lance journalist and professional photographer to write fiction. *Little by Little* is her third Superromance; she has one Harlequin Temptation to her credit, with plans brewing for other books in both series. Georgia and her husband, a firefighter, live with their two teenage sons in Northern California.

Books by Georgia Bockoven

These books may be available at your local bookseller.

Don't miss any of our special offers.
Write to us at the following address for
information on our newest releases.

Harlequin Reader Service
P.O. Box 52040, Phoenix, AZ 85072-2040
Canadian address: P.O. Box 2800, Postal Station A,
5170 Yonge St., Willowdale, Ont. M2N 5T5

Georgia Bockoven
LITTLE BY LITTLE

Harlequin Books

TORONTO • NEW YORK • LONDON
AMSTERDAM • PARIS • SYDNEY • HAMBURG
STOCKHOLM • ATHENS • TOKYO • MILAN

Published November 1984

First printing September 1984

ISBN 0-373-70138-1

To Steve, my "little" brother and biggest fan. Thanks.

CHAPTER ONE

"WITH A BODY LIKE HERS, she doesn't need a brain."

The throaty sound of male laughter drifted into the waiting room of the liaison office at Edwards Air Force Base. Caroline Travers looked up from the notes she was studying for the upcoming interview with Michael Webster, NASA spokesman for the space-shuttle program. Confused by the voices coming from what had been an empty room only moments earlier, she soon realized there must be another entrance to the office.

"I can't imagine how she ever convinced someone to make her a reporter," a second, deeper voice said. "I thought the television stations out here had more integrity than that."

"Why should Los Angeles be any different than anywhere else?" the higher-timbred voice asked. There was a slight pause. "You sound like you know the lady."

"She was what I believe they called the 'weather girl' at one of the Houston stations when I was still in the astronaut program. She was so unbelievably inept that we only watched her station when the news was really bad. We knew we could count on her for a little comic relief.''

Caroline felt a hot flush of mortification crawl up from her chest to her neck, to finally leave its bright red calling card on her cheeks. She glanced over to Randy Kavanaugh, her cameraman, to see if he was truly asleep in the torture rack of a chair he had chosen to collapse in, or just lost in his usual catatonic world. The lazy grin let her know he had not only heard everything, but he had also filed it away in his computerlike mind for use later.

"I remember one time...she tripped walking from the newscaster's table to the weather board. Her wand put a hole through Texas big enough to destroy the state's entire economy."

Again there was laughter.

Caroline relived that moment in a nightmare at least once a month. Without close competition, it was the single most embarrassing occurrence of her career.

"We can't be talking about the same woman, Mike. KMTV's Caroline Travers is pure East Coast finishing school—as cold as the business end of a penguin. At least when she's on the air that's how she comes off. I probably should add that that's how she seems from the neck up. Now from the neck down—" Caroline heard a lascivious groan "—that woman has a chest that makes my palms itch every time I see her."

It wasn't the first time she had heard a man describe her that way, and the words didn't sit any easier than they had the other times. Unconsciously Caroline folded her arms over a chest she had always considered too large for her frame, which someone had once referred to as "birch-tree" thin. At least it was nice to know that cutting her dark brown hair and having it clipped in a sophisticated, "businesswoman" style, so short that it barely brushed her collar in the back, had garnered the desired results. While television reporters had to be attractive, there was a fine line between projecting a "news" image and a sexual one. And while she hadn't been aiming to evoke the "business end of a penguin," that impression was better than "Sexiest Television Newsreporter in Seattle," a title she'd been given three years ago by a local paper.

"Oh, I'm sure it's her, all right," the somewhat tired, deeper voice answered. "I caught a glimpse of her on the late news last night. She's the Houston Hurricane, there's no doubt in my mind."

Houston Hurricane! She would be in her forties and plucking gray hairs before Randy let her live that one down.

"Gee, Mike..." the higher voice commiserated, but without any real sympathy. "I don't know what I can tell you 'cept, I'm real, real sorry you're going to be so miserable cooped up inside all morning. Especially with someone who looks like she should be doing centerfold work instead of wasting her time interviewing some idiot who can't appreciate what she's got to offer. I'd give up a month-long hunting trip to Idaho to switch places with you. Hell, I'd give up *two* trips to spend a morning with that broad."

Broad! Few words could push her buttons faster than that one.

"If all I had to do was to look at her, I'd agree. But once she opens her mouth, the rest is ruined. Inanity reaches new heights when she conducts an interview. I like my women with a modicum of intelligence."

The flush of embarrassment disappeared as anger narrowed Caroline's eyes. That he had based his opinion of her and her abilities on a job she had held almost seven years ago—a job that had obviously been her first in the industry—was grossly unfair. And then to go shouting it about....

The more she thought about the injustice of the man's summary dismissal of her abilities, not to mention her intelligence, the angrier Caroline became. She looked down at the basically innocuous questions she had prepared for the interview and drew a line through them.

Inane, was she? She would show him inane. When she was through with him he would forget all about hurricanes. From today on he would scan the skies for dark funnel clouds when she was in his vicinity. Teaching Michael Webster to qualify his judgments with a sprinkling of tolerance was going to be a honey-dripping pleasure.

Caroline heard footsteps inside the office. She glanced up just as the door swung open and a man with a receding hairline and rimless glasses, dressed in an air force uniform, peered into the room. He stared at the empty chair where the receptionist should have been. At almost the same instant that a scowl appeared on his face, his head swung to the left, and he discovered Caroline. In a frozen instant—one of those exaggerated moments that seem to go on forever—his face lost the scowl and registered a range of emotions from surprise to dismay to utter embarrassment.

The man attempted a smile, but failed; the corners of his mouth only twitching in abject misery, he murmured, "I don't suppose there's any chance that you arrived in the past ten seconds?"

Caroline met his pleading gaze. "None." From the corner of her eye she saw Randy Kavanaugh shift in his turquoise vinyl chair, recrossing his legs as if settling in for a long siege.

"Ah...uh...." The man in air force blue cleared his throat several times. At last, thoughts connected to speech. "Please excuse me for just a minute." His eyebrows arched comically in hopeful friendliness as he withdrew into the office, carefully closing the door behind him.

Seconds later the door opened again. Displaying none of his companion's chagrin, a man Caroline recognized as Michael Webster strode confidently into the room. He stopped in front of her and extended his hand. "Well, Ms Travers—" his voice was filled with suppressed humor "—if nothing else, this interview will be a first for me. I've never conducted one with my foot in my mouth before."

Before taking his hand, Caroline stood up, noting as she did that he was only normal size, after all, and not the giant he seemed on television. Neither did his hair seem so black, nor his eyes so blue. She guessed him to be six-one or -two at the most. And, she reluctantly admitted, while height might be ordinary, there was nothing else about Michael Webster that was. Even in faded jeans, tweed jacket and a nondescript shirt, he looked fantastic. He was not someone who needed to spend a fortune on custom-tailored clothes to hide a pot belly or sagging shoulders.

Caroline heaved a mental sigh of disgust. He was probably one of those people who wound up at the bottom of a ski run looking as good as he did at the top. Someone who could spend a day at the beach, and that evening not look as though he'd been dragged home through the sand—neither of which effect she had ever accomplished.

Their handshake was formal and firm and lingering, as if each of them was reluctant to be the first to back down.

Finally Caroline withdrew her hand. Purposely she moved aside so that she could glance down at his feet. She let her gaze travel up his lithe frame in careful assessment. "With a foot that size to talk around, I'll be sure to give you plenty of time to mumble your answers."

Michael Webster's slow smile exposed perfect teeth.

Lucky me, Caroline silently groaned. *I've just witnessed the smile that quickens millions of hearts every time NASA launches another shuttle. And wouldn't you know it, it's everything it's cracked up to be. Too bad it belongs to such a creep.* But then, wasn't that the way it always worked? If they were thirty-five and single and had dynamite looks, there was always something wrong somewhere.

"Would it help if I offered my profound apologies?" he said, his voice as smooth as a caress, as confident as a politician's on the campaign trail.

"For?"

"Perhaps for having such a big mouth?"

"Forget it." She reached down to retrieve her notes. "I'm sure this isn't the first time your foot's been there." Instead of the flash of anger she had anticipated, had hoped to arouse, there was only a glint of amusement in his eyes.

"I suppose this means you would prefer to skip the amenities and get right to the interview?"

"The sooner we begin, the sooner it will be over."

"Hot date tonight?"

It was her turn to smile. "Actually, there's a textbook on European economics sitting on my bedside table that has suddenly developed special appeal."

He chuckled. "You're not going to fall under my magical spell easily, are you?"

"Do polar bears live in the desert?" Ugh! Her repartee had been more clever in the sixth grade.

He studied her for an awkwardly long time, his dark blue eyes staring into her deep brown ones in a blatantly intimate way, daring her to be bold enough to meet his gaze. Finally, his words spoken so softly that no one else could overhear them, he said, "Actually, I have scientific-type friends who've often referred to the arctic as a vast desert."

In a voice as soft she replied, "I guess we all have friends who need humoring."

"How encouraging. We have something in common already—and we've just met."

"Something in common? Inanity, perhaps?"

With a grin and a slight nod of his head, Michael Webster intimated that she had at least held her own, if not won the first round. Then, as if it had never been, the look of carefree amusement disappeared. Michael Webster assumed the more familiar and serious demeanor of the oft-televised spokesman for NASA. Only fleetingly—almost imperceptibly—could the mischievous twinkle be seen in his eyes, like a capricious prisoner enticing all who saw it to try to set it free. And the reward? To be allowed to witness the devastating smile that had graced the cover of almost every national magazine at least once in the past half decade. Yes, the magazines had had a field day with similar exaggerated prose.

"Have you chosen your background for the interview?" he asked.

"Since most of the scenes for this piece are exterior, I'd like some indoor shots to balance. An uncluttered office would be perfect." Subtly her tone had taken on a commanding quality, implying she was accustomed to giving orders disguised as suggestions, and having them unquestioningly obeyed.

For an instant the repressed amusement shone through. He indicated the room he had just left. "I'm sure Captain Brown would be more than receptive to relinquishing his office for such a good cause."

Quickly glancing at Randy, still lounging with a smirk on his face, Caroline said, "You want to check it out?"

"Sure 'nuf, boss lady." He drew in his long legs and stretched his arms languidly.

Within minutes he was back for his equipment. "Looks good to me. I moved a few things around, borrowed some plants from down the hall, sort of made it cozy like. Didn't want any of the frostiness I seem to feel around here winding up on my tape." He leaned over to pick up his camera. "By the way, Webster, the captain said to tell you he had a meeting to attend and wouldn't be able to stick around for the taping."

"Coward," Caroline said to no one in particular.

"I'm sure it was nothing more than a tactical withdrawal," Mike suggested. "Discretion being the better part of valor and all."

"It seems to me that the discretion arrived about a half hour late."

"Or the reporter an hour early," he answered easily.

When Randy had again passed between them,

Mike stepped aside and indicated that Caroline should follow.

She hesitated an instant, seriously considering insisting that he go first, unsure of herself for the first time in a long while. Quickly glancing toward the door and judging the distance to be about the same as it had been between the infamous news desk and weather board, she stuck out her chin and stepped past him.

While her entry was not that of a Pavlova, it was at least uneventful. Once in the office, Mike Webster reached inside the pocket of his tweed jacket and withdrew a tie, which he casually knotted while talking to Randy about the technical aspects of the interview.

Caroline watched his movements. *I'll bet he's going to tie that thing perfectly the first time and never even bother to check the results in a mirror.*

He did just that. Sitting behind the desk so that his faded denims were hidden, he was completely transformed from California casual to business formal. He caught Caroline eyeing the change. "I had planned on greeting you in my standard three-piece, 'I'm real serious about what I do, folks,' pin-striped suit, but you arrived earlier than I had anticipated."

"Needless to say," she mumbled under her breath.

Webster's quick smile let her know he'd heard her. Caroline turned to her notes. "How about if I run over some bio information with you while Randy finishes with the lighting?"

"Sure."

Flipping back several pages in her notebook, she immediately found the information she had gathered about Michael Webster from the station's morgue. "Stop me if anything isn't correct." He nodded, and she began.

"Born in Bangor, Maine; father, career navy; mother, housewife—"

"Sorry to interrupt so soon, but I'm a little touchy about that. Any woman married to a military officer deserves recognition for two careers."

Caroline looked up from her notes. Her years of reporting hadn't left her completely jaded, but she had stopped being gullible a long time ago. To her, a man spouting feminist sentiments was as suspect as a kitten sleeping beside a broken vase. But even after a thorough scrutiny she was unable to detect any of the normal signs of a snow job.

"I didn't mean to throw you," he said when her skeptical glance became a puzzled frown.

Finding her place again, she continued. "Graduated from Annapolis; from there to flight school, where you graduated first in the class; became a test pilot; went on to astronaut program; left the program after a knee injury that happened while you were ejecting from a plane, which then crashed into the Gulf of Mexico...." She looked up from her notes. Unmistakable anger flashed in his eyes. "Everything all right so far?" She was probing for the problem.

"Certainly," he snapped. "I'm just amazed at how easily you rattle off the high points of a man's life—no matter how personal.'' The fire left his eyes as quickly as it had come. For an instant there was a look of weariness. Then it, too, was gone. ''You forgot to mention a tour of duty in Vietnam.''

''Yes, you're right.'' *Of course he's right, you idiot!* Nonplussed, she avoided his gaze as she turned to the next page. ''Moving on to the personal side...briefly engaged but never married; parents retired and living in Florida; a married older sister in Nebraska; a single younger sister in Washington....'' This time when Caroline glanced up, he leaned back in his chair and folded his arms across his chest.

''I can't imagine how or why you plan to work all this personal garbage into the interview. I was under the impression this was to be a somewhat serious piece on the shuttle program, not another bit of nonsense about me.''

There was acrimony in his tone, and Caroline carefully lowered her notebook. ''When in the public's mind a space program becomes so readily associated with the personality of one man, everything he is or does is an integral part of that story. Let's not play games, Webster. You are a marketable commodity for NASA. With your appearance on the scene five years ago, the public, which had become undeniably space weary and inflation weary, was again willing to invest its tax dollars in a program most people didn't even understand.''

''You're vastly overestimating—''

"Come off it. Don't try to tell me you're unaware of your mythical magnetism. It's been written about often enough. After all, in an age where sex sells everything from cars to toothpaste, why not the space program?"

His sudden hearty laugh broke the tension. "Please excuse my choleric behavior," he said without any real contrition. "It's simply hell when people love you only for your body, constantly overlooking your fine mind." His eyes flashed a challenge.

Caroline glared at him. "Are you ready to start the interview?"

"Fire away."

With pleasure, Webster. With real pleasure. She looked at Randy. "Ready?"

He nodded, flicked a switch and filled the room with glaring light.

Speaking crisply, always cognizant that the average television viewer was lost if a question or answer went beyond ten seconds, Caroline began. "Mr. Webster, when the idea for a space shuttle was first presented, one of the selling points was that it would pay its own way. It doesn't. Will it ever?"

Caroline was certain the question had to be familiar, yet he gave it a moment of thoughtful consideration, as if he were hearing it for the first time. Sincere concern radiated from him like rays of warm sunshine. He appeared genuinely disturbed by the space program's unbalanced financial statement. He was very good at what he did; she would have to give him that.

"Actually, it is a matter of when. We're working toward a target date of five to six years."

She went on to the next question, pretending the answer had been unexpected and not a rehash of information she had garnered earlier in her extensive research for the series. "And in the meantime the American public is continuing to carry the millions of dollars of deficit at each launch, even though the cargo on the shuttle might be for a foreign government or private industry?"

Without hesitation or the slightest suggestion of evasion, he answered. "Essentially, yes." There was a hint of that incredible smile. "You might say we are still in the process of delivering the payloads—satellites, that is—for the 'drumming up business' sales we offered several years ago. We gave special deals to those willing to launch with us in the beginning instead of waiting until we had proved ourselves. Those who were astute enough to sign up early got a real bargain. What costs them eight or nine million dollars today will, if our projections are correct, cost around twenty-two million five years from now."

Working to suppress the feeling that they were cat and canary, and to keep the sniping tone from her voice, Caroline asked, "But won't you have to continue to offer these bargain rates if you hope to get clients to 'fly American' instead of contracting with the European Space Research Organization? Going to the absolute bottom line. . . is it really all that important to become cost effective when you have the taxpayers behind you? Isn't most of the rhetoric we hear about financial independence simply lip service?''

A slow smile preceded his words. ''Perhaps to your first question, yes to your second and an emphatic no to your third.''

Caroline waited for him to elaborate. She wanted him to fill the chasm of silence she let grow between them. But he was too well schooled in the tricks of her trade to fall for her attempt to put him on the defensive. Without any sign of unease, he patiently waited for her to continue. The awkward gap would have to be edited from the tape later, or they would both come across like idiots.

''I'll put it another way, then. Do you honestly feel the average taxpayer, if he or she were polled, would agree to the continuation of the program through this indefinite deficit period?''

''I would answer that with an unqualified yes if the average taxpayer polled were also aware of how much his or her daily life is touched by the satellites that are now orbiting the earth.''

''Let's use me for an example. How is my life touched by satellites? Why should I care if the program continues?''

''A few of the obvious ways...there are computers that communicate the latest medical information to each other via satellite, making that information accessible to doctors...and of course, telephone calls are beamed off satellites, as well as television programs, not to mention long-distance weather reports.

''And you are affected in ways that are less obvious. Maybe the best example I could give would be to talk about one of the shuttle flights that didn't go as planned. Back in 1981, Columbia's mission had to be cut from 124 hours to fifty-four hours because of a faulty fuel cell.'' Mike shifted in his seat, leaning one elbow comfortably on the arm of his chair, inviting trust with that simple bit of body language. ''Before Columbia had to return home, the crew had scanned a fifty-kilometer-wide path through the Sahara with radar, looking for old buried riverbeds. They found them. Because of their work, archaeologists know where to dig to look for early signs of man, and geologists think they'll be able to use similar scans to locate deposits of minerals and oil.

''But personally, I feel the most important use of the scan in the future will be in the search for active underground rivers flowing through arid regions. If these rivers can be tapped, think of the food that can be grown for the world's hungry.'' He leaned forward in his chair again. ''And all this from a mission that supposedly failed.''

Once more, a hint of a smile. ''Now as to why you personally, Ms Travers, should care if the shuttle continues to place satellites in orbit—as well as eventually maintain them should they ever need servicing—the television-news industry is probably one of the most dependent users of the benefits. Without the satellites. . .who knows how many people would lose their jobs?''

This time she smiled. ''Now that we've taken care of me, let's get back to the average taxpayer.

What do you think he or she would say if given an option to channel the funds allocated to the space program into social areas?''

"Ms Travers—if the *entire* NASA budget were given to the Department of Health and Human Services, that department would run out of funds in a little over two weeks. I doubt any thinking individual would consider the trade-off worthwhile.''

The smile moved up to Caroline's eyes. He was very, very good. "All right...let's theorize for a moment that it's possible to convince everyone that the shuttle program should be fully financed, regardless of how it's operated. What happens in the 1990s when, according to projections, all the available orbital space for communication satellites will be filled?''

She listened carefully to his unavoidably technical explanation, despite knowing she would never be able to use the detailed answer in any of the segments of the five-part series. Her series fell into the category of "news entertainment"; only incidentally was it supposed to resemble anything educational. She doubted that, once edited, today's interview would result in more than a minute of air time. There was really no reason to keep up the verbal sparring she had initiated. She had all she needed. And since it was obvious that Michael Webster was as unflappable as he'd seemed, the personal satisfaction she had hoped to gain by making him squirm a little would have to be given up as a lost cause. Caroline signaled to Randy that the next question would be the wrap.

The cameraman had his equipment collected in a fraction of the time it had taken to set it up and was heading out the door before Caroline had her few things gathered. She glanced up to see Michael Webster, subdued now, unknotting his tie, purposely watching her. A slow, private smile curved his mouth when she had to make a grab for her notebook to keep it from falling from under her arm.

"You've improved," he said.

"I beg your pardon."

That brought a low chuckle. "How utterly charming that sounds. No one has begged my pardon in ever so long."

So much for the muddled sort of respect she had begun to feel for him. "I don't wonder. It's obviously a complete waste of time."

He came out of his chair and around the desk to sit on the corner, directly in front of her. "Now don't get in a huff. The compliment was sincere. You've become a pretty good reporter . . . and that catch you just made wasn't bad, either."

"I'm overwhelmed. Courtly manners, no less. You've exceeded my expectations."

He went on as if her sarcasm had been sugar. "How about forgetting your economics textbook for tonight? I know a place that serves fantastic Mexican food."

"You can't be serious."

"About the Mexican food? Surely you've been in Southern California long enough to realize what great—"

"About my going out with you."

"I'm only in town for a week. You have to catch me while you can."

Long seconds passed before she was composed enough to reply. "That's a rotten shame. And wouldn't you know it. The one week that it just so happens I'm booked solid. Any other week of the year—nothing. But come the middle of November, and it never fails. I have a date every night." A choreographed shrug, elegantly nonchalant, accompanied her words. "Happens every year," she sighed.

As she turned to go he reached out and took her free hand. Deliberately he brought it to his lips and lightly, gracefully kissed the tender flesh covering her knuckles. With supreme effort Caroline controlled an urge to snatch her hand from his grasp.

When he glanced up again his eyes sparkled roguishly, a perfect complement to his lopsided grin. In a deep, caressing tone, far more appropriate for the bedroom than the office, he said, "Boy, wait until I tell the boys back home that I actually met the Houston Hurricane. . . and in person, no less."

Damn him! She would not yield the parting shot to him. Her eyes narrowed. "I certainly wouldn't want the boys back home to be disappointed, Webster. If you're going to go to all that bother to remember li'l ole me, you might as well have a story worth the telling. . . ." Her voice dropped to a low, sultry drawl. "You might as well tell them about this, too."

Without stopping to consider her actions, or how unorthodox her behavior might seem, only knowing that she would not let him best her no matter what the consequences, she dropped her purse and notebook into the chair beside her, stepped between his outstretched legs and sensuously slid her arms around his neck. Her actions were accomplished with such speed and smoothness that she caught him completely off guard.

It had been a while since she'd kissed a man with the sole intention of arousal, and she was delighted to discover the skill didn't need constant practice to keep in good working order. His response was textbook perfect: first an instant of surprise, his lips rigid, then the softening and slight parting in invitation.

His hands went to her waist to pull her closer. She fitted herself into the planes of his body as easily as if he were the mold and she the prewarmed clay. As the kiss deepened, Mike began to assume the role of aggressor, and Caroline knew if she hoped to keep the advantage it was up to her to break the contact. She brought her hands to his shoulders and pushed, extricating herself from his arms as abruptly as she had slipped into them.

She blinked in surprise. Not even fleetingly had she thought she would feel anything. Yet there it was—a peculiar pleasurable sensation, a strange tingling inside her. Hiding her disquieting reaction with difficulty, she picked up her discarded belongings and walked across the room. When she reached the door, she turned and delivered an exaggerated wink.

What had gotten into her? She had never behaved like this before.

Hesitating a moment longer, Caroline met his gaze as he silently stared back at her, his arms folded lightly across his chest, a look of—what was it...challenge?—written on his face.

In the thickest Texan accent she could summon, she said, "Now you be sure to give everyone back in Houston all my love, you hear?"

As she hurried to catch up with Randy, her hand unconsciously went to her mouth. Touching her tongue to the still-tingling softness of her lips, she was startled to discover his taste had lingered. He felt...he tasted— *Well, go ahead, admit it...he felt good!*

Randy turned when he heard her approach. "What kept you?"

Caroline tried to bring her thoughts around enough to mumble a half truth that would satisfy his insatiable curiosity. "Uh...I was...uh, turning down a date."

He eyed her quizzically. "A date, huh? Want to tell me about it, Houston Hurricane?"

She rolled her eyes, glanced his way and caught his knowing smile. "Ha! Do I look like I've lost my mind?"

"I don't know about lost, but I gotta tell you, you had me wondering if maybe you'd misplaced it somewhere when you came out with that polar bears in the desert line."

Caroline groaned. "It sounded that bad, huh?"

"Only if it was meant to display a high degree of wit and intelligence. If not, you're okay."

She tossed him a disgusted look. "Thanks, Randy—I needed that. One must be careful about growing overconfident."

"No problem, boss lady. Anytime I can be of service."

MIKE WEBSTER left the desk and walked over to the window. He reached up and with two long, slender fingers, separated the Venetian blind, making an opening large enough to watch Caroline Travers walk across the lawn and get into a van with a large stylized eye and the letters KMTV on the side. He stood at the window for the few more minutes it took Caroline and Randy to leave, then turned and left the office.

Since the shuttles were finally being launched with something close to the predicted regularity, his job had become far more complicated. Between flights to Edwards Air Force Base in L.A., where crews were kept in constant readiness for landings that couldn't be made in Florida because of bad weather, between flights to Florida for the steadily increasing launches and his full load of routine work in Houston, Mike frequently felt as if he'd invented jet lag. Adding on the odd jaunts to the Jet Propulsion Laboratory in Pasadena, and to Washington, D.C., to testify at Senate hearings, he sometimes had to arrange a weekend just to catch up on lost sleep. Often his job seemed to border on the impossible. He was responsible for relaying the drama and excitement of a launch, for keeping up the public's enthusiasm while at the same time playing up the routine aspects of ferrying satellites into orbit. He also had to reassure the people who held the purse strings that efforts toward space travel and exploration were not Buck Rogers fantasies. But because Mike was exceptionally good at what he did, making the juggling seem little more than something any competent public-relations person might handle, few people outside NASA's inner circle were aware of his critical importance.

He was handsome, personable, and because he never lied and only hedged the truth in dire situations, he was trusted by both friend and foe of the space agency. If Michael Webster came on a television screen to announce a devastating failure or a rousing success on one of the shuttle flights, he did so in a way that insisted those watching share the tears or the joy. Using the rapport he had worked so hard to establish with the tax-paying public, he had managed to make them feel, once again, that they were personally involved in every flight.

As Mike walked down the narrow hall, his leather heels tapped softly against the asphalt tile. He nodded and smiled to those he passed, aware of their faces and greetings while at the same time in deep thought about the amount of work he still had to do that day.

It wasn't until he spotted Captain Brown leaning over a desk that he focused once more on externals. "If you're not in the middle of something, I'd like to finish going over that list of guests for the February launch," Mike said.

"That was quick. I thought you'd be most of the afternoon," the captain replied as he gathered up an armful of papers.

"I think the lady was in a hurry."

The captain looked pointedly at Mike, searching his face and then his body. "Well, I don't see any evidence of maltreatment. Does this mean you escaped unscathed after our little social faux pas?"

Mike felt an unreasonable surge of annoyance at the other man's conspiratorial tone. The feeling of irritation, particularly its strength, brought the hint of a private smile to his lips. Caroline Travers had obviously triggered a long-dormant protective instinct in him. His smile broadened as he considered what her reaction might be if she knew. He didn't doubt for a minute where she would tell him to put his feelings.

Beauty—charm—elegance. . . as far as he was concerned, they came in distant seconds to a woman with spunk. Give him a woman who would stand toe to toe with him, and he was as caught up in her as a two-year-old in cotton candy. Combine beauty and moxie, and it made what was, for him, a lethal combination.

You're one hell of a woman, Ms Travers, he told himself as he walked with Captain Brown back to his office. His faint smile became full-blown. *Be forewarned, lovely lady, we will be seeing each other again.*

CHAPTER TWO

BY THE TIME Caroline and Randy drove the eighty-odd miles from Edwards Air Force Base back to the television station in Pasadena, it was late afternoon. Her emerald-green silk blouse felt like a clammy second skin; her feet and head ached; her normally even temper was only slightly less ferocious than that of a mountain lion with a thorn in its paw. "It's supposed to be *cold* in November," she grumbled aloud as she tossed her notebook on her desk. Again she thought of all the beautiful wool suits, coats and boots she had worn last winter in Denver, suits still packed snugly in boxes.

Giving her warm clothing away was unthinkable. Two suits, purchased at an end-of-season sale, had never even been worn, yet keeping them was idiotic—no matter how desperately she wished that it would, it wasn't going to snow in the Los Angeles basin. More than likely, by the time she was working someplace where she could wear her lovely winter wardrobe, it would be out of style.

After checking the telephone messages on her desk, Caroline walked over to the long-range assignment board to see if anything new had been posted beside her name. It had. Two weeks before her Rose Parade coverage, she was scheduled to interview several astronauts who would be on a goodwill tour for the February launch. She glanced over to Sid Minkner, the assignment editor, her eyebrows raised in question, a look that said "Tell me it isn't so" on her face.

"Since you've become the expert, you were the logical choice," he told her.

"High praise for a piece of work still in the camera."

He chuckled. "See what faith I have in you?"

"Thanks. That almost makes me feel better."

"Don't thank me yet. I have another piece of news—this one will give you an even bigger thrill. Roger Harper is going to be your co-anchor for the parade."

Caroline groaned. Roger Harper was possibly the worst reporter she had ever worked with. But for some reason, once a year when the ratings race was run, his name consistently came up as a favorite among the viewers. Consequently, his contract was renewed despite his lack of talent. "Is this your way to get even with me for telling your wife you were cheating on your diet?"

"It would be fitting punishment," he said with a laugh, "but I can't take the credit for this one. Ed had to give up the co-anchor because his bypass surgery date has been moved up."

"Is he all right?"

"Yeah—it's just more convenient for the doctors this way."

Caroline shivered as a picture of a day spent with Roger Harper flashed through her mind. She wandered back to her desk. One more thing—that's all it would take. One more piece of bad news, one more obnoxious person, and she would count the day a total loss. Roger Harper was bad enough, but even thinking about running into Michael Webster again was worse.

"Caroline...."

She looked up to see Randy waving to her from across the newsroom. "Bill said to tell you you're taking over the anchor on the six-thirty and eleven o'clock shows."

Immediately an image she had caught of herself in the glass doors on her way into the building passed before her. She looked like a Saturday-night party on Sunday morning. "Did you tell him—"

"Yes, I told him you'd been up since the sun, but he said no one else was available."

Caroline glanced at her watch. If she hurried, she could run home for a change of clothes and a quick shower and get back to the station in time to go over her half the news. "Thanks, Randy," she called, pulling open a desk drawer to retrieve her purse. Why was it that since she had made her decision to avoid the anchor spot in favor of on-scene reporting, her time at the news desk had almost doubled? Obviously Murphy's Law covered television, too.

Later as she dipped her head under the shower to rinse shampoo from her hair, she thought about her day, carefully going over the details as if they were on a reel of film she could slow down and speed up at will. Unavoidably, she stopped the action at the interview with Michael Webster. She tried to concentrate on the questions she'd asked and what he'd said, wondering how and where they would fit into the series she would begin editing tomorrow.

But her thoughts kept straying to the man behind the image. What a hunk! She had to give him that much. He certainly lived up to his publicity. Since there was no shortage of men in the Los Angeles area who were exceptionally handsome, it wasn't as if she'd been out of the mainstream so long that she would overreact to this one. Too bad his appearance went for naught the minute he opened his mouth.

Caroline reached for the faucets; a slow, self-deprecatory smile touched her lips. Wasn't she as guilty of stereotyping as he?

MIKE WEBSTER'S RENTED COMPACT easily slipped into traffic as he left Interstate 5 to merge onto 210, the freeway that would lead him to Pasadena. He had planned to wait a while before contacting Caroline Travers, to give her a few days to recover from their first meeting and perhaps think of him in kinder terms. But with a free evening ahead of him and a message from NASA headquarters that he was needed back in Houston in two days instead of seven, he had opted to rush things a little.

As honorable as he kept trying to convince himself he was—after all, he had already decided he wanted to get to know her better *before* she had kissed him goodbye—he couldn't deny the warm glow that started inside him every time he thought of that fragrant body snuggled against his, her arms around his neck, her lips. . . .

Mike became so enamored in remembering that he almost missed the turnoff to Pasadena. It took fifteen minutes of traveling before he was passing through guarded gates into the parking lot of KMTV. Checking the time, he was delighted to see there was more than enough left to watch Caroline anchor the last segment of the early-evening news.

Leaving the car and heading for the back entrance to the studio, he spotted a meticulously tended rose garden. He detoured, stepping from the concrete walkway to one of gravel. The slight difference in height between the two surfaces was just enough to make Mike twist his ankle as he stepped sideways. He caught his breath as pain shot up his leg and deep into his groin. Incapacitated, he stood perfectly still, waiting for the punishment to lessen.

Of all the lingering effects of his accident, such physical weakness was the most obvious and disquieting, stripping him of the pretense of total normalcy, forcing him to acknowledge something he daily tried to forget. The dull ache that had become his usual companion he had learned to all but ignore; the gut-wrenching torment that sometimes seized him to the near exclusion of everything else he could only marginally control. When he became a slave to the pain, as he was now, he felt compromised. In this one instance, the strict self-discipline he had learned as a child did not serve him.

With the inevitability of a tide finally ebbing, the pain began to recede, leaving Mike covered with a thin sheen of dampness. He wiped the tiny beads of perspiration from his lip and forehead with the back of his hand, took a deep breath and again started toward the rose garden.

Not only did Mike take time to smell the flowers, he decided to share the pleasure with Caroline. Carefully, so that nothing was broken or disturbed, he chose only the most beautiful buds in an array of colors. To enable her to hold the flowers without being pricked by the thorns, he went to the front of the building to purchase a newspaper from one of the machines. With the roses carefully enclosed in the sports section of the *Los Angeles Times*, Mike headed for the back entrance once more. The familiar dull ache had returned to his limb.

He was sitting behind Caroline's desk watching the newsroom monitor when she came in, looking like a before-and-after picture that had been cut apart and the wrong halves pasted back together. She looked much as he had earlier that day. From the waist up she was dressed in a classically tailored rust-colored linen suit jacket, print blouse and gold jewelry. From the waist down she wore faded, paint-spattered jeans with bright orange running shoes on her feet.

"You—" she groaned. Mike Webster was at the very bottom of the list of people she wanted to see right then. He had probably heard her on-air stumble when she tried to report that the Pasadena Police Department's picnic was being postponed because the caterer had food poisoning. No doubt he would make the most of the blunder. When Mike smiled in reply to her cool greeting, she heard the woman technician behind her let out a tiny wistful sigh. Caroline looked at Mike again. Along with the smile, she could see a twinkle developing in his eyes.

"I called the station to see if they could get a message to you. I wanted to let you know I was able to make it for dinner tonight, after all. The receptionist said you would be here doing the news." He shrugged lightly. "I figured since I had to eat sometime, I might as well come by and pick you up, too."

He had made it sound as if *she* had asked *him* out—and in front of a newsroom full of people who never failed to note such things. He might as well have said it over the air. "How lucky for me. But I'm afraid you've come all this way for nothing. I have a hard-and-fast rule about never leaving the station when I have to anchor the late news." What was the harm in one tiny lie?

Mike looked at his watch. "We have exactly three hours and fifty-two minutes. Plenty of time, if you would get a move on."

Caroline walked over to her desk. Planting her hands on the top, she leaned forward so that her face was directly in front of Mike's. Slowly, as if speaking to a child, she said, "Read my lips, Webster—I-do-not-leave-the-station-when-I-have-to-do-the-eleven-o'clock-news."

"Do you realize how rigid you eventually become when you use the word 'never'? Life isn't exciting unless you make exceptions to rules."

"He's right you know, Caroline," said Bill Williams, the producer of the evening news, who had come to stand beside her. "There isn't any real reason you couldn't step out for a bite to eat."

Caroline sent her best "I'll get you for this" look to Bill and yanked open her desk drawer to retrieve her purse. "Anything would be better than making this a round-table discussion."

"See you later, then." Bill sauntered past them on his way to his desk, sending her a surreptitious wink of victory. He was paying her back, pointedly, for the religious cult leaders she had referred to him for possible coverage of their annual cleansing swim in the ocean.

Mike stood, a grin of satisfaction on his face.

They were on their way out when he remembered the flowers. With a sweep of his arm he gathered the bundle from the desk and handed it to a surprised Caroline.

She peeked inside. Her look of delight quickly escalated to one of panic as she folded the paper so that none of the roses could be seen. "Where did you get these?" she whispered, already knowing the answer but hoping she was wrong.

"Just outside. There is the most—"

"Don't say another word," Caroline snapped, grabbing his arm and steering him toward the exit.

Once they were outside she turned on him. "Being found in possession of just *one* of these roses could get me ambulance-chasing duty for a year. Walter Paulson has fired people for lesser offenses. These are his prize roses. He would let the station fall into ruin before he would let anything happen to his roses."

In the same hushed, conspiratorial tone, Mike said, "If we should get caught, I'll accept full blame." He reached up to tug on a curl that brushed against her ear. "When they question me, I'll tell them you told me I was to pick only the ugly ones, that it was my decision to go after the winners."

"You would, wouldn't you?"

He grinned. "You'll never find out, because we're not going to get caught."

Trying to hide the bulky package under her suit jacket, Caroline practically ran toward the parking lot. Mike followed. "You'd make a lousy spy, Caroline. Here, let me carry them."

"Gladly." She thrust the roses at him.

Mike carried the package openly, with casual aplomb. When they came to the curb, Caroline headed for her own car. "This way," Mike said, touching her elbow.

Somehow, in her haste to put as much distance as possible between her and the roses and the television station, she had forgotten the reason she was with Mike in the first place. "I have to stop by my apartment to change."

"I'll take you."

She hesitated, then sighed with resignation. "All right."

As he opened the car door, he asked, "Which half are you going to change?"

Caroline looked down at her blue jeans and scruffy orange running shoes. "I would prefer the jacket...."

"But?" he queried, getting in his side of the car.

"Since I have the eleven o'clock show to do yet, it would be prudent to leave the top of me alone."

Mike started the car, paused and reached over to clasp Caroline's knee lightly. "Let's begin again," he said softly, a playful twinkle in his eyes. "Hi, I'm Mike Webster. I've been watching you on television for years and years—ever since I was a little kid—really. I want you to know I sure am excited about finally getting to meet you. Not only are you a dynamite reporter, you have the neatest nose of anyone I know. And since I'm a nose man from way back, I know of which I speak. Sort of having a knack for knowing noses, if you know what I mean."

She smiled in spite of herself. He was making it difficult for her to maintain her pique. Being around him gave her the same eerie feeling she had had when staring into the Grand Canyon's mesmerizing depths—if she weren't very careful, she would fall from the precipice, taking a wild one-way ride to the bottom. The feeling made her extremely uncomfortable. Having already climbed out of one gigantic hole in her life because of a man, she didn't need to tumble into another.

"Glad to meet you, Mr. Webster," she said, deciding since she was going to spend the evening with him, she might as well be as pleasant as possible. "My name is Caroline Mary Travers. I'm a mustache person myself. I don't know what it is about hairy lips that turns me on, but it happens every time I see a man wearing one. I just love the fuzzy little rascals."

Mike held his finger under his nose. "Well... what do you think?"

She studied him for a moment. "Wrong color."

"It's the best I can do for now."

"Don't worry about it. Some men can carry it off. Others...." She shrugged. "It might help if you knew my nose wasn't always this cute."

"Surgery?"

"Childhood allergies. At least five months out of every year I resembled some crazy reindeer that was rumored to have the same problem."

He gave her knee a gentle squeeze. "I like you, Caroline Mary Travers. I like you a lot."

The sincere ring to his words and the warm smile he gave her made her bite back the retort that had immediately come to mind. Instead she gave him a little smile. "If one is to believe the Duchess of Windsor, one can never be too rich or too thin. I like to add—or have too many friends."

Mike stared at her a moment longer before starting the car. He had the strangest feeling about what had passed between them. It was as if Caroline had one of those invisible barriers surrounding her—the kind popularized in the science-fiction movies he had frequented twenty years ago—and for just an instant she had left it unattended and allowed him to enter.

They came to the intersection. "Which way?" Mike asked.

Caroline directed him to her apartment on Orange Grove Boulevard. Her building was unpretentiously opulent, as were the other apartments and homes lining the street once known as Millionaire Row. Stately trees, broad lawns and well-maintained driveways occupied by expensive foreign cars bespoke the stability and wealth of the neighborhood. It was the kind of place where people still went for evening strolls and stopped to talk to their neighbors.

"Nice," Mike said, looking around as he opened her door.

"And quiet most of the time."

"Rowdies move in every once in a while, do they?"

Caroline led him to her apartment, which faced a postcard-perfect formal garden filled with blooming flowers. "The Tournament of Roses Parade passes down Orange Grove Boulevard. For a couple of weeks each year, I understand the only way the owners can keep their property from being trampled or stolen is to put up temporary chain-link fences."

"I take it you weren't living here last year to witness this catastrophic event for yourself?"

She shook her head. "I was still working in Denver." Caroline stepped through the door and switched on the lights. Despite her sporadic attempts to add homey touches, Caroline's apartment had a temporary look and feel about it, as had all her apartments since her divorce. The furniture was sparse, the knickknacks few—packing was such a pain even if the movers did most of the work. For years she had been what was known in the trade as a "Gypsy," someone always on the move, forever seeking a station with a larger viewing audience, willing to go anywhere to advance her career. Consequently she earned an enviable salary, but never stayed anywhere long enough to use the money to create a nice home for herself.

"Have a seat," she said. "I'll be ready in a minute."

When he was alone, instead of resting his lanky body in one of Caroline's mismatched chairs, Mike went into the kitchen to look for something to put the roses in. He hadn't meant to pry, only to find a vase; nevertheless, his search yielded more than the vase. Not only were her cupboards bare of the traditional kitchenwares, there was very little food. It looked as if she ate out a lot, starved or fixed extremely simple meals.

In the last cupboard Mike found a large assortment of florist's vases. Judging by what else he could see of her apartment, he sincerely doubted that she had lugged these vases around the country with her. Therefore, she was going with someone who owned a flower shop, or a lot of someones who believed they really could "say it with flowers." He wasn't sure he liked either surmise.

While he waited for Caroline to return, he arranged the roses, filling in the empty spots with flowers and greenery he took from the small garden they had passed on their way to Caroline's front door. The arrangement, sitting on the dining-room table, was the first thing Caroline saw when she came out of the bedroom. Her initial look of pleasure changed abruptly as her eyes widened in horror. "Where did you get those— No! Don't tell me. I don't want to know."

"They look nice together, don't they?"

"Of course they look nice. You've purloined your arrangement from two of the most fanatically tended gardens in Pasadena. Why shouldn't they look nice?"

"I always did have this special ability to home right in on the best," he said with pride. His words intimated he was talking about flowers; his tone and the look he gave Caroline told her differently.

She was the first to break eye contact. "I assume you've decided where we're going?"

"A place that serves the world's best nachos and cheese enchiladas."

"And was this judgment made by Mobil's Restaurant Guide or the local automobile club?"

"Oh, m'lady, you do me a disservice." He sounded wounded. "Do you think I would trust the judgment of others on something this important?"

"How far away is this restaurant?" But Caroline missed his reply when she opened the closet to get her sweater.

"If we don't get on the road," he concluded, "we'll have to rush dinner."

Once they were traveling the freeway away from Pasadena, Caroline glanced at the digital clock on the dashboard. She was surprised to see so much time had passed already. "You do know I'm expected back by ten-thirty?"

"Everything's under control." Mike reached over to turn the radio on. After a few minutes of adjusting the dial, he settled for a soft-rock station. "Tell me something about yourself, Caroline Travers."

"Out of my entire twenty-eight and a half years of existence you want me to choose one highlight?" Her voice held a teasing quality that softened the words.

"Remember you've had an unfair advantage. I don't have a file somewhere so I can look up a bio on you."

"I concede. I did have an unfair advantage. All right. . . what would you like to know?"

"Pretend you're filling out a job application."

"Dare I ask what job you had in mind?" His answer was a quick smile and a wink. She leaned farther back in her seat, resting her head as she stared out the side window. "Born in Crossroads, Kansas. Father was a banker, mother ran a yardage shop. Parents divorced. No siblings. Graduated from University of Nebraska with a major in communications. Started working in television as a weather girl for a Houston station." She glanced over to see if she could detect any reaction to her reference to Houston. When she saw none, she went on. "After Houston I was at six other stations at various locations around the Midwest before I came to Pasadena. In April I will have been at KMTV a year."

"That's quite an odyssey for someone hailing from a small farming town."

"If you recall, Johnny Carson was from a tiny town in Nebraska."

"Could it be that the end of the winding road you're on is a network reporting job?"

Her dreams and ambitions were something she rarely discussed with anyone. "If a network job should happen my way, I could probably be talked into taking it," she admitted. Uncharacteristically, she went on. "But what I'm really aiming for is a foreign-bureau job." She studied his profile as he answered her, his voice low and serious.

"I've known several network reporters both here and overseas. The way they have to work reminded me of someone trying to keep both a wife and a mistress happy at the same time. Their time was never their own; their private lives were usually a shambles."

"No one gets to that position wearing blinders. It's impossible not to know beforehand what the job entails."

Mike took a moment to think about Caroline's remark. Why would a person purposely set out to get a job that would almost certainly prevent her from ever having a stable home life? There were plenty of status jobs in the television-news field that didn't entail such devotion to duty. Ambition he could understand; it had been one of his driving forces for as long as he could remember. But friends were also an important part of his day-to-day existence. As was the hope that someday he would find someone he wanted to share his life with. He couldn't imagine living without the hope, as Caroline seemed to do.

Flicking on the turn signal, Mike crossed a lane to reach the exit. Caroline looked around her. She had become familiar with most of the roads within a twenty-five-mile radius of Pasadena; she couldn't remember seeing a restaurant in the area he was heading for. "Are you sure this is the right way?"

"I'm taking a shortcut."

"Here? Through the foothills? A shortcut to where?"

"Relax. You're in safe hands."

As the suburbs disappeared and the land around them became more open, Caroline began to fidget. "Mike, did I emphasize how very important it is that I be back at the station by ten-thirty?"

"At least a dozen times."

"And you took me seriously?"

"Indubitably." The road suddenly narrowed into little more than a country lane. "Tell me about your father."

As always, when she thought of Harold Travers Caroline smiled. "He was the kind of father everyone should have. A perfect balance to my mother, strict where she tended to be lenient, lenient where she would have been too strict. They were like spotters for me as I walked the tightrope of childhood, each in their own way giving me a shove when I faltered, a boost back up when I fell.''

"Do you see your folks often?"

"No. . .not as much as I would like. If I spend a holiday with one, it seems I hurt the other. So I usually spend holidays by myself, and when I visit, I do it unexpectedly.'' She had never put those feelings into words before. How simple they sounded—what trauma they represented.

"I take it they weren't divorced until you had left home?"

"I was thirteen.''

"That must have been—'' The rest of Mike's sentence was lost as an explosive sound came from the right front tire. Gradually the car thumped to a halt as he guided it to the wide shoulder. He glanced at Caroline. "Probably just a flat.''

Caroline rolled down her window when Mike left the car to examine the tire. A quick look revealed it was indeed flat. He came over, leaned his elbows on the frame of the open window and gave her an apologetic look. "Want to hand me the keys?'' And when she did, "I hope you aren't ravenous—we may have to postpone dinner until after the newscast. Changing tires is not one of my specialties.''

Caroline closed her eyes and scrunched into the

upholstery. It was too soon to panic. One or two deep calming breaths, and she would be all right. She was on the third deep breath when she heard a muted "Damn!" and her heart lurched. Still she held in check the creeping sense of disaster.

Mike came to her window. "Seems someone has made off with the spare tire."

Don't panic, Caroline. You still have time to get back to the station. "Can we get the flat fixed?"

"Only if we melt it down and start over. It's in several pieces."

She looked out the window past Mike. They were miles from town. *Now* it was time to panic.

With great effort she calmly closed her eyes and leaned back against the headrest. Several seconds passed.

Confused by her peculiar reaction to the news, Mike asked, "What are you doing?"

She opened one eye to look at him. "I'm telling myself that pulling out my hair, screaming like a banshee and running around hysterically will only make me feel better about all this. It will do nothing to get me back to Pasadena."

This time it was a full-blown smile that Mike unleashed on her. Caroline groaned and closed her eye. Her future sped past on her mental editing machine. Banner headlines told of a promising reporter's career wiped out by a devastating smile.

"Caroline...." His voice was like a tubful of warm water after she'd been lost in the cold. "I told you I would get you back to the station on time, and I will. So roll up this window and lock the doors. Don't open up for anyone. I'll be back as soon as I can." He turned to go, then turned back. "Here, take these." He thrust the keys at her.

"You're leaving me here? Alone?"

"If you'd kept your running shoes on we might have made it together. But with those things you've got on now, we never could. Now is getting back to the station as important to you as I think it is?"

"Yes—"

"Then let me give it a try."

Slowly she rolled up the window before reaching for the door locks. When she glanced to the road again, he was gone. She stared outside. It was so quiet up here in the foothills. And so dark. But the view was spectacular. It always amazed her that the layer of smog hovering over the Los Angeles basin in the daytime seemed to disappear when the sun set and the valley supplied its own light source.

Caroline tried to see the hands on her numberless watch. When she couldn't, she switched the ignition key to accessories and turned on the overhead light. It was almost nine o'clock. Needing something to keep her occupied, she went through the glove compartment, looking for reading material. After finding and rejecting the rental agreement, she discovered a paper explaining how to change a flat tire. So much for the glove box. A quick look through her purse yielded nothing more interesting than a week-old grocery list of five items.

Reluctantly she doused the light. She could just imagine Mike returning with a new tire to find the battery dead. Without light there was nothing to do except sit and wait. Methodically she began to go over the past weeks of shooting and the research she had done for the shuttle series. The first program was a natural, a wrap-up of the past quarter century of America's space program. A nice angle might be to summarize the cost during those twenty-five years and compare it to the money spent on social programs over the same period.

It would all have to be done very carefully—she didn't want the program to smack of editorializing. From her earlier research she knew the money for the shuttle had been hard won. The disbelievers in Congress were backed by a general populace who had lost interest in supporting what they considered expensive toys for an elitist group of scientists. It was a time when the "competitive spirit" whipped up by the Sputnik launch, a decade earlier, had all but evaporated. Skeptics abounded, supporters were few. The Apollo program to put men on the moon had come to an end. There was nothing in the wings to catch the enthusiasm of a public weary of hearing about the millions spent on each launch.

As she had done since beginning the project, Caroline tried to imagine what it would be like to be an astronaut. What kind of person devoted years of his or her life to train for a flight that lasted only a few days? Now, since she had met Mike, she also wondered what it would be like to be on the edge of the reward for all those years of hard work, then to watch it disappear forever because of a freak accident.

If Mike Webster had sustained any emotional scars from the accident, she hadn't been able to detect them. Physically all she'd seen was an almost imperceptible favoring of the right leg that resulted in a limp no more obvious than that of a man with a blister on his big toe. If she hadn't been looking for some outward sign of the crash, she doubted she would have noticed anything at all.

Giving in to her growing feeling of impatience, she again turned the keys and looked at her watch. It was nine forty-five. A sudden chill made her retrieve her sweater from the back seat. At least the evening had had the decency to turn cool in acknowledgment of the upcoming winter season. In the distance she noticed amber and red flashing lights. Watching them a moment longer, she saw them leave the main road. They seemed te be heading toward her.

First to arrive was a black-and-white highway-patrol car, followed closely by a tow truck. Mike climbed out of the car, stood beside it a moment and then came over to her, his limp decidedly more pronounced. He motioned for her to roll down her window. "You okay?" he asked.

"I'm fine."

"Get your things. Your ride back to town is here."

"I don't understand—"

"Officer Hernandez is taking you to the station." Noting her look of alarm, he laughed. "Don't get excited—I haven't done something to get you arrested. You're being taken to the television station. He's promised to get you there in time if he has to use red lights and siren all the way."

"You're kidding."

"My word is my bond, remember? Now get a move on."

"But what about you?"

"I'll stay with the car and make sure it's taken care of."

"I—"

"Listen, Caroline, there's nothing I would like to do more than stand around here and talk to you, but since I made such a big deal about returning you to the station on time, I really think it would be best if you got going."

She picked up her purse. Mike took her arm to help her over the soft earth and coarse gravel to the patrol car. Once she was seated, he leaned down so that he could see inside and make the introductions. "Caroline Travers, this is Officer José Hernandez."

Caroline shook the man's outstretched hand. She guessed him to be in his early twenties and, judging from his enthusiastic smile, still new enough to police work not to be completely blasé about an oddball request. She turned back to Mike. He touched her chin, tilting it up slightly before giving her a kiss that was no more than a momentary meeting of lips. "I'll call you," he promised, then shut the door.

Caroline was too surprised to reply. As the patrol car made a wide U-turn she looked over her shoulder to see Mike watching her. Automatically her hand came up to bid him goodbye. He smiled and returned the wave. Suddenly, more than anything, she wished she could stay. She dropped her hand. *That's irrational, Caroline. Get hold of yourself.*

CAROLINE HAD PRAYED, because it was late evening, that she could arrive at the station unobserved. As it turned out, her hopes were as unfounded as those of a dinner-party guest desperate to camouflage the red wine trailing down the front of his white shirt. Half the late-news crew was outside the station, setting up for a live-action shot.

Caroline heaved a weighty sigh as she thanked Officer Hernandez and left the patrol car. At least they hadn't arrived with lights blinking and siren blaring. For one blissful moment she thought she might make it into the studio before anyone cornered her with pointed questions about her mode of transportation. But just as her hand closed around the door handle, she heard a chorus of voices call out, "Somebody stop her!" Realizing escape was impossible, she turned and faced the curious crew.

CAROLINE ENDED THE NEWS that evening with a story about a Long Beach couple who were in the process of building their dream home with cement-filled aluminum beer cans. Even though her day had been almost eighteen hours long, she wasn't tired. It usually took her a while to come down from the high of doing a live show. She was busy removing the earphone and unhooking the microphone from around her neck when one of the cameramen told her she'd received a package.

The minute she opened the newsroom door, she knew what was inside the flat white box lying on her desk. The smell of pizza hit her with the force of a freight train. Her stomach let out a low rumbling growl. The pizza attracted anyone and everyone within smelling distance like bees to a flower. Caroline detached the note she found on the outside and stuffed it in her pocket before she opened the box.

At first she could only stare. How could Mike possibly have known sausage and pepperoni were her favorite pizza ingredients? That the pizza was from Mike, she had no doubt. Caroline looked up at the people around her desk. "Dig in. There's no way I can eat all this by myself."

Bill Williams took a bite, closed his eyes and released a long, eloquent sigh. "I don't know about your heart, Caroline, but this guy sure knows his way to mine."

"I'll give him your address," she answered, reaching for a piece.

"Thanks, but no thanks. The last thing I need is someone around my wife who looks like that man does. I've got her believing I'm the handsomest thing walking upright."

Caroline smiled. Bill was a few years past fifty, had just a little over half his soft brown hair remaining, a rounding stomach and the makings of a double chin, but from all accounts his wife did think him the most handsome man she had ever known.

When the pizza was only a pleasant memory and everyone was back to work, getting ready for the early-morning shift to come in and take over, Caroline pulled the note from her pocket, sat back in her chair and started to read.

Caroline,

Just wanted to convince you I'm a man of my word. I said I would feed you, and one way or another, I was determined to do so. Need I say that I'm sorry I couldn't deliver this in person? Or that because of a crazy mix-up I won't be able to see you again this trip?

I'll be back next month, and we can take up where we left off. But then . . . maybe we could start over yet again . . . you know, keep practicing until we get it right. Either way, save some time for me the next chance I get to come to town.

Mike

P.S. We have a rain check for the nachos and enchiladas. My friends the Gonsalveses are terrific people. Juanita said the kids were disappointed that they didn't get to meet the famous television lady, Joan Rivers—Caroline Travers, Joan Rivers—I can see how they could mistake the two of you. When I told them they would get to meet her next time, they were satisfied. So better polish up a few jokes—don't want to disappoint them. Also, you might look into a blond wig.

Caroline sat and stared at the note. She had known Michael Webster less than twenty-four hours, yet it felt like a lifetime. She thought about her crazy, tumultuous day, the incredible range of emotions she had experienced, the steamroller force of his personality. Slowly she refolded the note.

No, Michael Webster, I will not save time for you. Like a wild animal once snared in a steel trap, she would bypass this enticement—no matter how hungry she was for what he offered, no matter how lonely she felt.

Fatigue hit her like a sudden summer storm, washing away all but the strength needed to get home and crawl into bed. When she stepped inside her apartment it seemed colder than usual. Maybe there was hope for a winter, after all. She would have to find out tomorrow how to go about starting the heater. Yawning, she mechanically moved through the living room.

A faint scent of roses stopped her. She glanced at the table and the bouquet of flowers. She should throw them away before anyone saw them. But not tonight. Tonight she was too tired. In the morning. Yes, she would get rid of them in the morning.

A WEEK LATER, when the last of the roses on Caroline's table had finished blooming, a package arrived, postmarked Houston. Because it was too large to fit into her mailbox, she had to go down to the post office to pick it up. The package, wrapped in plain brown paper, sat on her table all afternoon, through the evening and into the next morning while she tried to decide whether to send it back unopened or check the contents first.

Finally curiosity won out. Inside she found a faded, leather-bound book, dog-eared and loose at the spine. Its title—*European Economics 1935–1937*—brought a smile that had long been absent. She looked at the flyleaf, at the bold handwriting: "To Caroline, Something to keep you busy nights until I can take over. Mike."

CHAPTER THREE

CAROLINE ROLLED OVER IN BED and peered at her alarm clock. It was seven-thirty in the morning on the day after Christmas. Who could be so inconsiderate as to ring her doorbell this early on the one day she had promised herself she would sleep until noon?

Again came the maddeningly cheerful "ding dong." Fleetingly she wondered if she was the only person who had had murderous thoughts about a doorbell. Ready to transmit those thoughts to the person standing with finger pressed to the damn bell, she stumbled from bed and reached for her robe.

"I'm coming!" she yelled in answer to the third summons.

"I'm glad!" came the baritone reply.

Her tailored satin robe half-tied, her hair standing on end, her feet bare against the cold tile of the entranceway, she flung open the door. "You!"

Mike Webster gave her his most devastating smile. Only it was not the same—it was enhanced by a month-old mustache. "I'm thrilled to see you again, too. Can I come in?"

"Didn't we have a long conversation on the

phone about a week and a half ago, during which I told you it would be impossible for us to date and you said you understood?"

"Yes, I seem to recall the half hour."

"Then what are you doing here?"

"Let me in, and I'll tell you."

"What if I say no?"

"I love a challenge."

Caroline rolled her eyes in frustration, noticing as she did that she and Mike were attracting an audience, older residents of the building who were habitual early risers. She had not only provided references to get this apartment, she had given a long, impassioned speech on single women and the unfairness of stereotyping them. The man in front of her now could destroy all her work with minimal effort. "You can have ten minutes."

He eyed her suspiciously. "You're giving in too easily."

She reached for the arm he held behind his back. *"Will you get in here?"*

Once inside, Mike pulled his arm the rest of the way forward and offered Caroline a single, perfect cattleya orchid.

Automatically she accepted the fragrant white flower, bringing it to her nose to catch more of the elusive scent. Glancing past the waxy petals into Mike's grinning face, she felt a sudden sense of unease. Twirling the flower around so that she could see it better, she realized there were none of the florist trappings indicating it had come from a shop. Only a small glass vial, filled with water and attached to the stem, proved he hadn't broken into someone's greenhouse on his way to see her that morning. "Where did you get this?" she asked.

"It's a secret."

"Most likely *your* secret...the owner's mystery."

He put his hand over his heart. "Thou dost fling such cruel arrows, fair maiden."

Caroline put her hands on her hips and glared at him. "What are you doing here?"

"In Pasadena?"

"Don't be obtuse. Why are you here, at my apartment?"

"I've come to take you to Disneyland." He moved her aside and went into the living room. "I'll bet that even though you've been here almost a year, you've never been to Disneyland."

"Mike, I told you I didn't see any point in our dating. You said you understood."

"This isn't a date. No one over twenty-one is allowed to call a trip to Disneyland a date. We're simply going to spend a day together—a couple of friends—having fun."

Caroline laid the orchid on an end table and walked over to the built-in bookshelves, withdrawing a dictionary. She started to hand it to Mike to have him look up the meaning of "date," then stopped and let her hand fall heavily to her side. "What's the use?"

"I'm not interfering with any other plans you'd made for today, am I? You weren't going to do battle with the-day-after-Christmas crowds in the shopping malls?''

''Would it bother you if I did have other plans?'' She sighed, exasperated. ''Actually, what I had in mind was spending a marvelous twenty-four hours doing absolutely nothing. I wasn't even going to get dressed. This was to be my one day of decadence, a fitting way to celebrate the closing of the year.''

''Boy, I'll bet you're glad I came along to rescue you.'' He sat on the couch, stretching his legs out in front of him. ''Now get a move on. The park opens at ten. By the time we get something to eat and drive all the way to Anaheim, there'll be a long line ahead of us.''

Caroline slipped the dictionary back into place on the shelf. She knew she should try, once more, to rationally explain to that mound of manhood sitting on her sofa that she really didn't want to see, become involved with or even become casual friends with someone who not only marched to a different drummer, but who also seemed to be conducting the entire offbeat band. Mike Webster was... what exactly was it about Mike Webster she didn't like? *Be honest,* she told herself.... Could it be that she knew if she entered into a relationship with him, she wouldn't be the one who held the power? Was she afraid of him because of that?

Almost angrily Caroline snatched the orchid from its resting place. *She was afraid of no one.* ''It will take me about a half hour to get ready. If you'd like to make yourself some coffee while you wait, the pot is in the kitchen cupboard by the stove. The coffee is in the refrigerator.''

"Thanks, but I think I'll just take a nap here on the couch, if that's okay with you. The flight in was even earlier than I'm used to.''

"Of course—why should I mind if a virtual stranger sleeps on my couch?''

Mike's eyes sparkled. "When two people have shared a kiss that nearly knocked the socks off one of them, they're no longer strangers—virtual or otherwise.''

Caroline tried to hide the smile of pleasure his words evoked, quickly turning and heading for her bedroom. It was nice to know her kiss had been as potent as she had intended. "There's an afghan in the chest under the window.''

Once in her bedroom, she listened a moment at her closed door, hearing Mike open the chest and return to the couch. She gave full rein to her smile. Yes, indeed...it was nice to know the Houston Hurricane hadn't lost her touch.

LESS THAN THIRTY MINUTES LATER Caroline reappeared, wearing a pair of dark brown slacks and an ecru blouse. Because Anaheim was closer to the ocean and usually a few degrees cooler than Pasadena, she also wore a dark brown alpaca sweater, the sleeves casually tied at the neck.

Sleeping as peacefully as if he were in his own living room, Mike lay sprawled on the couch, his stocking feet poking out at one end, his head at the other. Caroline walked over to wake him, but stopped before her hand touched his shoulder. She studied him for a minute. The new mustache had changed his appearance, giving him an air of mystery when he had seemed an open book before. Perhaps she got that impression because the mustache wasn't artful, wasn't carefully and precisely grown. It was naturally shaped and looked as if it had always been there.

Being awake brought a certain animation to Mike's face, but in repose several small scars were visible—one at his temple, one that ran parallel to his eyebrow and one that curved like a minihorseshoe just below his chin. Caroline wondered if they were remnants of an adventuresome childhood, or reminders, along with his leg, of the crash that had ended his career as an astronaut.

"Are you by any chance thinking about giving me a repeat performance of The Kiss?"

Caroline cried out in surprise. He had looked sound asleep. "What?" she said with startling originality.

"You know—the infamous kiss."

Regaining her wits, she said, "Those are strictly one-to-a-customer kinds of things."

"And I suppose—" he shook his head in mock sadness "—the next thing you're going to tell me is there's no Santa Claus."

"We all have to grow up and face these things sooner or later."

A lazy stretch and a fluid movement had him off the couch and standing directly in front of her.

Mike clasped her shoulders and gave her a quick kiss of his own. It was a gesture of greeting, easily and naturally given, something shared between two old friends. "I happen to have a little inside knowledge about this Santa Claus thing," he said. "I stood in for the old guy the night before last at my sister's house. If you can believe the sworn testimony of my five-year-old nephew and three-year-old niece, Santa Claus is as real as I am."

"Did you really?" The idea of Mike Webster, dynamic spokesman for NASA, dressed up like an overgrown elf was more than she could imagine.

He nodded.

"Red suit and whiskers and everything?"

"The entire get-up."

"I'll bet you didn't use the chimney."

"Couldn't . . . someone had started a fire."

"Tell me about it," she coaxed. "Were they surprised?"

He chuckled at the memory. "I think I even had my sister, Peg, going for a while." Mike released her shoulders and began folding the afghan. "I waited out in the car until everyone had been in bed for about twenty minutes—damn near froze to death in the process. When I was confident all was quiet, I let myself in with the key Peg had given me on my last visit. It only took a few ho ho's and a little stomping around before I had the whole family downstairs."

"You're lucky they didn't call the police—or shoot you. I can just see the headlines now . . . 'Santa Gunned Down as Suspected Prowler.'"

"Not a chance. What prowler ever robbed a house while ho ho'ing at the top of his lungs?"

Caroline had become pretty good at making it through holidays without feeling sorry for herself. Not even a fellow employee's excited plans or a detailed recounting of the day that had passed bothered her too much anymore. So why this surge of melancholy at Mike's tale?

Once the afghan had been folded and put back in the chest, Mike turned to her, a puzzled frown drawing his brows together, and for some odd reason, making him even more handsome. "You don't celebrate Christmas?"

Caroline was startled. "What makes you say that?"

"I just looked around your apartment. Unless you're someone who likes to spend her Christmas taking down all the trappings, I'm assuming there were never any put up."

She busied herself readjusting the sweater that had started to slip from her shoulders. "It's such a hassle for one person. I rarely spend a holiday at home, anyway. Since I'm one of the few single reporters at the station, I make it a habit to offer to work 'family' days so that someone with kids can be at home."

And you don't have to face being alone, Mike speculated. So Caroline Travers hadn't quite finished building her protective shell around herself. She still had a few vulnerable spots.

Uncharacteristically, Caroline rushed in to fill the silence. "I spent my Christmas interviewing people who also had to work. It made a good human-interest piece. Nothing original, but I like to think I handled it with a fresh approach.''

"If it was anywhere close to the quality of the series you did on the space program, I'm sure it was outstanding.''

Quick anger shot through her. Or was it disappointment? How could he possibly know how the series had turned out? KMTV was one of the largest Southern California stations, but it stopped short of reaching Houston. Insincere compliments were a hundred times worse—no, a million times worse—than no compliment at all.

As if reading her thoughts, Mike came over to stand in front of her. For a minute, while her anger and disappointment continued to bubble, he gently straightened her sweater. "I had a friend tape the series for me," he said softly. "He's not only a very good friend; he's an avid news watcher. Thanks to him, I've seen every report you've done for the evening news since I left last month. I'm sure I'll find this week's tape of you waiting when I get back to Houston.''

She couldn't find the words to express the conflicting emotions surging through her. Finally she centered on one question. "Why?''

His arm went around her waist as he guided her to the front door. "For a hundred little reasons, but really only one important one. I was unfair to you that day in Captain Brown's office. The only way I could offer the kind of apology I felt you deserved was to offer it with some authority. Now that I've seen your work, I can sincerely tell you that I feel you have become one of the best reporters I've ever worked with—and there have been quite a few. My opinion, for what it's worth, is that there is only one thing that will ever get in your way—your beauty. There will always be people who won't be able to see past it.''

It was senseless to try to hide the flush of pleasure his words provoked. "Perhaps I should grow a wart on the end of my nose.''

"Don't even suggest it.'' He touched the end of her nose with his finger. "It would be a desecration to mar such perfection.''

She picked up his teasing tone. "But if it were to help further my career....''

"If you feel a compulsive need to do something, at least try blacking out your teeth first. Then if that doesn't work—''

Caroline laughed out loud. How delightful it felt.

AFTER LINGERING OVER COFFEE in an out-of-the-way restaurant that served homemade bread and rolls, then a leisurely drive to Anaheim, they arrived at Disneyland after the first influx of tourists had entered and before the second wave had rolled in. Walking down Main Street, Caroline was as enchanted as Walt Disney had intended visitors to his Magic Kingdom to be. They stopped to stare at a Christmas tree decorated with ornaments from basketball to tennis-ball size. After careful consideration and mental calculations, they estimated the tree to be more than fifty feet tall. Carolers dressed in turn-of-the-century costumes sang beside the tree, while people outfitted like the classic Disney cartoon characters posed for pictures with children and adults alike.

Taking Caroline's hand, Mike gently tugged her along the festooned Main Street, telling her he was afraid the park would close before they had left the entrance area. "What would you like to see first?" he asked.

"You mean after we've gone through all these wonderful little shops?"

"No, I don't mean after we've gone through all the shops. I don't want to disillusion you, but shopping is not a primary reason for coming to this place. I'll make a deal with you...how about if we come back here tonight when there's a parade to watch and the lights are turned on?"

She eyed him suspiciously. "Are you sure the stores will be open after dark?"

"Trust me."

"Okay, you're on. I don't know what I want to do first. I've never been here before."

"I was hoping you'd say that." There was a note of triumph in his voice. "Can I assume you have neither a weak heart nor a bad back?"

Puzzled, she nodded.

He grinned. "Well, let's go, then."

It took only one wild ride down Space Mountain, an enclosed roller coaster, to understand the weak-heart, bad-back question. It took two more before Caroline was able to completely discard her tendency to remain aloof at amusement parks. She became more open, suddenly eager to spend the day with Mike in childlike pursuit of pleasure.

They worked their way through Tomorrowland, journeying into a microscope and on a submarine, then on to Fantasyland, where they stood in line with toddlers to ride in the Mad Hatter's tea cups. They were serenaded by bears and attacked by wild hippos and taken on a ride through a haunted house. Lunch was eaten in bayou country, with cool breezes and fireflies lending a feeling of authenticity to the waterside restaurant.

By the time they were again back on Main Street, Caroline felt the muscles in her legs threatening to mutiny. She and Mike found an empty spot on the curb, and they sat down to watch the Christmas Parade. When she shivered with a sudden chill, Mike slipped his arm around her. He did so as easily and comfortably as if his arm had been there a hundred times before. In the beginning Caroline held herself stiffly, not yielding to the warmth he offered. Soon realizing it was warmth and nothing else he wanted to give her, she snuggled gratefully into his side.

After the parade they went into an old-fashioned candy store, where Mike bought a cinnamon stick, which he offered to share with Caroline. When she hesitated to take a bite, he intuitively unwrapped the other end and held the candy out to her. "Have you always been so proper?" he asked gently, standing close beside her.

"Always," she sighed. "There are dozens and

dozens of ingrained dos and don'ts that still haunt me from my childhood.''

"Tell me a few." He wanted to understand her. To know why she sent him such contradictory signals. Hold me, touch me. . . stay away.

She tilted her head in thought. "Never lend or borrow a comb, never use someone else's lipstick, never drink from the same straw or bottle—" Still holding the candy stick, she glanced up at Mike. "Never eat off the same piece of candy." Her eyes sparkled then. Purposely she turned the candy over and took a bite from his end.

His smile was hidden from her as he took her hand and started walking again. "Does this mean we're friends at last?"

"Eating off the same candy stick is as close as I'll ever come to having a blood brother."

His laugh was low and intimate. "Caroline. . . you have to know by now that brother was not the role I had in mind for you to play."

Nor, she was beginning to think, was it a role she wanted him to play. What would be the harm in dating Mike Webster occasionally? Hadn't she enjoyed being with him today? With him it felt natural to do things she normally never would— ride automated cars through a maze, or sit in a boat that was swallowed by a whale—rides where they were the only adults not accompanied by children. He made her laugh. He was easy to talk to.

"I'll give you the last bite of candy if you tell me what you're thinking right this minute."

She stopped beside an antique lamp post decked

with swags of garland and bright red ribbon. "I was thinking about you. . . ."

"And?"

"And wondering if I was wrong when I told you I wouldn't go out with you. I've come to the conclusion you're not as bad as I first thought."

"Thanks—I think."

"You're welcome. And you can be sure."

They left the park hand in hand.

It was after eleven by the time they reached Caroline's apartment. Mike walked her to the front door. "Would you like to come in?" she asked.

"I'd *like* to, but I'd better not. I'm due someplace very early tomorrow morning."

She leaned against the doorframe. "I have tomorrow afternoon and evening off. Want to do something?"

He gave her a warm smile. "Am I hearing this right? *You're* asking *me*?"

"I have a large block of time off this week because of the long hours I'll be working on the parade. We could—"

Mike pressed a finger to her lips. "Don't make this any harder for me than it already is. I won't be able to see you again until the afternoon of the parade. I'm sorry, Caroline, but I'm completely tied up until then."

Unexpectedly she smiled. "If this is what it feels like to be turned down for a date, I can't say I'm too crazy about it."

"Remember that the next time I call."

"I will." She slipped her key into the lock. When the door was open she turned back to Mike. "I guess I'll say good-night, then." Before going inside, she lightly brushed his lips with her own.

"Good night," he said softly, watching as she closed the door behind her.

Caroline leaned back, her head resting on the cool oak. She liked Mike Webster. She liked him a lot. Occasional dates with him would be a welcome diversion. He would be a nice balance to the kind of men she normally dated. She thought about the day just past, the fun she had had, the warm feeling he had left her with. A breath of unease brushed against her like an errant puff of wind. Suddenly she was grateful that Mike lived as far away as he did. She had a discomforting feeling that she couldn't handle seeing him on anything close to a steady basis.

The doorbell rang.

Caroline looked through the peephole. Even with the tiny window distorting his features, she recognized Mike. "Did you forget something?" she asked, opening the door.

For an instant he only stared. Then, his voice low and husky, he said, "Yes...almost...." He reached for her. His hands went to her waist. Gently he urged her to come to him of her own volition.

When their lips met, he kissed her with all the fire and passion she had simulated a month earlier. Instantly she responded, knowing as she did that she had been wanting this since he had first walked through her door that morning.

The feel of his lips—the faint spicy smell of his after-shave, the breadth, the hardness, the warmth of his body—all were as she had remembered. The only new sensation was the faint touch of his mustache against her lip. This time, when he gently sought entry into the intimate recesses of her mouth, she welcomed him. With coaxing passion, his kiss methodically made love to her, taking her on an erotic journey, letting her lead when she would, becoming the leader when she would follow.

Finally, reluctantly, he broke the kiss and looked down at her. "When I was walking away just now, I told myself I'd go crazy until I saw you again if I didn't come back here and tell you good-night properly. I'm wondering now if it was such a hot idea."

Caroline tried to make her trembling lips smile. She half succeeded. "It will certainly make the next week interesting."

He kissed her again, only this time it was no more than a faint caress. "Save the afternoon of the parade for me."

She nodded. When he released her she reached out and touched his arm. He looked at her questioningly. "Did you grow the mustache for me?" she asked.

He smiled. "It was the least I could do."

"Well, it must have worked. But then...I suppose your willingness to share your candy stick with me might have done the trick."

His smile deepened. "When my charm failed, I had to try something else."

"Don't give up on the charm yet. With a little polishing, you might have something."

"Do you realize how dangerous the combination might be—the Houston Hurricane and Mr. Congenial?"

Oh, did she ever! "I'm sure you'll learn to cope."

The smile faded. "Don't give me too much credit for control, Caroline. I'm standing on the brink right now. And after saying that, I'm going to leave before this goes any further." He stepped outside, quietly closing the door behind him.

Caroline went to her bedroom, only then realizing her legs felt like twin mounds of gelatin. Switching on the light, she saw the orchid on her nightstand. Brilliant white with a touch of yellow at the throat, the flower somehow reminded her of herself. The orchid was a flower aloof from all others, even in areas where it grew commonly. Her aloofness was an emotional safeguard she had purposely cultivated after her divorce from Tom, a shield that was supposed to protect her from ever feeling such pain or hurt again.

She had dated dozens of men in the past four years, and not one of them had been able to reach past her defenses to the hidden place where she was still vulnerable. It was as if an alarm went off inside when someone got too close, and she immediately pulled back. Mike was wrong. She knew exactly what she was doing with her career. Becoming a bureau reporter, someone who lived out of a suitcase and called no city home, was the ultimate protection.

Caroline walked over to the bed. She picked up the orchid and brought it to her face. If she were as tough and had it as all together as she told herself she did, when she could hear her alarm ringing louder than it ever had, why was she still planning to see Mike Webster again?

CHAPTER FOUR

MIKE SAT AT HIS DESK scanning launch-insurance-coverage figures for the afternoon's interview with a reporter from *Newsweek*. He had received a call in Los Angeles early that morning asking him to return to Houston for the last-minute taping. While he had long ago become accustomed to having breakfast and lunch in different time zones, in this instance he was having trouble. He had spent the entire previous day with Caroline at Disneyland. For some mysterious reason, the day seemed far away, the distance sharply accentuated by his overwhelming desire to forget everything else and be with her.

The figures in front of him kept fading to soft focus as he remembered. It took a rapid, coded knock announcing Cory Peters's arrival to snap Mike out of his daydream.

Dressed in astronaut coveralls Mike considered only marginally distinguishable from an auto mechanic's, Cory poked his head in the door. With freckles that faded a little more each year and hair that had turned from screaming red to strawberry blond, Cory had finally reached a point in his life when people no longer ignored every other physical feature save his hair and freckles when describing him.

Mike had called Cory his friend at each stage of their adult lives. They met in high school when Cory was playing center on the football team, Mike quarterback. And then again in the fraternity of pilots. Mike came to the navy as a graduate of Annapolis; Cory went the route of private college and enlistment. Mike was Cory's best man at his wedding, which took place right after high school, accompanied by grim predictions from just about every guest. Sixteen years and one or two bumpy roads later, the Peterses' marriage was the best union of two people Mike had ever seen.

Cory and Mike reached another milestone in their friendship when they learned that out of almost nine thousand applicants, they had been chosen as two of the thirty-five people for the astronaut training program.

And it was Cory and his wife, Ann, who endured the long hours at Mike's bedside with him, waiting to see whether he would keep his mangled leg. Afterward the friendship had weathered its most formidable test: Cory realized the dream of piloting a shuttle, while Mike was forced to stay behind. If possible, they had drawn even closer during the shared tragedy.

"If you're busy, I can come back later," Cory said now.

Mike shuffled the papers in front of him into a central stack. Ever since the crew for the February launch had been announced a little more than a year earlier, he had hardly seen Cory. Most of his friend's waking hours were spent with his crew of five, with a small amount of time left for his family. "I have a feeling I'd better make time right now," Mike said. "*Later* could be sometime in March."

Cory sauntered into the room. In all the years Mike had known him, Cory had never just walked like everyone else; he had a natural swing to his hips that made him look like a swaggering cowboy. "I came in to see what you know about the new cracks they found last week in the shuttle rockets. All us peasant crew members seem to be getting are rumors so distorted they haven't even brushed past the truth on their way into the training center."

Mike motioned to a chair. "Have a seat." He leaned back in his own, lazily stretching his arms over his head. "It just so happens you have come to the right man for your information." He grinned. "The truth was in Florida only last week. In short, it seems the designers and efficiency people have not only ignored our cherished, unofficial motto here at NASA, they have trod all over it. Don't Screw Up has been turned and twisted so many times, it now reads, Let's Keep Tinkering with It until It Stops Working." Mike leaned his elbows on the arms of the chair, his hands in front of him, tent fashion.

"The problem is similar to the one they had in '83 when they were trying to improve the rocket thrust. Someone in design decided the additional vibration the ship would be getting from the new thrust would mean the hydrogen fuel pipes were going to be under greater stress and would therefore require more support welds. The welds created their own stress, and cracks developed. They're going to try fixing the cracks the same way they did in '83, by using computerized welds, which, as I understand it, make the tubes more flexible than brazing would.''

Cory looked as if Mike had given him a present. "That's the same story we've been getting," he admitted, his words tinged with relief.

"The holidays have created a lack of communication, and with no one taking the time to send out reassurances, people were bound to begin to feel a little edgy.'' Unable to resist a friendly jab, Mike added, "I'm sure if you had hopped a plane over there, they would have given you the same tour I had.''

"Easy for you to say. It's been hard enough finding some extra time for Ann and the kids this past week. If they had discovered I'd gone to the Cape just to chase down a rumor, they would have hung me up by my thumbs.''

Under normal circumstances Mike would have given Cory a harder time about his uncustomary nerves, but the launch date had drawn too close for any incident not to be taken with deep seriousness. As one of only twelve astronauts qualified to pilot the shuttle, Cory had a good chance of being chosen for future flights if he proved himself on this one. Even though he was the epitome of "cool under pressure," the astronaut's cardinal rule, there was too much at stake to take even rumors lightly. Mike doubted anyone else could detect the trace of nervousness in his friend. Before being given his own shuttle flight, Cory had served as capcom, the person on earth who communicates and relays instructions to astronauts in space. He had performed the job with remarkable coolness through more than one troubled flight.

Changing the subject to one Mike knew would elicit a relaxed smile, he asked, "How was your Christmas?"

"Great. The kids loved your presents—as usual, you overspent but managed to get them exactly what they wanted. Ann would like to know how you outguess her every year."

"It comes from still being a kid at heart myself. By the way, you might pass on that the kids have already called to thank me for the presents, so Ann can relax."

"I'm surprised they reached you. You've been harder to track down than a trap-wise coyote," Cory said. "We tried to get in touch with you yesterday to ask you for dinner. Ann fixed home-made bread and minestrone."

"I was in California."

Cory waited a second, absorbing the information. "Just being in California doesn't jibe with that look in your eye or that stupid grin on your face." He thought another moment. "And where was the groan of protest over missing Ann's bread and soup?"

Mike sat forward in his chair. He picked up his pencil and tapped it against the desk. "Do you remember the Houston Hurricane?"

Cory frowned as he sought long-stored information. "Wasn't she that television reporter—the one who destroyed Texas with her weather wand?"

"I ran into her in California—"

"On purpose?" He grinned. "Or was it just another unfortunate freeway accident?" His grin faded when he got no reciprocal smile. "You weren't kidding around about meeting her, were you?"

Mike was surprised he had given himself away so easily. "No..." he said slowly, trying to decide how much of his feelings he wanted to reveal. "I wasn't kidding."

Cory sat straighter in his chair. "How about giving me a few of the particulars here?"

Mike filled him in on the meeting he had had with Caroline.

"I hate to tell you this, old buddy, but it seems to me you've either fallen or jumped overboard. Whether you know it or not, it sounds like you're hanging on to the gunwale by your fingertips."

Mike let the pencil slide through his fingers. "You're not telling me anything I don't already know." He sighed. "If someone were paying me to think about her by the hour, I'd be a rich man."

Cory let out a soft whistle. "Wait until Ann hears about this. Just the other day she said she's been anxious for you to find someone for such a long time that she's damn near given up hope." He stood up and headed for the door.

"Hey," Mike protested, "stick around. I don't have to be at the interview for a couple of hours yet."

"I'm going to call Ann. This news is too good not to share."

"Hold on a minute." Mike held up his hand. "I don't want you to go out and reserve the church just yet. I'm still in the process of trying to convince the lovely Caroline I'm not the jerk she has every right to think I am."

"I have no doubt you'll succeed beautifully. She'll come to her senses. And if your glib tongue doesn't do the trick, just being around you for a while will eventually convince her you're harmless."

"You realize you're not high on my list of references, don't you?"

Cory laughed. "How can you say something like that after the blind dates I've tried to set you up with. You must realize by now that I'd do anything to get you married off—even lie!"

Mike shook his head. "Get out of here—and give Ann my love."

"Will do," Cory called over his shoulder as he closed the door.

Once again Mike tried to concentrate on the figures in front of him. He wanted to be able to give quick, precise answers about the problems involved in private insurance coverage for the clients sending up satellites. At the early stages of the program, when the shuttle had carried only two satellites, the underwriters hadn't been concerned about handling the coverage. But with more cargo, the third-party damage insurance had far exceeded the billion-dollar mark, and NASA had been forced to look into new ways to handle the risk, including the possibility of providing the insurance itself.

Even though it was a dry subject to start with, Mike was having what was for him an unusual amount of trouble wading through the information. Caroline constantly resurfaced in his memory, promptly erasing everything he tried to file away.

To have waited so long to find someone who made him feel the way she did, to have watched others from a distance secure in their loving cocoons of family life, to have lived so long with a lonely ache inside him.... He feared even contemplating the possibility that the wait could be over lest he jinx himself. Despite his steadfast insistence to friends that a special woman would come along someday, Mike had privately begun to doubt that there was such a person.

Just what was it about Caroline Travers that made her so different? Why, how had she made him feel euphoric? Even to himself he was hesitant to describe the feeling as love. Infatuation? Perhaps. But not love. The word "love" represented too much; it was too special to be bandied about so casually. That emotion had to be nurtured in

rich soil; it had to be given room to grow, to pros-
per.

The thoughts swirling through Mike's mind
were intensely private, a part of him that few people even knew existed. His nomadic childhood,
spent traveling from one military base to another,
always being the new kid in the neighborhood or
in the school, constantly developing friendships
while knowing all along they would have to be
abandoned later, had made a sensitive child
develop a thick shell of protection to survive. The
craving for stability—for a bedroom that was truly his own, where he could put nails in the walls to
hang pictures without causing his parents to for-
feit the rental deposit, or for a grandmother, aunt
or cousin who didn't live thousands of miles
away—had created an ache in him. It had been a
lonely life, accentuated by his eventual reluctance
to let anyone get too close because of the painful
parting he knew would follow. Despite a life now
rich with friends, some of that loneliness still
resided in Mike. The home he went to after an evening with friends was always empty.

He couldn't take it in, that he might have finally
found someone to share his life, to erase the life-
long lonely ache. Reason told him to go slowly,
cautiously. He must examine his feelings to find
out if they were real or just the product of his
overwhelming need to make them real.

Mike glanced at his watch. Still two hours before the interview. He thought about calling Caroline but discarded the idea in favor of restraint. He

sensed that to push too hard, too soon, no matter the provocation, was the wrong way to convince her she couldn't live without him.

Again there was a quick coded knock on the door. Not waiting for a summons, Cory peered inside. "Ann insists you come for dinner tonight."

Mike's smile was immediate. "Tell her thanks, but I'm flying back to Los Angeles later this evening. And I'll be gone for the rest of the week, so she'll have to wait until after New Year's to buttonhole me."

Cory opened the door wider, leaned against the frame and stubbornly crossed his arms. "I don't think you understand the situation here—the invitation wasn't a request, it was a command. She emphatically told me I couldn't come home without you in tow."

Mike scooped the papers in front of him into his desk. There was no way he was going to memorize any more insurance figures that afternoon. If the reporter needed anything beyond the basics, Mike would refer him to the man who was actually handling the issue for NASA. He glanced up at Cory. "I'm starved. Have you had lunch?"

"Answer me first—are you coming to dinner?"

"I have a better idea. Have Ann meet us, and we'll go out to eat. The hop I'm catching out of Ellington doesn't leave until eight-thirty."

"That should do the trick. I'll give her a call after lunch."

"I'd call before, if I were you. She may have to find a sitter for Mindy."

Cory shook his red head in disgust as he came over to Mike's desk and reached for the phone. "It's a good thing I'm not the jealous type. If I wasn't convinced Ann couldn't live without me, I'd resent the affinity you two have." The complaint had been voiced so often it had become a standing joke among the three of them. Over the years Ann and Mike had developed a bond stronger than that of most brothers and sisters.

The call made and arrangements finalized, Mike and Cory left for lunch.

As WITH ANY TWO PEOPLE caught up in their work, the conversation over lunch centered on just that.

Cory and Mike had filled their trays, found an out-of-the-way table and immediately slipped into discussion about the newly announced crew members for shuttle flights scheduled the following year. They openly wondered about the choices, curious to see how the personalities would mesh over the fourteen months the men and women would be forced to spend sixty hours a week together.

The space program was a subject the men never grew tired of discussing. Cory's mind was so focused on the upcoming launch that he could concentrate on little else. The extended hours he spent with the other crew members, constantly rehearsing their flight, going over and then over again the smallest details of the experiments they were to perform, had become the controlling force in his life.

Mike listened and commiserated, laughed at the jokes and examples of sophomoric humor the astronauts used to break the tension when it became particularly thick. He sympathized with the frustrations that were an intrinsic part of the job.

During the devastating period after Mike's crash when he had learned he would never pilot an aircraft of any kind again, he and Cory had come to a critical understanding; without it their friendship couldn't have continued. Mike had insisted there never be any holding back on Cory's part to spare Mike's feelings—no tempering of the astronaut's enthusiasm for or about his job anxieties. Mike had convinced his friend not to close him off from such a part of his life.

Mike's recovery period had been filled with difficult decisions; leaving the navy had been the hardest. Becoming a civilian for the first time in his adult life had given him an odd feeling of being cut loose. Eventually he had grown to like the freedom. Remaining at NASA had been a tactical and obvious choice—it was the world he knew best. Because of his background and reputation for honesty and his ease with the press, Mike was a natural choice to fill William Dawson's job as spokesman for the space-shuttle program when the longtime NASA employee went into private industry.

Mike was making more money than he ever had in the military. But the money meant little to him beyond allowing him to live in a nicer apartment and drive an obscenely expensive car he had purchased on impulse one weekend when his ten-year-old Mustang had thrown a rod.

Through his job he met influential and famous people, had dated titled women as well as Hollywood stars. He traveled extensively and attended parties that were written up the next day in the society pages. Seemingly, he had it all.

Only he knew he would trade everything he had, everything he would ever have, for the opportunity to look down at his home planet from a place far into space. . . if just for one orbit.

Oblivious to what was happening around them, the two friends were taken by surprise when they were unceremoniously interrupted by Frank Jenkins, one of the mission-specialist astronauts on Cory's flight. A scowl animated his normally expressionless face.

"Mind if I disturb your lunch for a minute?" he asked, hauling another chair up to the table.

Though he'd been perversely nicknamed Sunshine by the other astronauts, Frank Jenkins was highly respected by them all for his mechanical genius. Not waiting for a reply from either man, he directed his question to Cory. "Have you noticed any problems yourself, or have you heard anyone else complain about the way the manipulator arm is working?"

Both men's relaxed body attitudes changed subtly. The February shuttle flight involved using the manipulator arm extensively. It would figure in several of the major experiments, including retrieving and trying to repair a satellite that had been taken up by shuttle the year before. The arm was more than just another object of testing; it was a basic function for the shuttle. NASA had prophesied, ever since the inception of the program, that the arm would be one of its best features.

Cory spoke first. "What is it doing?"

"I've spent all morning trying to figure out what's wrong, but I still can't put my finger on anything specific. I thought if someone else had mentioned they were having a problem, I might be able to draw some conclusions."

Mike glanced from Frank to Cory. The only sign that the news had affected his friend at all was a slight shuttering of his eyes as if he were deep in thought. Looking back to Frank, Mike said, "Have you talked to anyone else about this?"

He shook his head. "It's so nebulous—just a feeling, really. Everything I tried to get the arm to do, it did. I don't know how to describe the problem to anyone. I'm only bringing it up now on the off chance someone else has said something."

"They haven't," Cory said slowly. "Why don't you check with Teresa to see if she's noticed anything. I'm pretty sure she was the one who worked with the arm yesterday. It seems to me she should be more sensitive to a malfunction than anyone, after all the time she operated it while preparing for her last flight."

Frank stood up abruptly, sending his chair skittering across the tile floor. "As soon as I find out anything I'll get back to you."

When he had gone Cory leaned his arms wearily on the table, clasping his coffee cup with both hands. "I knew I shouldn't have smashed that spider," he said with disgust.

"Or helped Mindy open her umbrella in the house," Mike added, a half smile acknowledging his friend's superstitious nature.

Cory swallowed the last of his coffee. "You'll know where to find me."

They cleared their dishes and left, heading in opposite directions—Mike to the Project Management Building, Cory to the Mission Simulator and Training Facility.

Several hours later, as they walked together into the Steak and Rib House where they were to meet Ann, it seemed their conversation had never been interrupted.

"I can't figure it out," Cory said. "Frank's right; there is something peculiar about the arm. But I'll be damned if I can find out what it is."

Ann came up behind them in the foyer. Dressed in an electric-blue silk shirtwaist that made her shoulder-length black hair seem darker than it was and her waist impossibly narrow, she looked far younger than the thirty-six she readily admitted. The soft beginnings of the lines that would eventually "reveal her character," as she said, showed around her eyes, accenting their impish sparkle.

Slipping between Cory and Mike, she took an arm of each, stood on tiptoe and gave first one then the other a kiss. "Listen up, fellas, I'm giving you two fair warning. There will be absolutely no shuttle talk at our table this evening. We have far more important things to discuss."

The two men exchanged glances. To spend an evening without the shuttle as the main topic of conversation was about as conceivable as running a marathon backward—possible, but highly improbable. The hostess led them to a quiet table at the back of the restaurant. Ann nodded her approval.

Again Mike looked at Cory. "I think I'm being set up."

"Count on it," Ann replied. "Now get busy and look at your menu and decide what you're ordering so Mike can concentrate on telling me all about Caroline Travers."

"Everything there is to know about her?" Mike laughed. "In one fell swoop?"

Ann's eyes narrowed ominously. "Mike Webster, you are either going to tell me what I want to know or not leave this restaurant unless it's over my dead body."

Mike held his hands up in mock surrender. "She has short dark hair that she wears swept up on the sides in curls...stands around five-five or -six...." He warmed to his subject immediately. By the time their dinner arrived, he had told Ann everything he knew about Caroline Travers.

She looked at him incredulously, her knife and fork suspended over her steak. "Do I have this right—you've gone out with this lady exactly one and a half times?"

Mike nodded.

Ann glanced at Cory, then back at Mike. While she listened to his enthusiastic discourse, her earlier smile of pleasure had slowly disappeared, to be replaced by a worried frown. "Do you think it's possible that everything is happening a bit too fast?" she asked gently.

"Hell, yes. But I haven't the vaguest idea how to slow it all down."

"Maybe one way would be to wait for a while before you go back to Los Angeles," Cory suggested.

Ann stopped eating, laid her fork down and reached for Mike's hand. "I'm sorry, Mike...I don't mean to sound like a pessimist. It's just that—" She squeezed his hand tighter, as if trying to communicate with touch something she didn't know how to say with words. "Dammit, it's just that I want this to work out for you."

"You're not saying anything I haven't already told myself, Ann. After I've waited all this time, it's tough for me to fathom or believe that I've come across someone who makes me feel the way Caroline does. I keep bracing myself for the punch line."

Ann thought a minute, then went back to cutting her meat. When she looked up again she had a sheepish gleam in her eye. "Forget everything I just said. I've been sitting here searching through ancient memories and just recalled that I fell in love with Cory the first day I saw him in biology class. I'm the last person who should give advice about slowing down and doing things the sensible way."

Registering Cory's smile, Mike said, "Maybe it would ease your mind somewhat if I told you I'm not going back to Los Angeles to see Caroline—at least not right away. I have a job I promised I'd do for someone. It'll keep me tied up from the time I get back there until New Year's Day."

Ann sent him a face-splitting grin. "So—" she popped a piece of juicy steak into her mouth "—how's the shuttle coming along?"

CHAPTER FIVE

RANDY KAVANAUGH slouched against Caroline's desk. The Rose Parade was two days away, and the station was in turmoil. "Sid said to tell you I'm your camera operator for today."

Caroline looked up from the clippings she'd been studying. "I'll be with you as soon as I've finished these. Why don't you get a cup of coffee while you're waiting for me?"

"You want one?"

She smiled.

"That's what I thought." He turned and ambled toward the lounge.

Caroline went back to her research. She could remember watching Tournament of Roses parades on television as a child. Then, when she was old enough to notice such things, she could remember thinking there must be a list of questions used by reporters year after year. She had wondered at their lack of originality and had made a solemn vow that if she ever had the opportunity to interview for the parade, she would look for a fresh approach. Today, she would put the finishing touches to a half-hour program airing the night before the parade, with segments being shown early the next morning as fillers for the live coverage.

She had forced herself to put even more energy than usual into her work this past week in an attempt to keep thoughts of Mike Webster from dominating every waking hour. She couldn't believe what a lustful creature she'd become. Just thinking about the kiss he'd given her...the feel of his thighs pressed against hers...the warmth of his breath against her cheek—

"I'd like to go wherever your thoughts are taking you." Randy stood in front of her, holding two take-out cups, steam rising from the tops.

She could feel a blush burning her cheeks. "I haven't been there myself in quite a while."

He handed her one of the cups. "You say the most provocative things with such innocence. I take it you're still seeing Michael Webster?"

"If one date—well, kind of a date—counts for still seeing Mike Webster, I qualify."

"You mean it wasn't Webster who put you in orbit—pardon the pun."

"I didn't say that."

Unwilling to stand if there was a place to sit, or to sit if there was a place to lie down, Randy perched on the edge of Caroline's desk, stretching his lanky legs far out into the aisle. "This guy must be even better than he looks. Do you suppose you could give me a quick rundown on any particularly effective attributes I might adapt for myself?"

Caroline leaned back in her chair, ostensibly

giving his question careful consideration. "You might grow a mustache."

"You think a mustache will do it for me, huh?" He took a sip of coffee. "What else?"

"Develop a wacky way of looking at the world."

"No problem. I'm half there already."

"Refuse to get uptight about anything."

"That's me."

"Smile a lot."

"I'll have to work on that one. I'm a better frowner."

Caroline began gathering the clippings. "Is there anyone in particular you're honing your skills for?"

"I take it you haven't seen Cindy Hamelin, the new camera operator Bill hired? The tall, statuesque blonde with the peaches-and-cream complexion, legs that go all the way up to her hips, lips like rose petals and a waist hardly larger than the span of a man's hands? Caught a glimpse of her."

"More like ogled, I'd say. Did you get caught?"

Randy laughed. "With my tongue hanging down to my knees."

"It sounds like you're going to need more than a mustache and a course on how to smile. Take it from someone who's been there, Randy. The best way to handle a woman like Cindy is to be totally unintimidated by her appearance. When she's around, look at something else once in a while. Try to convince her that you can see, and that you actually *like*, what's underneath the fantastic covering."

"I don't know, Caroline. That sounds kinda hard. How about if I just lust after her body?"

Caroline laughed. "Sometimes that works, too." She slipped the clippings into an envelope. "Come on, let's get going. I can finish these in the van."

THE FIRST INTERVIEW was to be with one of the Rose Parade officials. When they arrived and found him still in a meeting, Caroline and Randy began rummaging around the headquarters building and the grounds, looking for anything that might make a human-interest story. The stately, cream-colored Tournament House, once the home of William Wrigley, Jr., of chewing-gum fame, was also a museum housing memorabilia from earlier parades.

Caroline wandered over to talk to one of the guards about the mansion's security. Out of the corner of her eye she saw Randy signal to her. She excused herself, crossing the expanse of lawn to the side of the house, where a young woman was playing with a puppy. The girl was strikingly beautiful, with shining ebony hair and lagoon-blue-green eyes. The puppy was a plump mass of curling black-and-white hair.

"Caroline," Randy said, "this is Tina Gregory. Tina, Caroline Travers." They shook hands. Randy turned to Caroline. "Tina is one of the princesses. She's been telling me what the experience has been like for her."

Caroline sensed Tina's withdrawal. It was one

thing to talk casually to a friendly cameraman, quite another to speak to a reporter. She prodded her memory for details about this year's queen and her court. "Tina Gregory...aren't you from Edgemont High School?"

An immediate smile came to the girl's face. "I'm a senior there."

"We have a reporter at KMTV whose son goes to Edgemont. I think his name is David...David Parker." Caroline laughed when she saw a flicker of dislike cross Tina's face. "He must be a chip off the old block. I'm not too crazy about his dad, either."

"I didn't mean—" There was alarm in Tina's voice.

"Don't worry. Your secret's safe," Caroline assured her.

This time it was Tina who laughed. "Oh, it's no secret. Everyone knows I think David is a nerd, and that he thinks I'm a snob."

"Sounds as if you two have all the ingredients for a romance."

"Oh, gag!" With that Tina gave up her carefully cultivated princess image.

"Would it be all right if we talked for a while?" Caroline asked.

"I guess so." Tina glanced nervously at Randy, who was preparing his camera to record the interview.

Caroline diverted her attention. "Tell me about the puppy."

"Her name's Rosy." She scooped the puppy up

in her arms, and it immediately began nipping at her chin. "My boyfriend gave her to me. He said she would help me remember this time in my life." She laughed. "Not that I'm likely to ever forget something like this."

"Have you been kept pretty busy?"

"It seems like it hasn't stopped since September, when the judging first started. This past month, there's been something scheduled every day."

"I'll bet it gets awfully tiring after a while."

"Not really. When I think about the nine hundred girls who tried out and didn't make it—well, I can imagine what they'd say if they heard me complain."

"What's been the most fun so far? Maybe something you didn't anticipate?"

Tina offered the puppy her finger to chew on to distract Rosy from the lace on the front of her blouse. "Unexpected? That would probably be all the professional people who came in to teach us about makeup and hairstyles and getting the clothes that are designed especially for us. Right from the first day it was made very clear to all of us that when we were chosen, we moved into a fishbowl, and that we were supposed to look our best at all times."

"And what's taken the most adjustment for you?"

Tina thought a moment, then smiled. "I guess my answer would be the same."

They talked for a few minutes more before

Caroline signaled Randy. When he was ready, they both thanked Tina and left her playing with her puppy.

Out of earshot, Randy asked, "Any ideas where you might use it?"

"How does just before the queen's float sound? I think it would humanize the whole thing a little."

"The puppy being there lent a nice touch."

"Yeah...it did."

"So what now?"

"We look for our tournament official, and then head out to the barn where the college kids are building their float."

"I thought they weren't allowing anyone near their creation, that only the tournament people had seen their plans and they wanted to keep it that way until the great unveiling."

"They decided to let the press in today with the proviso that nothing would be aired until judging tomorrow."

When Caroline and Randy went into Tournament House they were told that Thurmond Johnson was waiting for them. Once Randy had set up his lights in the oak-paneled room, Caroline began the interview.

"Mr. Johnson, I've decided I'd like to put a float in next year's parade. What do I do now?"

The meticulously outfitted man sitting across from her, dressed in the traditional white suit of the parade officials and looking as if he'd be perfectly at home at a lawn party, gave her a tolerant smile. "First of all, you would write to the tournament office requesting an entry packet. Should you decide you want to pursue your application, you would be asked a barrage of questions along the lines of who you are and why you want to enter the parade. I suppose I should add that there is a waiting list of over sixty applicants, and that someone must drop from the established parade lineup for someone new to be accepted.

"But let's say we can bypass all that and go on as if you'd been accepted. Your first step, after you've paid your promotion fee—$500 for a noncommercial applicant, 1,500 for a commercial one—would be to contact a professional float builder. This you would do approximately a year before the parade. The float builder will then submit plans for not only your approval, but the board's. Should everything progress smoothly to this point, actual work on the float would begin sometime in early spring."

"How much should I plan on spending?"

"Between $110,000 and $350,000."

"A third of a million dollars for a two-hour parade?"

Almost imperceptibly Thurmond Johnson straightened in his chair. "Ms Travers, this year we have bands visiting us from as far away as Australia. I can assure you the cost to bring them here is far greater than that of the most expensive float. Being a participant in a Rose Parade is an experience of a lifetime. The money is spent quite willingly."

Caroline forced a smile, reminding herself where she was and what she was doing there. This was the Tournament of Roses Parade, not a criminal investigation. "And I'm sure they consider their money well spent."

"Indeed. For the commercial builders, the goodwill promoted by being in the parade is incalculable. For the colleges that design and build their own floats each year—not to mention growing most of their own flowers—well, how can you put a price tag on pride? What more wholesome way can you imagine to send your message to 125 million people from Europe to Venezuela?"

Each person does his own thing, and in the process sometimes becomes blinded to any other way. Caroline had seen and heard it a hundred times. The fiery enthusiasm, the rhetoric. "Thank you for sharing that information with us, Mr. Johnson."

"Thank *you*, Ms Travers."

She had caught Randy by surprise, but he quickly recovered. When they were outside he turned to her. *"Thank you for sharing that information with us?"*

"It sounded that bad, huh?"

"Worse. It sounded like something Roger Parker would say."

"You could easily find yourself walking, Randy. Remember, I've got the keys to the van."

"I calls 'em as I sees 'em."

"A little judicious editing, and it will sound fine."

"In other words, you want me to lose the tape."

"No, don't do that. Most of it's fairly good stuff we might be able to use as filler."

CAROLINE AND RANDY took an hour and forty-five minutes to find the "barn" where the college students were building their float. After discarding their useless directions, they drove around looking for places large enough to accommodate such a project. If Caroline hadn't been especially fascinated by the idea of students building their own float, a float that would compete with those built by professionals, she would have headed back to the station after the first hour. Finally, only determination drove her on. When at last they located the building, they faced another challenge to get in. After unsuccessfully trying two doors, where even they couldn't hear their own knocking over the din of rock music, they finally succeeded at a third. A young man answered, wearing a T-shirt with the message, Petal Pusher.

"Hi. What can I do for you folks?"

Caroline identified herself and Randy. He checked their IDs carefully before letting them inside. Then he led them to a small waiting room and told them someone would be in shortly to give them a tour.

When the teenager had gone, Randy looked at Caroline. He shook his head in wonder. "He can't possibly think we're here to steal secrets at this late date."

"Who can understand the mysterious workings

of the mind of a college student? I'm just glad the only thing we have left for today is the 'street people' interviews.''

A girl with long blond hair who barely came up to the third button on Randy's shirt, dressed in jeans and a Petal Pusher T-shirt, joined them. "Hi. I'm Kathy Wilson. I understand you'd like a tour.''

Again Caroline introduced herself and Randy. "Perhaps it would be better if I asked you some questions in here first. The music might make voice pickup a little difficult out there.''

"Sure.'' She stuck her hands in her back pockets and rocked back on her heels. "Fire away.''

Caroline looked at Randy. "Ready?''

He smiled. "Fire away.''

"Kathy, can you give me a brief history of your school's participation in this year's parade?''

"As you probably know already, this is our first time. We wanted to be in the parade mainly because of the other college that participates....'' She grinned. "A college that shall remain nameless. Anyway, every year they walk away with an award, and every year people at our school grumble that they could have won if they'd entered. Well, two years ago a bunch of us got tired of listening to the grumbling and told everyone to put their time and energy where their mouths were. Ergo...our float.''

This didn't quite mesh with Thurmond Johnson's version of how to go about entering a float. The puzzled thoughts must have relayed themselves, because Kathy Wilson quickly added, "We were given special consideration and allowed to bypass some of the normal procedures. The board thought the rivalry between the two colleges would lend an added interest to the parade."

"Why all the secrecy, when the parade committee, the official programs and several newspapers already have a sketch of the float?"

Kathy laughed. "I think the cloak-and-dagger business got a little out of hand. In the beginning we just didn't want the other school to know what we were doing and how we were progressing. Like you said, to keep it up now does seem a little silly—but we do have one surprise left. No one except the officials is aware of who we have riding on the float."

"And when will that be announced?"

"Sometime tomorrow."

"Since I have to wait for the big news, how about giving me a few of the humdrum details behind all this—the cost and how you raised the funds, who designed the float, who's working on it—that kind of thing."

Kathy leaned against the wall. "The design came from a committee. Because it's animated, we needed engineering and electronics students as well as artists and architects. The money we also acquired by committee. We went into the community and asked for donations, and when we ran short, we went back again. It wound up costing about $15,000 more than we'd figured; that's when the alumni chipped in. But we'll be able to do it cheaper next year, because we'll already have the steel and the driving mechanism.''

"And the total cost?''

"Oh, yeah. The bottom line was $132,000. Of course all the help was volunteer—you have to be a full-time student to be involved with the float, and you have to keep your grades up. It wasn't too bad last spring, but carrying the load has been a killer this winter.''

"I assume, since that other college involved in the parade hasn't been quite as secretive, that you have an opinion about who might come out the winner?''

"We haven't actually seen our rival's float, but the information we've received makes us think we've got a good chance at an award.''

"What are you going to do when this is all over?''

"First comes a huge party, then a week in bed. Then it's starting work on next year's float.''

Caroline smiled. She didn't doubt the week Kathy planned to spend in bed; she looked exhausted. "Do you suppose we could see the float now?''

"Sure. Follow me.'' Kathy opened the door.

When word spread that there were television people present, the radios and tape decks were turned off. Caroline looked around and smiled. Had the music been switched off out of courtesy, or because the workers were collectively curious about the kind of coverage they would be getting? Probably a bit of both reasons.

Her gaze swept the room, taking in the smiling faces, the clutter, the seeming confusion and lastly the float. She could see very few places where flowers still needed to be applied; barring a catastrophe, the students were certain to be ready for the judging, now less than twenty-four hours away.

Peering past the obstacles, Caroline tried to get a clearer impression of the float. Finally, unable to understand it fully, she asked Kathy to tell her more. Kathy beamed with obvious pride. "Since the theme for this year's parade is explorers, we decided to use explorers of the future. We've sent an astronaut to Mars."

Caroline studied the portion of the float she could see. The Martian landscape, covered in craters, had been decorated with rust-colored chrysanthemums to depict the red planet's surface. Sticking out of the largest crater were two Martians, dressed in party finery. Toward the front of the float was a rocket ship, the top open, a chubby astronaut poking his head out.

Kathy directed Caroline's attention to the six-legged "dog" standing beside one of the cones, and to a strange-looking bird perched on the edge of one of the craters. "I really like the little touches we've added, but it's the hydraulics that make our float special. At the beginning of the show, all you see is the dog, the bird, the land-scape and the rocket landing. The rocket lowers about eight feet with blasts of carbon dioxide go-ing off all the time, looking like smoke. We had to get special clearance, because when the ship is up we're over the eighteen-foot height limitation.

"Anyway, when the ship lands the top opens. At precisely the same time that the astronaut begins to come out of his ship, the Martians come out of their home in the crater. They see each other, scream, throw their hands in the air, and then they all disappear again. In the final segment the ship blasts off."

Caroline smiled. If everything worked for the kids when the judges came, she had no doubt they would indeed be taking home a trophy.

LYING ON HIS STOMACH on scaffolding some thirty feet in the air, Mike looked up as the door opened. He had taken the time to note Kathy Wilson as she came through, then looked down again to place another carnation. Glancing away from his work a few minutes later, he caught his breath in surprise. Caroline now stood beside Kathy. Even half a float away and thirty feet below him, she looked stunning.

God. . . but she appealed to him. She was feisty, stubborn and standoffish, someone who must be carrying around and protecting a cache of hurts as though they were precious jewels. She was such a contradiction—one minute self-assured and boldly aggressive, as she had been when she'd kissed him at their first meeting; the next, timid to the point of shyness, as she had been when he'd put his arm around her at Disneyland.

She was all wrong for him—he needed a woman

who wanted to settle down. But every time Caroline stuck out her chin, or gave him back better than he'd given, she sparked a feeling in him close to the elation he used to feel while flying. No woman had ever done that before. He hadn't imagined that was even possible.

Flying jets, the navy jets that tore through the sky at 500 mph with ridiculous ease, had been like soaring in a constant high. Having it all disappear after coming so close to the ultimate flight had made Mike think he would never have that soaring sensation again. He had learned to live with the knowing, learned to go on...only feeling the loss when he happened to look skyward to a beckoning message written in a lingering jet trail. This woman had brought that incredible feeling back to him.

Mike took a puffy carnation out of the box and tossed it down. It landed behind Caroline. He tried again. This time it hit her shoulder. Startled, she looked around. Discovering nothing, she went back to talking to Kathy. The next time Mike took aim more carefully, and the yellow carnation landed on her notebook.

Caroline made a grab for the flower as it started to fall. She turned, her gaze sweeping the groups of workers nearby. When she saw someone looking up at Mike's perch, her eyes followed. She spotted him sitting on a wooden beam looking down at her.

He felt the smile she gave him all the way to his toes. The way her face radiated pleasure, the way she brought the flower to her mouth to let the petals caress her lips provoked a warm wave that washed through him. Gone was the fatigue, the product of eighteen-hour days spent helping to get the float ready.

As easily as a construction worker, Mike descended, landing beside Caroline. "We meet again," he said warmly.

Kathy Wilson looked from Mike to Caroline, alarm clearly written on her face. "You two know each other?"

Mike gave her a reassuring smile. "Caroline and I are old friends, Kathy. She won't give away our secret."

A puzzled look furrowed Caroline's forehead, then as quickly disappeared. "You're the surprise?"

"All six feet two inches of me."

"*This* is where you've been all week?"

"Here and at the dorm where we go periodically to crash." He looked down at his glue-encrusted jeans and Petal Pusher T-shirt. "No one told me you were coming."

He could have been covered in mud, and she still would have gloried in the sight of him. "Someone called the station this morning and said we could stop by. Since I'm out in the field today doing the parade, anyway, Sid sent me."

"How have you been?"

How simple his words, how complex the answer. Should she tell him how often he had entered her thoughts each day, her dreams each night? Warmth flushed her face as she remembered the dream she'd had just last night. "Busy. And you?" She looked down, concentrating on working the stem of the yellow carnation through her buttonhole. When the stem got stuck, Mike reached over to help her. Where their hands touched she felt as if he had caressed her.

"We've been working round-the-clock shifts to get the float finished on time." Suddenly it seemed there were only the two of them, standing alone in sharp focus, their surroundings fading into a soft blur.

"How did you—"

Kathy chimed in, "I asked him," and reality returned.

"Kathy's father is a friend of mine," Mike said, making a final, unneeded adjustment to the flower.

"He's an engineer for NASA." There was an unmistakable note of pride in Kathy's voice.

Caroline looked around the room at the dozens of float workers surrounded by boxes and buckets and huge sprays of flowers. "I didn't know the person who rode on the float also constructed it."

Mike followed her gaze. "When I asked if they needed any help, they told me they could use all they could get. *At the time* I figured the week between Christmas and New Year was usually so uneventful that I might as well be doing something worthwhile."

Randy came up to stand beside them, his camera ready for shooting. "How ya doing, Mr. Webster?" he said, extending his hand.

"Not bad, Randy. And make it Mike, please. At least I've kept my foot where it's supposed to be since the last time we met."

Randy laughed. "I wish I could say the same." He turned to Caroline. "We're running kinda late, boss lady."

Caroline glanced at Mike. "It seems duty calls," she said softly, then turned back to Randy. "Where do you want me?"

"How about over there—" He indicated the back of the float. "I'll use the crater with the bird on it for backdrop." After Caroline was in place, Randy directed Kathy to where he wanted her to stand before he turned the camera on Caroline for the intro.

Once she had told the when, where, why and who of the story, she walked over to Kathy. "Kathy, I understand all the flowers for this float were grown on campus."

"Almost all of them. There were a few things we didn't know we'd need, and the orchids we've used require a greenhouse to grow. They, the orchids, that is, were all donated by an alumnus who lives in Hawaii. He even had them flown over for us at his own expense."

Caroline looked up to the Martian lady in her finery and saw that her blouse was made of white cattleya orchids—white with a touch of yellow at the throat. One mystery solved. "What were some of the things you had to buy?"

"Onions—we used those for the Martian lady's pearl necklace. And to get the proper look and feel on the faces, we had to buy gallons of ground spices. Cherry tomatoes spell out USA on the side of the spaceship, and the letters are outlined in dried beans.''

"Did you have help from any of the professional float builders? Words of advice or anything like that?''

Kathy looked surprised. ''We never thought to ask anyone. Our research was all done after last year's parade when the floats were parked around the high school. We took seven rolls of pictures and a folderful of notes.''

"Is there one particular award you're shooting for?''

"There are two possibilities. The Isabella Coleman Trophy for most whimsical and the Animation Trophy for . . . well, animation.''

"Can you tell me something about the person you've selected to ride on the float?''

Kathy rolled her eyes. ''He's handsome. He's exciting, and he's just about the neatest guy I've ever met. Real friendly and all. A super person.''

Out of the corner of her eye Caroline could see Mike shift uncomfortably from one foot to the other. She knew she wouldn't get Mike's name from Kathy, but asking was almost obligatory. And besides, what good was a mystery if no one whipped up any interest?

An impish smile curved Kathy's mouth. ''But that's all you'll get from me until parade morning.''

"Well, maybe this is something you can tell me. Who's going to be driving the float?''

"Ed Patterson—he's our mechanical genius. He's the one who tore the truck apart and put the parts back together to make it fit under the float. He's also responsible for the hydraulics we're using for the people and the space ship. Ed even set up the bottles of carbon dioxide that go off when the ship is landing and taking off."

This interview, combined with the one they'd done a few minutes earlier with Kathy, would provide Caroline with enough material for her piece. She put her free hand behind her back, her wrap-up cue to Randy, thanked Kathy and did a short sign-off. As she handed the microphone to Randy, she asked, "How long do you think you'll be?"

"Twenty minutes, maybe a little more. I want to get some footage of the workers and try for an uncluttered shot of the float."

"See if you can get one of the driver, too."

"Gotcha."

Caroline turned to Mike. "Could we find a cup of coffee somewhere?"

He was watching her with an intensity that made her feel she was the spy and he the government agent.

He took her arm. "*Coffee* was not what I had in mind," he said, his voice low so that only she could hear. He motioned to Kathy. "If Randy Kavanaugh should ask where we are, tell him we'll be right back."

Mike guided Caroline out and around to the sheltered side of the building. Stopping, he placed his hands on her shoulders and turned her to face him.

"I'm going to do something I've been aching to do since the minute you walked into that room." He kissed her. Longingly, deeply, thoroughly, he kissed her. His mouth met hers with a wild and wonderful passion, unbridled, naked.

Caroline forgot about the things that should have bothered her—wrinkling her suit, ruining her makeup, Randy. She forgot everything about her job as heat swept through her, burning her loins, making her breasts ache. Her heartbeat pounded in her ears; a yearning gripped her with the force of an avalanche, burying all practicalities with its awesome force. If he had asked, she would have made love to him then and there. She couldn't remember ever having felt such hunger for a man. Nor could she remember ever being so completely and unabashedly wanted in return.

When Caroline responded in kind, Mike's control suffered a near fatal blow. Primitive urges stirred inside him, telling him to gather her in his arms and flee to a quiet, sheltered place where they could finish what they had naively started. Here they were taking such foolish chances that someone might see them. Her professional reputation...his. Reluctantly, with great effort, he broke the kiss and pulled back from her. For long seconds they stared at each other, stunned by their own passion.

Finally, determined to break the silence, Caroline smiled nervously and said, "I hope you don't think I kiss all the guys like that."

It was meant to be humorous, a light remark to

make their descent into the real world easier, but
as soon as she said the words a picture flashed into
Mike's mind. Again he saw the only full cupboard
in Caroline's apartment, the one filled with flower
vases. She didn't have to tell him what had passed
between them was new to her, too; he knew they
had shared something unique. Still, the thought of
her with another man made him unreasonably
jealous. Jealousy? Was that really what he felt? It,
too, was a new feeling—one he didn't care for.

Mike reached up to run his hand along her
shoulder. Slowly, lovingly he touched her neck;
his thumb softly caressed her jaw. "I don't think
you've ever kissed anyone like that before," he
said. "I never have."

A warning bell went off in Caroline's mind.
"Mike, surely you don't believe I've lead a
celibate life." Never to date just one man at a time
was one of her most important rules. Relationships were demanding, and they took more from
her than they could ever return. Besides, the investment of time and emotion was more than she
wanted to give. She could go on seeing Mike only
if he knew and agreed to this. "We have to come
to an understanding before this goes any further. I
will not make any commitments to you—not even
a small one. My life will go on essentially as it has.
I think we should recognize what is happening between us for what it is." Her gaze fell to the printing on his T-shirt, but all she saw were fuzzy blue
letters. "We are physically attracted to each
other—that's all."

Mike watched her closely as she gave her little speech. He was certain she was unaware of the slight trembling of her lower lip as she spoke, a trembling that told him far more than her words. What in the hell had happened to her to make her want to live in isolation? He pulled her to him, softly pressing his lips against her forehead. "All right. We'll play the game by your rules." *But in the end, Caroline, I'll still be the one who winds up the winner.*

She tried to convince herself that the feeling sweeping over her was relief. "Thank you for understanding—"

"I didn't say I understood. But I want to go on seeing you. If the only way I can do that is to affect your life as little as possible, then that's the way it will have to be."

"I know it sounds—"

"Caroline, you don't have to explain. At least not now. Let's save it for a day when we've nothing better to do than get drunk and share maudlin secrets from our past." He felt her stiffen.

"My past has nothing to do with how I feel. It's my future I'm concerned about. Ties, no matter how loose the tether, wouldn't give me the freedom to go where I want to go."

He looked down at her, staring deeply into her expressive brown eyes. "I wonder if you haven't said that so many times that you've finally come to believe it yourself."

She drew away from him. "When you feel it absolutely necessary to tread on someone's aspirations, you might find it to your advantage not to wear hobnailed boots.'' She turned and started to leave.

"Caroline—'' he caught her arm ''—I'm sorry. I was out of line.'' Reaching into his pocket, he withdrew a nickel. Handing her the coin, he also gave her a coaxing smile. "I'm returning my psychiatric fee.''

She took the nickel. "Unless I should happen to give this back to you someday, promise you won't try to psychoanalyze me again. It's a waste of energy, anyway. I'm exactly as you see me, nothing deep, dark or mysterious.''

"And I very much like what I see.'' Mike slipped his arm around her shoulders, and they walked back inside together.

CHAPTER SIX

CAROLINE BEGAN WORK on parade day before the sun was a faint glimmer in the sky. It was cold; however, the sky was clear and the weatherman had promised a high of eighty-five degrees today. The good weather was only a bonus for the people on the floats and in the stands—if a raging storm had been predicted, the parade would still have gone on. Only when New Year's Day fell on a Sunday was the routine in any way changed; the parade was moved to Monday, a habit adopted in 1893 in deference to the many churches located on Colorado Boulevard.

KMTV's media booth faced Orange Grove Boulevard, with the camera set up across the street to catch the floats as they made the big swing onto Colorado. The small wooden structure where Caroline would spend her morning sequestered with Roger Harper was located above the top row of bleachers. Although the show was a far cry from the reporting jobs she hoped to have one day, she enjoyed the special challenges it presented. It was live, and because it was live, anything could happen. There were almost always delays, usually caused by floats breaking down along the parade route. Since tournament policy determined that every float be allowed to finish the parade, delays could stretch into several minutes or more while a tow truck was summoned to pull a float. These awkward times had to be filled smoothly as if they were a planned part of the show.

Caroline had learned that one year a float not only broke down, it caught fire and completely burned before passing the judge's stand. During such unplanned pauses good reporting skills were mandatory. Good reporting skills and solid preparation. When the time frame became too long to fill with ad libs, she would use the human-interest pieces she and Randy had been putting together over the past week.

On her way to the booth that morning, practically in the dead of night, she had been surprised by the number of spectators already lining the streets. The crowd had tripled since Caroline and Randy's shooting sequence two nights before. Sleeping bags carpeted the sidewalks; old couches, later to be abandoned, enjoyed status as front-row seats; fires burned in oil drums, keeping those huddled around them temporarily warm.

Banners were strung from trees and campers parked on side streets, proclaiming allegiance to one or the other college football team playing later in the day at the Rose Bowl. Soon the hearty parade enthusiasts would be joined by those less willing to sacrifice a night's sleep for a good view, and by those fortunate enough to have reserved seats on bleachers lining the parade route in every conceivable location, including the insides of buildings with windows large enough for viewing. By the time the festivities began, at exactly 8:20 A.M., the route would be lined with one million people. Add to that another 125 million watching on television, and it was apparent that in every way possible, the Tournament of Roses Parade had become a big-time operation.

Settling into her chair, Caroline began going over the notes she had made on each of the bands, equestrian groups and floats. Coming to the fifty-ninth entry, she stopped reading. She had spent several sleepless hours during the past two nights trying to decide whether it was the best thing for her to see Michael Webster again. Every time she came to the conclusion that she would see him, but on her own terms, an inner voice challenged her, telling her she was afraid to put herself to a real test—that she was taking the coward's way out. It wasn't until the early hours of the morning that she would finally admit her inner voice was right—she was afraid of Michael Webster. Yet in the bright light of day, her fears seemed groundless. Still, she hadn't been able to come to a decision.

She looked up to see Roger Harper climb into the booth carrying a sheaf of papers. "I have the judging results, if you're interested."

Roger Harper was fifty but looked thirty-five. He dyed his hair, submitted to periodic "lifts" and "tucks" and worked out daily at a health club only used by people already in shape. He believed the public decided the worth and talent of a reporter, and therefore, because of his high popularity, was convinced he was the best. Caroline had known at least one person like him at every television station where she'd worked.

Caroline held out her hand. "I assume you brought me a copy?"

"I didn't think we would need more than one," he said, handing that one to her. He gave her a lascivious smile. "I keep telling you life is too short not to share. One shouldn't keep things all to oneself—especially if the things they're keeping happen to be such spectacular specimens." Purposely his gaze swept over her, settling on her breasts.

"Well, one thing a chauvinist should keep to himself is his innuendo, especially when it's not a spectacular specimen of wit!" Giving him a disgusted look, Caroline turned her back and began reading. It was going to be a long day.

Finding the judges' sheet, she quickly scanned the list of eighteen awards, looking for SCR University. There it was! They had won the Animation Trophy. She could just imagine how that barnful of kids had reacted to the news. The thought brought a smile. There would be some earnest celebrating at tonight's party.

As always before a broadcast, time seemed to vanish. KMTV was on countdown, then on the air. The intro went smoothly—a brief history of the parade, a few anecdotes about the people involved—and then the coverage began. Roger was to take the lead.

"Here they come, ladies and gentlemen, boys and girls. I can see Old Glory waving in the air now. By the way, an interesting little fact I learned just before air time about the Boy Scouts who are carrying the flags this year—these fellows were created especially for the Tournament of Roses Parade."

Caroline mentally let out a scream. *Created especially for the parade? In someone's back room? Were the boys going to be dismantled after they'd marched their 5.5 miles and saved for next year?* Smiling into the camera, Caroline tried to cover for her colleague. "That's right, Roger. I understand these young men are from troops located all over Southern California, and that this is their first time marching together as a unit." It was going to be a very, very long day.

As the parade progressed, Caroline found herself constantly glancing down Orange Grove Boulevard. When at last she caught sight of the tip of the spaceship, her heart lurched. She felt a tightening behind her eyes that indicated she was one step away from misty vision. Her wide streak of sentimentality, her tendency to support the underdog—no matter the odds—her belief in the "little" man doing something monumental were traits few knew she had. Because most of her acquaintances over the past few years thought such feelings unsophisticated, she had kept them hidden rather than have to constantly defend herself or put up with teasing.

But today, for just a moment, she allowed herself a swell of vicarious pleasure when she thought of the odds those college kids had beaten and the euphoria they must rightfully be feeling. Briefly she wondered how the people who had spent small fortunes to hire a professional float builder, and hadn't won awards, felt. She hoped they wished the upstarts well, at least for this year.

At last entry number fifty-nine was in front of the reviewing stand and ready to put on its show. Caroline breathed a quiet sigh of relief when everything went without a hitch. The dog wagged his tail and turned his head, the bird flapped its four wings, the rocket landed in a puff of smoke. When the astronaut popped out of his capsule and the Martians out of their home, and when all three threw up their hands and screamed, the appreciative audience laughed and broke into spontaneous applause.

While Caroline could see every detail, it was the lone figure standing on the back of the float that she zeroed in on. As she watched Mike's gaze swung up to meet hers. Even across the distance separating them, the chemistry was so strong it made the crowds, the noise, the confusion around them disappear. When the float began to move again he waved to her. The smile he flashed was a silent message, as intimate as a touch.

An hour later, after the final float had gone by, a new parade immediately began. Haphazardly organized clusters of people, carrying banners and homemade signs espousing a dozen causes, shouted slogans and warnings about the earth's imminent demise. For the most part they were ignored as the spectators calmly went about the business of packing up to leave.

Caroline was amazed at how quickly the streets cleared of all but a few stragglers, and stunned to see the amount of garbage left behind. As usual, after participating in something that required her to be constantly keyed up, she was having trouble coming back down. Once the excitement had worn off she would be exhausted; right now she needed something to do.

Spotting Randy, she went over to him. "You want to go to lunch?"

He grinned. "Can't, boss lady. I've got a hot date for this afternoon."

"It wouldn't happen to be with Cindy, would it?" She had seen him talking to the woman earlier that day.

"She's consented to let me go jogging with her. She has her own special trail—five miles long."

"Five miles!"

"She runs it every day, rain or shine. Says it's the only way she can keep in shape. Otherwise she'd never be able to lug around all the gear we have to in this job."

"I didn't know you were a jogger."

"I'm not."

"And you're—"

"Hey, look, I figure it this way—I'm young, healthy, reasonably in shape. How hard can it be?"

"Are you serious? It's damn hard."

"Aw, if she can do it, I can."

Caroline slowly shook her head, biting back a skeptical smile. "I'll look forward to hearing the details tomorrow."

Randy gave her a wink. "Censored, of course."

"Oh, by all means. I'm not sure my aging heart could stand to hear *all* the details." She waved goodbye and started walking down Orange Grove Boulevard, turning to wish him good luck. To herself she added, *you'll need it*.

Although she had agreed to spend the afternoon with Mike, they hadn't made arrangements to meet anywhere. She was confident that if she wasn't at the booth when he came looking for her, he would try her apartment. And if he didn't—they would just miss each other, that's all. The thought didn't rest as easily as she pretended it did.

First thing when she arrived home, she headed for the kitchen to get something to eat. She couldn't remember her last full meal. Other than a few staples—flour, sugar, salt, pepper—she had a container of yogurt a week older than the date stamped on the bottom, a wilted carrot, party crackers that had gone stale and a fried-chicken TV dinner. She settled for the TV dinner.

While waiting for it to bake, Caroline changed clothes—three times. She went from overdressed to too casual to somewhere in between. She ended up with slacks, a long-sleeved blouse and a sweater vest. The timer on the stove went off just as the doorbell rang. She went to the door.

Standing on the step was Mike, almost hidden by a huge spray of flowers. "They're from the grand marshall's car," he said, peering between two triangles of fern. "Aren't they beautiful?"

Despite herself Caroline laughed. "They're magnificent." She stepped out of the doorway. "How did you manage—"

As he passed he gave her a quick kiss. "Charm...pure charm." He placed the spray on the table. It covered the surface in a mounded profusion of green and white, draping down the sides, almost touching the floor. He looked at Caroline, who stood with her hand on her hip, her elbow leaning on the wall, staring at him. He shrugged. "I couldn't stand to see them go to waste."

She nodded slowly as if in agreement. "I can understand that...now should anyone I know happen to die in the next few days, I'll be able to send them one hell of a floral tribute."

"Ah, Caroline, my love. There are times when one must look beyond the obvious. Dismantled, there are enough mums, carnations and roses to brighten every room in your—" He gave her a puzzled frown. "What's that buzzing?"

"Oh, my God. I forgot my chicken." Caroline rushed into the kitchen.

Mike followed. He watched her as she grabbed a dish towel, folded it twice, then reached inside the oven. By the time she made it to the counter and let go of the aluminum tray, she had burned her fingers. She swore and brought the throbbing tips up to her mouth to blow on them. When that didn't help, she went over to the sink and stuck them under cold running water.

"We're eating out, I take it," Mike said.

"You only said we would see each other this afternoon." Mike noticed her chin raise a quarter of an inch, a sure sign that she was on the defensive. "You said nothing about food." Realizing she had come on stronger than she had intended, she added, "Do you want to join me?"

He gave her a warm smile. "You're willing to share your TV dinner with me? I'm impressed. You must like me a whole lot." He crossed the room to her, took her hand from the water and brought it to his lips, where he gently blew air across her fingers.

The gesture caught Caroline by surprise, and it took her several seconds to respond. She pulled her hand away, grabbed the towel and concentrated on drying the water that had dripped down her arm. "It feels better," she offered by way of explanation.

Leaning against the counter, Mike reached for her. He brought her to him so that she stood between his outstretched legs. "Are we to start over from square one every time we get together?"

Caroline resisted him, trying to keep her thighs from pressing into his. "I don't understand what you mean."

"How long are you going to hold me at arm's length? You make me feel like a blind date you've been coerced into going out with."

She pulled away from him and stepped back a

few paces. "What did you expect? Did you think just because we happened to share a couple of kisses, I would greet you at the door today with open arms?"

"It would have been nice—but no, that's not what I expected or even what I'm talking about. It's the mental barrier I have to hurdle every time we're together that's driving me crazy. Can't we at least pick up where we left off last week? If you recall, by the time I brought you home, you were actually letting me hold your hand without that look of panic in your eyes." He shoved his own hands in his pockets. "I don't understand, Caroline. For someone who professes such sophistication where men are concerned, you act as if I'm your first date. You can't possibly think I'm going to attack you."

"Frankly, I'm never sure just what you might do next."

He met her gaze, staring at her so intently she couldn't look away. "You don't believe that," he said softly.

She caught her breath, then let it out in a deep sigh. "No...I don't believe you would ever do anything I didn't want you to do."

"Come here, Caroline," he gently coaxed.

She hesitated.

"Please...."

She moved over to stand in front of him, careful that their legs didn't meet. He reached for her hands, bringing them to his shoulders. He put his own hands on her waist. "Kiss me, Caroline."

Again she hesitated.

"Nothing fancy... just a simple kiss."

Slowly she came forward, unavoidably making contact with his legs as she did so. Tentatively she touched her lips to his, feeling him respond only to the pressure she applied. It would be up to her if the kiss were to deepen. Did she want it to, or did she simply want to get past the awkwardness of the moment so that they could get on with their day?

Caroline pulled back and looked at him. "Hi..." he said softly.

She smiled. "Hi, yourself."

"Are you ready to go out and get something to eat? I'm starving."

"Does that mean you're turning down my offer of a chicken dinner? How ungallant."

"Not at all. I'm just wondering what you would eat."

"Have no fear, Webster. I'd get my share." She kissed him lightly on the end of his nose. "Wait right here. I'll get my purse." As soon as Caroline reached the doorway she saw the spray. "The flowers... we have to do something with the flowers. They'll never make it if we wait until we get back."

"I'll bring the vases," Mike said, his tone implying that he'd been struck by inspiration.

Equipped with vases lined up on the shelf and scissors and knives for them both, they began disassembling the flowers and greenery from the wet florists' foam. They made stacks of pompom mums, carnations, roses and baby's breath.

Caroline brought a carnation to her nose. "My mother used to grow these. They weren't nearly as big, but hers had the most wonderful smell. Kind of spicy." Caroline stopped a minute to stare out the window. "I remember my Aunt Cordelia wore a perfume called Blue Carnation. My father said she smelled as if she had a perpetual toothache."

Caroline sniffed a perfect white rosebud. She glanced at Mike. "Nothing."

"I suppose that in order to reach the stage of perfection these flowers have, it's not surprising that they've lost something along the way." He scratched the tip of his chin with the stem of a mum. "I've heard it can happen to people, too."

Caroline chose to ignore the parallel. "Did your mother have a flower garden?" she asked.

"She told me she started one a couple of times, but she was never around long enough to see the results of all her work. New orders would come in before blooming season, and she would have to leave her labor for someone else to enjoy."

"That must be a hard life—being constantly uprooted, losing your friends, learning about new neighborhoods over and over again."

Mike stared at her. "You should know how hard it is. Six stations in five years couldn't have been easy."

"It's different with me. It's only me; there are no kids or pets or anything that would make the move as difficult as what your mother faced."

"Her comment to that when any of us would

complain was that we were lucky because we had one another.''

Caroline turned back to her task of adding ferns to a vase filled with roses. She would have to agree; when she had had someone to share the journey with, even if only in spirit, it had indeed seemed easier. Until she'd discovered one day that she'd been making the journey alone all along.

Working together like seasoned veterans of the florist trade, they had seven vases brimming with flowers and greenery in little more than half an hour. When Caroline suggested they save the last of the spray for her own funeral, which was imminent because of her impending starvation, Mike went into the kitchen and returned with a piece of the pathetic-looking chicken. He fed it to her in morsels he took off the bone with his hands. By the time they had left for the restaurant, they had recaptured the warm and familiar mood they'd shared at Disneyland.

After a long leisurely lunch that was really an early dinner, they headed to the party, which was in full swing. As soon as Mike opened the door to the barn, now surprisingly large and spacious without the float, a chorus of cheers went up. Before they could move Mike and Caroline had been handed glasses of beer and ordered to ''drink up.''

Music and laughter and shouts of unbridled exuberance rose to a level only slightly less deafening than the roar of a jet engine. There were tears and smiles, hugs and horseplay. And there were toasts to the winners. Mysteriously, each time Caroline thought her glass empty she found it full. When she began to feel light-headed and tried to put her beer aside, another toast would be proposed and another glass found.

Because Caroline was essentially an outsider, she was able to view the goings-on with objectivity. She could observe Mike and his interaction with others. He was open and friendly with everyone; never once did she detect the slightest hint that his goodwill was faked. And the outpouring of affection that came his way, the easy banter always tendered with respect and just a touch of awe let her know he was considered "one of the guys," albeit a very special one.

Beautiful young women who came up to Mike with challenging eyes and meaningful swaggers to their walks were treated with an amused smile and a kind tolerance. Whereas Caroline, by his side throughout the evening, was conscious of being treated with particular deference.

Mike was discussing the advisability of using humor on next year's float with Kathy Wilson and several other designers, when he caught Caroline trying to stifle a yawn. He leaned over so that his cheek brushed the top of her head. "Sleepy?"

"No, I'm doing fine," she lied.

"Having a good time?"

"Yes, I am," she said with a smile. "Thank you for asking me to come with you."

"Anytime." His lips pressed against her hair. He turned back to Kathy. "Do you suppose there's some way to quiet this group enough for me to say a few things before I leave?''

"No problem." Placing two fingers in her mouth, she whistled shrilly, bringing almost instantaneous silence from the crowd. Once the music had also stopped, Mike jumped up on a table and motioned for everyone to come closer.

"Before I leave, I want all of you to know that I've had more fun working with you on this float than I've had since I was eleven years old and leaped into Horvath Canyon with eighty helium balloons tied to my waist. I was honored when you chose me, and I was doubly honored today when I rode on one of only eighteen award-winning floats." He waited for the cheers to die down. "Thanks again—for the good times, for the good friends I've made and for one hell of a memory." He waved and vaulted from the table, carefully landing on his left foot.

They could still hear the cheering as they made their way through the crowded parking lot. The car Mike had rented this trip was a midsized model with a bench seat in front. After he'd opened Caroline's door, he was startled to see her slide across so that she would be sitting very close to him. Startled, but not displeased. When he was behind the wheel Caroline reached for his arm.

"Mike, there's something I have to tell you."

Several seconds passed and the silence only became more pronounced, so he prodded her. "And?"

"I'm trying to think of a proper way to say what

I want to say." She spoke slowly, taking time to form each word. Laying her head against his shoulder, she sighed deeply. "I'm not absolutely sure about this, because it's never happened before—but I think I'm drunk!"

An amused smile lighted his eyes. He wasn't surprised. He had watched her consume beer with the best of them that night. "You want to tell me the symptoms?"

"My legs...feel funny, kind of tingly. My tongue seems to have enlarged...and when I close my eyes, everything starts going around faster and faster." She giggled. "It would be absolutely perfect if I wanted to dream about whirlpools."

His smile broadened. "Well, my dear, I would say with those symptoms there's little doubt you have the disease—despite your remarkable control."

So much for control, she thought. Now that she was away from the party, she seemed to have forgotten how to pretend to be sober. "What about you?" she mumbled.

"Not even light-headed."

"Good." She gave him a satisfied grin. "I was afraid I might have to call us a cab, or that we would have to walk home." Once again she nestled her cheek into his arm.

When they were out on the main road Mike said, "Let me know when you begin to feel like everything is spinning too fast." He waited for her reply. "Caroline?" Still nothing. She had fallen fast asleep.

THE NEXT MORNING a shaft of sunlight fell across Caroline's eyes, making her groan in pain and roll over in bed. Her headache wouldn't go away. Maybe if she stayed perfectly still...maybe if she moved just a little.... Maybe if she got up and shoved her head in the oven.

She tried to lick her lips. Her tongue all but stuck to them. Maybe if she opened her eyes.... Ow... could she possibly function all day with her eyes closed? She had no doubts about the source of her discomfort; she had heard enough tales about the mornings after from seasoned veterans. Intoxication had set in so fast. And with so few.... She tried to tally the beers she remembered drinking. She groaned again.

Maybe if she stayed in bed all day—she couldn't. She had to go to the bathroom. Carefully she plotted the route, counting the steps, trying to estimate the seconds the trip would take. When she could wait no longer, she began.

Coming out of the bathroom, she leaned against the door. Aspirins. That's what she needed. Kitchen. She must work her way to the kitchen. To avoid jarring her now throbbing head, Caroline didn't walk, she shuffled.

She was about to make the turn into the kitchen when she stopped. Something wasn't right. She faced the living room again. A small, blanket-covered mound protruded over the arm of the couch. Since the back of the couch was toward her, she couldn't see anything else without going into the living room. Curiosity won out over pain.

Mike Webster had made a bed on her couch. Made a bed, and obviously slept in it.

He opened his eyes. They were filled with amusement mixed with concern. "How are you doing?" he asked, his voice purposely soft.

She winced. "Were we in a wreck on the way home last night?"

"That bad, huh?"

"Worse." She reached up to rub her temples.

"I've heard of a hundred cures, but not one that really works. Do you have any aspirin? We could start there."

"I was on my way to the kitchen...." She stopped rubbing her head. "Uh...what are you doing here?"

"I stayed because drunks have been known to get sick in the middle of the night. I thought you might need someone to hold your head just in case."

She tried to concentrate. "I don't remember getting sick...but then, I don't remember anything at all after we left the party."

"That's because you passed out."

She groaned. It was getting to be a habit. She looked down at her rumpled clothes and ran her hand over her hair. A tiny smile touched her lips. "Well, now that you've seen me at my best, what do you think?"

Mike propped himself up on his elbow. The blanket fell to his waist, revealing that, unlike Caroline, he hadn't slept in his clothes. He reached up to gently touch her cheek. "If this is

the worst you've got to offer, kid, I'm sold."
Wrapping the blanket around his waist, he came
around the couch to stand beside her. "Let's work
on making you glad you're going to live through
all this."

After getting her aspirins and a cup of strong
herbal tea, Mike dressed. He checked the refrigerator and a few cupboards. "Don't you ever
eat?"

She looked up from the steaming mug. "I go
out a lot. Grocery stores intimidate me—all those
ingredients that I have no idea how to put together."

"No wonder you're so thin."

She gave him a wounded look.

"Beautiful. . . but still thin."

"You mean, in spite of."

"I mean in spite of, in addition to, besides,
moreover and also." He leaned over to kiss the
top of her head. "I'm going to leave you now. I'll
be back in about an hour. If you can make it that
far, a shower might help your spirits. I can't guarantee it will do much for your head."

"Mike?"

"Hmm?"

"Thanks. . . ."

"You're welcome." He went to the door.

"Mike?"

"Yes?"

"Take my keys. I'm not sure I could live
through the sound of the doorbell."

CHAPTER SEVEN

AFTER MIKE LEFT Caroline, he went to his hotel and cleaned up before going to the store. When he arrived back at Caroline's apartment she met him in the hallway, wearing her tailored satin robe and drying her hair with a fluffy yellow towel. "Welcome back to the world of the living," he said.

"It was touch and go there for a while." She reached out to take one of the three bags Mike carried, then followed him into the kitchen. The bags on the counter, Mike turned to Caroline and looked at her. He let his gaze take in the length of her in leisurely perusal. "You really are beautiful," he said simply. "Makeup and clothes do so much for some people—you don't need either."

She gave him a suspicious frown. "I hope you're not suggesting—"

"Aw, Caroline...you've just shot me with another one of your poison-tipped arrows. Stop thinking I have ulterior motives for everything I do or say. Take my compliment at face value; forget double or hidden meanings. I said what I did because your job requires you to wear heavy makeup—I always thought it was the makeup that made your eyes seem so full of mystery and mischief. Now that I see you au naturel, I realize the shadows and liners hide more than they reveal. Did you know there are times when your eyes say things radically different from your words? It seems they're the one part of your body you haven't learned to keep under tight control."

She crossed her arms over her chest. "Are you through? This is getting embarrassing."

"No, as a matter of fact, I'm not through. Now that I'm at it, I want to say something about your body. I've never known anyone who looked as good as you do who fights so hard to hide it. I haven't seen all your clothes, but from what I have seen, I've come to the conclusion that you've either lost twenty pounds in the past few months, or you purposely buy everything at least a size too large. Why?"

Caroline felt herself reach the point just below boiling without even the preliminary simmer. Mike was intruding where he had no right. "For some insane reason, even though it is absolutely none of your business, I'm going to answer you. Do you have any idea—can you even begin to imagine—what it's like to go through puberty and suddenly have boys—and men—look at your chest instead of your face when they hold a conversation? What should be as natural and inconsequential a part of my anatomy as my arm or my leg too often elicits crude remarks in public from people who think themselves immensely clever. Now I suppose if what I wanted to do for a living was to enter wet T-shirt contests, or mud wrestle, I'd have it made. But being full-breasted can be a hell of a problem when you're trying to do your job, which both you and your employer take very seriously, and you can't get the man you're interviewing to look you in the face.'' Having blown off some steam, she felt she could breathe more freely than she had in a long time.

A conspiratorial smile warmed Mike's eyes. "Do you suppose," he said softly, "having someone say to you that sex sells everything nowadays, so why not the space program, would produce a similar feeling?"

Caroline winced and closed her eyes. Forcing herself to meet his gaze again, she said, "I really did say that, didn't I? Well, you have me on that one, Webster. There's not one thing I can say in my defense. It was a cheap shot."

He turned back to the grocery bags. "No, it wasn't. You were simply returning the fire that had been directed your way earlier that morning."

He was right about that, but she was being unfair to him in another way. She had made him the target of anger that had festered in her for years. Despite his conversation with Captain Brown, he was one of the few men she had ever dated who hadn't made her feel she was chest first, person second.

Mike tugged on her sleeve. "Tell me where this stuff goes," he said, indicating the groceries, giving her a graceful way out of the corner she had backed herself into.

I like you, Michael Webster. She gave him a

smile that she hoped told him as much. Forcing herself to concentrate on the practical, she said, "All this can't possibly be breakfast."

"I got a little carried away," he admitted sheepishly.

"A little?"

She started going through the bags, stopping to pull out a box of cereal. She looked up in disbelief. *"Chubby Chocolate Bears?"*

He shrugged. "They're fattening. I checked all the cereals, and Chubby Chocolate Bears had the highest percentage of sugar. Damn near one hundred. There are, of course, added minerals and vitamins to make sure you get a good dose of nutrition with your white death."

"Ugh! I can think of a lot more pleasant ways to gain weight."

"Name three."

She considered a minute, reaching up to fluff her hair. The motion drew her satin robe tautly across her breasts, clearly defining them. "Cheesecake for one...." Her hands continued to brush through her hair. "French fries, for another—"

"Caroline..." Mike interrupted, his voice almost stern.

"Don't you want to hear the third?"

"I want you to get dressed." He was suddenly very serious.

She was so surprised at the abrupt change of topic that she simply stood and stared at him. "Why?" As soon as she asked the question, she knew the answer. She saw it in his eyes. Looking down at her robe, she realized it had worked loose from the belt and now hung provocatively open. A nervous smile twitched at the corners of her mouth. She pulled the wide V closed and readjusted the belt. "I've never entertained in this robe before," she said, trying humor to ease the tension that had so quickly come between them.

He walked over to her, reaching up to tuck a curl behind her ear. "Caroline," he said huskily, "either leave right now, or...."

"Or what?" she breathed.

"Or... I will take you in my arms and hold you to me so that I can feel the heat of your body against mine." He touched her cheek. "And then I will kiss you... slowly, thoroughly, tenderly, but without restraint this time." His hand moved to cup the downy flesh at the nape of her neck. "I will touch the curve of your hips... the roundness of your buttocks... the flat of your stomach." His thumb gently stroked the side of her neck. "And I will touch your breasts because they are part of you, a uniquely feminine and beautiful part. I will learn their feel... as I will learn the feel of your thighs, your knees, your elbows... first with my hands and then with my lips."

Even as he spoke, her arms left her sides. She reached up to place them around his neck. No longer able to deny the ache, the longing that they had created in each other, they began what had been destined from their first meeting. He lowered his head to meet the kiss she would give him. Their lips touched, yielded and then parted. A tiny cry came from the back of Caroline's throat when he probed the sweetness she offered. Her arms tightened around his neck; she stood on her toes to better return his kiss, pressing the length of her body against him, feeling his thighs meet and eagerly return the pressure.

Mike's hands left her shoulders to travel down her back, slipping smoothly across the satin of her robe, coming to rest on the gentle curve of her hips. He pulled her closer to him, mutely telling her of his own need for her.

When Caroline sought access to Mike's mouth, to gently, shyly explore and then boldly caress, he caught her up, lifting her to turn and set her on the counter. His hands went to the tops of her legs, touching the outsides in long sensual strokes that stopped at her knees. He traveled the same course again, only this time his hands moved up the inside of her thighs, gently separating them. When they were open to him, he stood between them, pulling her close.

He found the knot in her sash and worked it loose. The robe fell open. Just as he had told her he would, Mike touched her. His hands went from her waist to her belly where he gently pressed his open palm against the heat he felt radiating from there.

His hands left the flat of her stomach to stroke her thighs. He bent and traced a thin moist line around her navel with his tongue. Caroline caught her breath. She ran her fingers into the thickness of his hair, holding him, not knowing which urge she should give in to, to pull him closer or push him away.

Gently Mike began to knead the insides of her legs, moving higher with each stroke. And as he had promised, his lips traveled this new course that his hands had traveled. Caroline's breath came out in a heavy sigh. "Mike—" she pushed him away "—you mustn't do that."

He straightened to look at her. Cupping her face in his hands, he made her look at him. "Caroline...I won't do anything you don't want me to do. But don't tell me no out of some sense of modesty—something that has no business between us." She started to speak, but he stopped her. "If the way I want to make love to you embarrasses you, consider the reasons." He watched her closely; there was a terrible conflict in her eyes. *"They don't count,"* he said slowly, insistently. "Whatever you're thinking, there isn't one valid reason why you should feel hesitant to let me make love to you in every way I know how."

Caroline struggled. She couldn't find the words to tell him how she felt—why she had told him no. She had been a virgin when she'd married Tom Ferguson. Their three years of "conjugal bliss" had involved straightforward sex. Tom had held strong convictions about foreplay and afterplay— there wasn't any. Whenever they made love, and it had been frequently, the act had consisted of a few minutes in the missionary position—the amount of time, she was quick to learn, depended on how long it took him to climax. A pat on the rear and a "That was really good, babe" was as close as he ever came to asking her how it had been for her.

Her relations with men since then had been as unsatisfactory, probably owing in great part, she had finally, reluctantly admitted, to her inability to deviate from the pattern Tom had established. In her mind certain things just weren't done by nice people, regardless of how passionately the body demanded differently.

"I can't, Mike . . . it's something I've never . . . I don't think I'm able. . . ." The words were carried on a sad sigh. No longer able to look at him, she dropped her eyes to the front of his shirt. "Can't we just . . . do it?"

He propped her chin up with his hand. "No, dammit, we cannot just . . . do it."

She tried to smile. "This is another first for me. No one's ever given me a flat no for an answer."

Before he could bite them back, the words tumbled out. "Oh? And how many times have you asked the question?" As quickly Mike shook his head in disgust. "I'm sorry, Caroline. I had no right to ask that." Wearily he rubbed his forehead. "It seems old standards die hard, no matter how unfair or double they happen to be."

In a voice barely above a whisper she said, "I've gone to bed with several men since my divorce. I stopped sleeping around when I realized I wasn't proving anything either to myself or to anyone else. Sleeping with men didn't make me feel any more independent, or that I was the sophisticated woman I wanted to become—I only felt used. Worst of all, the experiences weren't even satisfactory—not to mention the strain my 'loose' behavior put on my puritan sense of morality." She pulled her robe closed. "With you—" she shrugged "—with you, well, somehow it seemed different."

Mike caught her hands. "That's because it is different." Never would he have guessed that beneath Caroline Travers's granite exterior she was as fragile as pond ice in spring. His deep protective instinct made him want to take her in his arms and shelter her from any more hurt, while he didn't even know what that hurt might be. Yet he sensed she wouldn't welcome the gesture—if she suspected that he'd seen past her protective trappings, she would pull away from him, fighting and clawing all the way, like a wounded wild animal.

Caroline tugged her hands from his. "I think I had better go in and get dressed."

Placing a hand on either side of her legs, he blocked her from getting down. "Would you stay if I asked?"

"Mike...I don't think...."

"I don't want you to think. I want you to feel." He pressed his lips to the base of her throat. "I told you before, I won't do anything you don't want me to do." His mouth moved up her neck, across her chin then to her mouth. "But are you sure you don't want me?"

"Mike...." She caught her breath. "I do want

you...." Her arms went around his neck. "Show me how...to let go."

Caroline slid off the counter, and hand in hand they walked to her room. Standing beside the bed, she automatically started to remove her robe. Mike stopped her. "Me first," he suggested softly. "I want you to undress me, Caroline."

She looked at him to see if he was serious, and found the answer in his eyes. She had never undressed a man before—the idea pleased her. Where should she start? His polo shirt? She grasped the loose material at the waist and gave it a tug. After initial resistance it came free from his snug jeans. She let her hands brush against his bared back as she pulled the shirt up his long waist and over his head. Carefully she folded the green cotton and laid it aside. The smile she gave Mike then betrayed lingering nervousness. "There's one."

"It's a good thing I didn't come prepared to play strip poker," he gently teased.

She barely listened to his attempt to put her at ease. Her mind was on the broad expanse of flesh she had exposed. He was built leanly, muscled like a gymnast with a dusting of dark hair tapering to a V that disappeared into his jeans. She flushed as she mentally followed that V.

"I take it the lady approves," Mike said slowly.

"Yes," she breathed. "The lady likes what she sees very much."

Caroline reached for his belt, but instead of simply releasing the buckle, she illogically pulled it through all the loops. Next came the top button on his jeans. With difficulty she finally forced the metal button through the hole. Seeking the zipper, she was momentarily taken aback when she realized there wasn't any. Mike wore the kind of jeans with an all-button fly. The best way to cope with the stiff denim would be to slip one hand in behind. She hesitated. Plunging her hand down the front of Mike's jeans seemed to need more aggression than she felt she could pull off gracefully. Finally, angry at her timorousness, she just stopped thinking about the mechanics and went ahead. She was so surprised to hear Mike's sharp intake of breath that she immediately pulled her hand away. A private smile lighted her eyes. So...Mike was not as detached about what she was doing as he appeared.

The thought pleased her immensely. When she again reached for the buttons, it was in a decidedly different manner. She maneuvered her hand deftly, seeming to come only accidentally into contact with his shaft of heat. She had nearly finished when she looked up to see Mike watching her with passion-hooded eyes. Purposely, meeting his gaze all the while, she reversed the pressure she had been exerting, moving her hand against him. Mike caught his breath, and then returned the pressure.

Slowly she wiggled her hand. For the first time she understood the special joy associated with giving someone pleasure, not because she had to, or was expected to, but because she wanted to. Seeking more freedom for her movements, she reached up to slip his jeans from his hips.

He smiled at her. "First the shoes," he said.

Finally the last of his clothing was gone; he stood before her unabashedly naked. "Now what would you like me to do?" he asked softly.

"I would like you to lie down," she answered as softly.

Shrugging out of her robe, she immediately joined him on the bed, touching his shoulder with her hand, pushing him so that he went from his side to his back. Yielding to her newfound curiosity, Caroline propped herself up on her elbow and stared at him, letting her eyes do to him what her body wanted to. She saw how the hair curled softly on his chest, making tiny swirls around his nipples. Running her hand lightly over the fuzziness, she discovered it was soft and springy.

Mike relaxed, putting his hands behind his head better to watch her. He had gone through so many examinations in the military, physicals for flight training and then the astronaut program, that any sense of modesty he might have had once had been destroyed years ago. He was comfortable with his body; he knew its strong points and weaknesses. He wasn't reluctant to be the object of Caroline's curiosity. He only wanted to share another part of himself with her.

Flushed with success—she had never before so purposely looked at a man without clothing—Caroline grew bolder. She sat up, snuggling her legs into his side, letting her fingers trail lightly down his waist and over his hip before going on to his leg. She stopped when she saw the long surgical scar that ran along the outside of his thigh and around his knee. It was obviously several years old. Relatively inconsequential as injuries went, yet so terrible when she considered its significance. So little to mark so permanently the end of a man's dream.

Caroline tenderly traced the scar with her finger. "Does it ever hurt?"

"Mentally or physically?"

She caught her lip between her teeth. It had been a stupid question. "I'm sorry—it's none of my business."

He answered as if she hadn't apologized or withdrawn the question. "There was a period of adjustment I had to get through emotionally, but I'm all right now. Physically it only bothers me when I try to play too many innings of baseball." Mike felt a twinge of guilt about giving Caroline his standard reply to a question he had fielded all too often. But now was not the time or the place to go into how he coped with broken dreams. His burden was light compared to others he had known, his disappointments minor.

Caroline didn't indicate that she'd detected more hurt in his words than he'd intended. Impulsively she bent and began to tenderly kiss the trail she had just traced with her finger. She followed its course high onto Mike's thigh, but she didn't stop where the scar ended. Hesitantly at first, unsure of herself and only knowing how deeply she wanted to give something of herself to him, she continued until her lips felt the heat of his need for her. She heard him moan and call her name; her uncertainty changed into a wondrous confidence.

Mike reached for her, pulling her up to lie beside him. Long seconds passed while he looked deeply into her eyes. Faint traces of the fear he had seen earlier remained. He kissed her, a quiet kiss meant to reassure. "Now, it's my turn," he said softly. He felt her muscles grow taut. He gave her a teasing smile. "I promise you it will be no more painful than a trip to the dentist."

She tried to return his smile. "Bad comparison, Webster. The dentist I went to back home was a sadist."

"Caroline, did looking at me or touching me bother you?"

"No."

"Did it make you feel dirty?"

"No." She could feel a blush warm her face. "Actually...I liked it."

"Why?"

"I don't understand what you—"

"Why did you like touching me?"

She thought a moment. "Because I can tell that you like for me to."

"Oh...I more than like it, beautiful lady." Mike eased her onto her back, covered her legs with one of his own, then propped himself up on his elbow to look down at her. "Tell me how you feel when you climax." He had thought to distract her with words, never guessing the words would wound.

"I don't think that's something—"

He caught her chin. "You mean you've never—" *What in the hell is the matter with me? Didn't she tell me as much earlier without using the actual words?*

"I understand some people never do," she said defensively. Her voice grew cool. "It doesn't necessarily mean they're freaks."

"Caroline, stop it." He felt her muscles relax, as if she'd been hanging on to a rope and had suddenly let go.

"My automatic defense mechanism doesn't seem to want to disengage," she said.

Mike pulled her into his arms and held her. He wasn't sure precisely when it had happened—whether it was that first day when she had stood toe to toe with him, or later when he'd seen through to the vulnerable woman she was inside—the exact moment didn't matter, only that it had happened. He had fallen completely, unequivocally in love with Caroline Travers. And that knowledge brought with it a protective streak as enormous as the swell of his heart when he thought about the hurt she carried. "Caroline," he said softly, nuzzling her hair, "we can do this another time. It doesn't have to be now."

She pulled back to look at him. "You would do that for me? You would stop? Now?"

He frowned, puzzled. "If that's what you wanted, of course we would stop."

"But what about you?"

"What about me?"

"You mean you could just get up and walk away? You wouldn't—"

"Wouldn't what? Suffer the pangs of untoward frustration and walk with a funny gait the rest of the day?"

"More or less."

"I don't know what kind of tales you've been told about male libido, but there are still a few of us who can handle a woman changing her mind at the last minute." Mike rolled over to his back. "My God, Caroline, male sexual arousal isn't synonymous with raving lunacy." He swung his legs over the side of the bed and sat up.

She touched his back. "Mike...I really don't want you to go."

He turned to her. "Caroline, *it's all right*."

"Not for me it isn't," she finally admitted. "You've revived something in me I thought had died. There's a feeling in the pit of my stomach I don't know what to do about. In my stomach and in my...." She swallowed.

A slow smile crept across Mike's face. "Do you have any idea what you just did to my self-righteous male libido?" he asked, his voice husky with wanting her.

She returned his smile. "Bring it here and let me see."

Mike took her in his arms, holding her to him, covering her mouth with his own in a kiss that was filled with deep plundering need, a prelude to their lovemaking. Caroline moved against him, the burning in her loins long forgotten yet somehow poignantly familiar. How many times had she felt such desire long into the night, only to be frustrated? Silently she prayed that wouldn't happen to her again.

Mike kissed every inch of her face, pressing his lips to her eyes, her nose, her chin. His hands stroked her back, following the curve to the roundness of her hips and buttocks. Grasping her thigh, he brought it up so that he was able to slip his own leg between hers. His hand moved to her belly, then lower to the triangular mound of soft brown hair. As he felt her begin to pull away from him, he held her, whispering against her lips and then her ear.

"Let me touch you, Caroline..." he urged. And when she stopped fighting him, when he felt her forcefully hold herself still for him, he gently touched her. Slowly, lovingly he led her, teaching her and then letting her show him the way. After a time she began to move against him. A soft sigh, a caught breath, a low moan. She called his name and pulled him to her. But she was wary. She had been here before, but never beyond. She began to struggle, momentarily more afraid of going on than retraveling old paths, no matter how painful or frustrating denial would be.

Suddenly what she was feeling changed—as if she were caught up in the torrent of a white-water river—and then wave after wave of blinding delectation swept over her, leaving her gasping in surprise. She tried to catch her breath. Softly Mike called her name, and she heard him from a great distance.

Later, inexplicably, Caroline felt an overwhelming need to cry. She bit her lip and squeezed her eyes shut, trying unsuccessfully to stifle the tears. Mike cradled her in his arms, and when the tears finally won they came in deep, shoulder-shuddering sobs.

"The s-selfish bastard," she hiccuped against Mike's shoulder. "He made me think there was something wrong with me."

Mike kissed the tears from Caroline's cheeks. There were no words to lessen the hurt, the betrayal she felt, so he offered none. She turned her face up to meet his lips with her own. What began as a tender exchange turned explosive as rekindled passion swept them away.

"Mike," Caroline cried out, "I want to experience—everything."

Mike's mouth closed over hers. He rolled to his back, taking Caroline with him. Catching her thighs, he brought them up to ride the sides of his waist. He raised his hips; she met his thrust, and he was inside her. When Caroline shyly admitted she didn't know what to do, he helped her. More than anything she wanted to give him back the gift he had given her.

Sensing that need in her, Mike eagerly took the pleasure she sought to give, only hesitating long enough to be sure she traveled the final journey with him.

Afterward, as they lay together, arms and legs entangled, Mike pressed his lips to her forehead. "Who was the man you called a bastard?"

"Someone I was once married to—Tom Ferguson."

"How long were you married?"

"A little over three years."

"What happened?" he gently asked.

She disentangled herself and rolled to her side. "I would rather not talk about Tom, if you don't mind. I try not to let thoughts of him intrude on the life I've built for myself."

Mike ran his hand across her shoulder. "Why?" His tone invited her to share confidences.

"He isn't important. I'd rather forget that part of my life ever happened."

"For him to make you want to forget several years of your life, he must be very important to you still."

"Mike—" her voice held a warning "—I haven't returned your nickel. Don't start analyzing me again."

"Things have changed between us since then."

She twisted to face him. "No, they haven't. Nothing between us has changed."

His eyes narrowed. "Would you like to tell me what you're talking about?"

"Just because we've made love doesn't mean we're in any way committed to each other. I will continue seeing other men, and I would hope you would see other women." Why was it suddenly so hard to tell him what she had often said to others? "I never gave you a reason to think it would be any different between us. You've known all along that my career comes first, Mike—this is just my way of making sure things don't get too complicated." She reached out to touch his arm. "It's better this way...really it is. You'll see."

The look he gave her stripped her of the warm glow that had lingered from their lovemaking. "If I thought for a minute that you sincerely believed what you've said, you wouldn't have to worry about dating this man, at least. I will not make love to you on a casual hit-and-run basis, Caroline. I have more respect for myself than that. Whether you like it or not, in my mind a commitment was made between us this afternoon. I have no idea how deep or lasting it is, but it was made." He swung his legs over the side of the bed, got up and started to dress.

"I'm due back in Houston tomorrow—I think it would be better if I left now. Think about what I said and let me know if you change your mind."

She sat up, pulling the covers up to her chin. She didn't want him to go, but she couldn't say the words to make him stay. "Mike...I can't...."

Her words, the hurt he saw in her eyes, the hurt he knew she carried in her heart, cut into him with the ease of a scalpel, leaving him exposed, defenseless. Suddenly he knew that if he pushed her on this, he would lose—they would both lose. She needed time, time only he could give her. His pride, his feelings had to be secondary, at least for now, or it would be all over for them before it had really had a chance to begin. He ran his hand down her cheek, bent and kissed the top of her head. "I'll call you sometime next week. We'll talk then."

She caught his hand. "No one ever grew a mustache for me before.... Thanks."

She didn't believe he would call her, Mike realized. She was saying goodbye. "By the time we see each other again," he said, "it will need to be trimmed. Maybe you could do it for me? I've never been much good with scissors."

"Such trust you have in me." She could not let go of his hand.

"I doubt there's anything you couldn't do."

"Don't be too sure." Why couldn't she ask him to stay? Why this masochistic streak that demanded she push him away? "Remember, you've seen my kitchen."

Mike pulled his hand from hers. To stay any longer would be torture. He had to get away to think. "Don't forget the groceries—"

"I won't." *Please stay with me.*

He went to the door. "Goodbye, Caroline." Suddenly, overpoweringly, he wished she would ask him to stay.

She raised her hand in a tiny wave. "Bye," she said softly.

He turned and was gone. At the sound of the front door closing, she pulled her legs to her chest and rested her forehead wearily on her knees. If she ever wrote her life story, she would title it *Goodbye.*

CHAPTER EIGHT

UNABLE TO COPE with an apartment that had grown oppressively quiet, or the numerous floral reminders of Mike in every room, Caroline decided to go into the station on her day off. She had put in a request several days earlier for information on battered wives and was relieved to see that the young man handling the station's morgue had come through with his usual thoroughness. Her story would focus on the halfway houses recently established throughout the Los Angeles area to provide shelter for abused women and their children. The statistics were gruesome. This was precisely the kind of assignment she needed to make her own problems seem insignificant.

Several hours later she came to the end of the file. Raising her eyes from the papers scattered across her desk, she caught a glimpse of someone who looked a lot like Randy Kavanaugh limping into the back room. Deciding some aspirin might help the dull ache in her head, she took two from her desk and headed for the lounge, which also happened to be in the general direction of the back room. Randy might be a good sounding board for the things preying on her mind.

Opening the door, she immediately spotted his legs dangling over the arm of a couch. After a quick swallow of water to wash down the aspirins, Caroline went over to sit next to him.

He acknowledged her presence by opening one eye. "How's it going, boss lady?"

"All right. And with you?"

"Word has it that if I've lived this long, I'll probably make it."

"Care to explain yourself?"

"It's a little-known fact—due to a complex conspiracy among the manufacturers of running shoes and flimsy-looking nylon shorts—but jogging is a deadly sport."

Caroline laughed. "Ah, now I understand. All did not go as planned, I take it?"

"*Au contraire*—as far as the fair Cindy knows, she has met her athletic match." He tried unsuccessfully to cross his legs. After a deep groan followed by a pain-filled sigh, he went on. "You would have been proud of me. Not only did I make the full five miles, I did it with a smile on my face. She was a little confused when I told her I couldn't stay for dinner—said she wasn't aware that I had an elderly grandmother I took out every week, rain or shine."

"And how are you going to produce this sweet old lady should Cindy want to meet her?"

"Ever hear of rent-a-grandmother?"

"I hesitate to ask, but how did you explain the condition you're in today?"

"You didn't hear about the horrible accident I had when I fell off my racing bike last night?"

Caroline laughed and shook her head. "You're weaving one hell of a tangled web. You're going to get caught up in it so tightly one of these days that you won't be able to maneuver at all."

"I've got that possibility covered."

"Oh?"

"Should the you-know-what hit the fan, I plan to prostrate myself at her feet and tell her I was overcome by her incredible beauty and brains. She'll forgive me. She'll have to. I think I'm falling in love."

"How many times is this now?"

"None of the others count. This time it's the real thing."

"How can you tell?"

The playful look disappeared. "I'm not sure. All I know is that what I feel for her is special."

Caroline sighed to herself. Randy was obviously not the person to talk to about career first and commitment second. She told him good-night and headed for home.

WITH EACH PASSING DAY Caroline's arguments in favor of continuing to live precisely as she had been grew stronger. Her career was the one known in her life; it would be insane to disrupt or threaten it. If she worked with single-minded devotion it would always be there for her, in one form or another. It would never grow bored or out of love or betray her. Mike might promise the same, but he was only human. What someone said in the throes of passion one day didn't in any way bind him to feeling the same way the next. Especially men.

Forever echoing in the back of her mind was her mother's stern warning: all men are the same—creatures of such weak character that they shouldn't be trusted with anything as fragile as a heart. All through her teens Caroline had heard the warning repeated before every date. Yet somehow she had survived her mother's pessimism to fall madly, deeply, completely in love with Tom Ferguson.

Possessing Tom's love, she had felt sorry for her mother, whose life had become controlled by bitter memories. Caroline had truly tried to understand, to imagine what it would feel like to find the man she loved with another woman, what the hurt would be like if she were to walk the streets of the small town she called home and see the man she had lived with and loved for so many years strolling hand in hand with some other woman. She had tried to imagine these things, but she hadn't been able to. Not until they had happened to her.

Now she was no longer surprised to hear of a marriage breaking up, only curious when one didn't. She was constantly amazed, too, that the stampede to the altar never seemed to diminish. Well, it was not for her. She wasn't built of such stern stuff that she could survive another round. To think of herself first was a matter of survival. If Michael Webster couldn't, or simply refused to, understand how she felt, then they would not see each other again. Before she could change her mind, she picked up the phone and called John Wakefield, a reporter for the *Los Angeles Times* who had asked her out several times during the past year.

"John—this is Caroline Travers. I was wondering if you would like to go to the symphony with me next Friday."

"How did you know I was thinking of calling you with the same idea?"

She suddenly remembered why she had stopped seeing John Wakefield. He was "cute"—in what he said, how he dressed, the way he acted. "I take it that means yes?"

"I'll pick you up at six. We'll get something to eat first."

She replaced the receiver. Why did something so right feel so damn wrong?

MIKE CALLED three days later. Their conversation was stilted, awkward. Caroline sought a place in the pauses to tell him she had made a date with someone else, but somehow the words never formed. They discussed her job and his. He told her that because of the preparations for the upcoming launch, he wasn't sure when he would be back in Los Angeles. She told him the carnations they had arranged still looked as good as freshly picked.

When they finally said goodbye, Caroline felt a terrible sense of loss. She should have told him about her date with John Wakefield. Yet...she was glad she hadn't.

THE CLOSER FRIDAY DREW, the crankier Caroline became. Each time she thought of her upcoming date, the larger John Wakefield's negative qualities loomed, until she was visibly surprised when a strikingly handsome man arrived to take her out.

He tried and she tried, but it soon became evident to both of them that the evening wasn't going to succeed. After the concert Caroline demurred when he halfheartedly suggested they go somewhere for drinks. The way their date had gone, it seemed eminently preferable for them to spend the rest of the evening watching television. When they arrived back at her apartment, John insisted on walking her to the door despite her protests. Had she been just a little firmer in her refusal, she would have been spared the terrible look of disappointment in Mike's eyes.

Seeing him standing on her porch watching her walk toward him with another man sent a shock of pain through her chest. How desperately she wished she could erase the past five minutes of her life. It wasn't so much to ask—just five minutes. She turned to John. "Maybe we should say goodnight here," she said, a catch, a plea for understanding in her voice.

John Wakefield looked from Caroline to Mike and then to Caroline again. "At last the evening has started to make sense—"

"Please, John," she whispered.

"All right, Caroline. But do me a favor, will you? Lose my telephone number. I'm not real crazy about being used to make someone like

Mike Webster jealous.'' He turned and left, his heels striking the concrete walkway of the quiet courtyard like crashing cymbals.

Caroline looked at Mike; her chin rose as she walked toward him. Self-preservation frequently meant using an offense as the best defense—never more so than now. "I told you I would continue seeing other men. If you'd learn to call first, this wouldn't happen." She could no longer look in his eyes, so she began searching her purse for her keys. *Why didn't he say something?*

Intellectually Mike had accepted Caroline's insistence that she would go out with other men; emotionally he had not. He had fallen in love with a woman who couldn't let herself return that love. If he wanted her enough, if she was important enough to him, he had to give her time, time without pressure.

He reached out to catch her arm. "I think it would be best if I left now. You were right—I should have called first." He released her, turned and started to walk away.

She couldn't let him go. "Mike—" she called, and then more softly, "Don't leave."

He stopped and stared at her. "You're asking a lot, Caroline. I need some time to think about—"

"Please." She went to him. "You must believe that if I'd known you were coming I never would have—"

"Let's not beat it to death. From now on I'll call before I come. Let's just leave it at that."

"Will you stay now?"

He shoved his hands in his pockets. For the first time Caroline noticed the pillowlike bundle in a plastic bag tucked under his arm. "Actually, I never intended to stay. When I tried to reach you at the station they said you were off this weekend. I've made arrangements for you to come back to Houston with me." He shrugged lightly. "It was presumptuous of me. I should have realized you would have made plans of your own for your time off."

"There's nothing I can't change. Is the offer still good?" She stared at the brown-and-white object he had shifted higher up under his arm. It had an oddly familiar look about it.

Long seconds passed while Mike considered Caroline's conciliatory gesture. He had wanted the weekend to be special, a carefully laid foundation stone in their relationship. But he couldn't shake the feeling that it would be a mistake to let something that had started on such a sour note go on. He met her gaze. Who was he trying to kid? He could no more walk away from her now than a skier could ignore fresh snow after a long summer. "Of course the offer is still good," he answered softly.

"Then come inside with me while I pack."

In preparation to follow her, Mike grasped the bundle he held under his arm. Once the object was out of the wrapping its identity became obvious—it was a stuffed animal. More precisely, a teddy bear. The questioning look Caroline gave him brought a cryptic reply.

"It's for a friend who happened to lose hers."

"Here? In Pasadena?" she prodded, pursuing what she hoped would be a less volatile path of conversation.

"In Houston." Mike forcefully twisted the bear's leg, wrung its ear and scrunched its nose.

Caroline looked from the bear to Mike's face, then back to the bear. "I take it the friend didn't leave the bear with you for a little tender loving care?"

A hint of a smile made the corners of his mustache twitch. "I have less than twenty-four hours to make this brand-new bear look as if he's been in the care of a child for the past few years."

"It can't be done. There's a special patina that comes only after three thousand hugs by arms that are less than a foot long. I happen to know this because I had my own bear when I was a child."

"I refuse to be discouraged."

She flashed him a smile. "Oh, how well I know."

Mike reached behind her to push open the door. "If we don't get a move on we'll miss our flight." He waited in the living room for Caroline to pack, pacing, trying unsuccessfully to keep the image of her with another man from intruding on his thoughts. The feelings the image evoked were new to him—new, uncomfortable and unwelcome.

To distract himself he went to the bookshelf and, not bothering to look at the title, reached for a volume. He flipped open the leather-bound edition of *Paradise Lost*; several photographs dropped to the floor. Bending to retrieve the snapshots, he was unprepared for the mixed feelings that swirled through him when he discovered the woman dressed in the old-fashioned lace wedding gown. Caroline. Standing beside her in a formal maroon tuxedo, his arm possessively across her shoulders, was a darkly handsome young man with the soft features of youth.

Mike looked at the next photograph. Caroline stood in the center of six bridesmaids, her smile radiant. He looked at the next and then the next. There were photographs to capture the tradition and ceremony of a wedding, from cutting the cake to throwing the bouquet. In all of them Caroline wore the same look of childlike faith, of innocent trust in the promise of happily ever after. It was a look he had never seen on her face since knowing her.

She came up behind him. "Where did you find those?" she asked, her voice cool.

He stood up and handed her the book.

Slowly Caroline turned the volume over in her hands. She ran her fingers across the lettering. "I'd forgotten I'd put them in here. At the time it seemed fitting." She returned the book to the shelf and held out her hand for the pictures. Mike gave them to her. With studied casualness she tossed them on the table.

Mike watched her actions closely. She would have pulled it off if her hand hadn't trembled. Turning back to him, she gave him a dazzling smile. "Ready?"

"That's it?" he asked softly.

Her smile faded. "What would you like to know?" She didn't wait for his answer. "I told you once before that I'd been married. It failed. There's nothing so unusual about that these days." She reached for her purse, impatiently slipping the strap over her arm. When Mike didn't fill the silence, she flashed a fierce, protective look at him. "I haven't noticed that you've rushed to fill me in on your past affairs of the heart." Her strap started to fall; she yanked it back into place. "Well, dammit, say something. Don't just stand there staring at me."

"Since it's obvious your ex-husband is the one who put that great big chip on your shoulder, and that your wedding took place years ago, I would think enough time had passed for you to have shrugged free of the burden."

Her eyes narrowed. "If I had a chip on my shoulder—which I do not—did it ever occur to you that it might not be any of your business where it came from or who put it there?"

"Everything about you is my business."

"Since when?"

"Since I fell in love with you," he said quietly. There it was, out in the open. He immediately knew by the expression on her face what a horrendous mistake he had made in telling her so soon. As he watched, the color left her cheeks, and her eyes grew wary.

"You don't mean that." He couldn't. She didn't want him to love her. Their relationship was supposed to be free and open, without the stifling confusion of emotions out of control. She had honestly believed they could pull it off—until now. Dammit! She felt so cheated.

"Why don't I mean it?"

"You can't possibly love someone you don't even know." Her hands opened toward him in an oddly pleading gesture. "There are a thousand things you don't know about me for every one you do. Don't you realize how insignificant you make love seem when you treat it so casually?"

"Would it be all right for me to love you after I know you better?"

No, she wanted to scream at him. *It would not be all right.* But how could she tell him that? He would never understand. She needed time to deal with what he had just told her. In a calm voice that belied her raging conflict, she finally answered. "If you really knew me and still felt the same way, I guess I would have to believe you, wouldn't I?"

He walked over to her. Catching her chin with his hand, he made her look at him. "Does that mean you'll let me get to know you, that you'll stop throwing up roadblocks every time I get close?"

She stiffened. "You have no right to expect carte blanche privileges."

"I not only expect them, my love—" his voice was like a firm caress "—I demand them."

She tried to pull away. "No one—do you hear me?—absolutely no one has a right to any part of me but me. I'll choose whether or not to share part of myself with you."

"Then make that choice now, Caroline." He spoke with deceptive calm. "Decide now whether you want to continue seeing me. But be fore-warned, I will not be a yo-yo to be pulled or flung away depending on your particular feelings of the moment."

Did she want to continue seeing him? Could she put up with more of the disruption he'd already created? She started to tell him no, yet a stabbing sense of loss made the words catch in her throat. "But I don't love you," she said instead.

His look was warm. "That's all right. Someday you will."

"No, I won't," she said, her words wooden, her tone one of defeat.

"Trust me," he answered gently. "I'm a lov-able guy."

She raised her eyes to meet his. There was no hope or humor in her expression, only a terrible sadness. "You must not believe that I will ever fall in love with you in return. If you do, you'll only end up hurt."

Unable to stand seeing such sorrow on her face, Mike pulled her into his arms, rubbing his cheek into the softness of her hair. "How would it be if I settled for good friends for now?"

She put her arms around his waist and buried her face in his shirt. How desperately she wished the world were different or that she were stronger. If only people weren't human, so eager to make promises, so easily breaking them. "I would like to be your friend."

He pressed his lips where his cheek had been. "We have a plane to catch. Houston waits for no man—or woman."

BY THE TIME they landed at Houston Intercontinental Airport it was well after midnight. The trip had been quiet as they both sought refuge from the effects of their bruising argument at Caroline's apartment. Mike left her to get the car, a midnight-blue Porsche 911 Turbo.

When he pulled up to the curb she gave him her best long, low whistle. "Nice car you've got there, mister."

Mike grinned; it was the first true smile of the weekend. "You know how the old saying goes. The only difference between a man and a boy—"

"Is the price of his toy." Caroline knew there weren't too many more expensive toys than the one he'd chosen. He had surprised her. She had always assumed that someone who drove a car as ostentatious as a Porsche had a real fixation about his image. Yet the vehicles Mike rented in California were almost generic, they were so ordinary.

On the way into town Caroline told Mike that in the short time she'd lived in Houston she had never been able to drive the freeways—a group of roads the natives affectionately referred to as the Spaghetti Bowl—without being terrified she would never find her way home again. Roads that spiraled when logic dictated they should follow an orderly east-west or north-south route and freeways that changed names depending on the direction they went had transformed her glove box into a storeroom for city and county maps. Eventually she had started marking the success of her weeks by the number of times she didn't get lost.

Expecting to stay at Mike's apartment, she was surprised when he pulled up to the front of the Hyatt Regency Hotel. "What are we doing here?"

"I've reserved a room for you." When her only reply was a puzzled frown, he added, "I didn't want you to think my motives for bringing you to Houston were less than honorable."

Only then did Caroline realize how much she'd been looking forward to sharing Mike's bed. She hid her disappointment by hurriedly gathering her things to leave the car. While Mike finished registering Caroline wandered around the atrium lobby, winding up at a hanging sculpture entitled *Garden of the Mind*.

Mike came up beside her as she studied the piece. "Ready?"

She nodded.

Her room was lovely, with a spectacular view of the lights of downtown Houston, but it was still a hotel room designed for function, not warmth. She didn't want to stay, but she didn't know how to tell Mike. So she smiled when he went around turning on lights for her and simply said "Thank you" when he handed her the key.

"I'll pick you up in the morning." He looked at his watch. "Would you rather I made it around noon?"

"No. I can always catch up on my sleep at home."

"How about if I call before I come?"

How about if you never leave? "That would be fine."

"Well. . .good night, then."

She clasped her hands behind her back. "Good night."

He walked to the door.

"Mike?"

He turned. "Yes?"

"Friends kiss each other once in a while, don't they?"

He slowly walked back to her, a smile of pleasure making his eyes a deep liquid blue. "Sometimes even twice in the same day if the weather's cooperative." He took her in his arms.

"What if the forecast is for sunshine?"

"The rate of frequency could go as high as three, maybe even four—" His mouth closed over hers, and she unclasped her hands to slip them around his neck. Standing on tiptoe, she matched the hunger of his kiss. Without urging, her mouth opened, inviting him to explore the velvety interior.

He knew she wanted him, that she needed physical release and reassurance as a substitute for the emotions she kept in such tight rein, but he couldn't shake the feeling that if he settled for what she would give him physically, she would never give him anything else. He also knew the ache he fought in his loins whenever she was near was nothing compared to the ache he would feel if he should lose her. He had to find a way to make her love him. Now that he suspected how special life could be with a woman's love, he would forever know emptiness without it.

Mike gently pulled Caroline's arms from his neck. "I'd better go now. I meant what I said about not putting pressure on you."

"Mike...I'm a big girl. If I wanted to say no, I would."

"This has not been the best of days for us."

She stepped away from him. Studying his face, she crossed her arms over her chest. "You haven't given up, have you? All your talk about being friends was just talk."

Mike shook his head. "If I'd left when I first tried, we would have avoided this conversation."

Her shoulders slumped. "I'm sorry, I'm being a real bitch." Her smile was weak. "Stick around long enough, Webster, and I'll have you completely convinced that falling in love with me was probably the biggest mistake you'll ever make."

"Even if it happens to end eventually, Caroline," he said softly, "loving someone is never a mistake." He suddenly realized that if she were ever able to feel that as strongly as he did, she would be able to love him. "You learn something, you grow a little with everyone you come to know. If you also happen to love them, it's like a bonus."

Never a mistake? If only he knew. It was never a mistake unless what you learned was pain and what you came to know was fear.

CHAPTER NINE

MIKE ARRIVED THE NEXT MORNING a little after nine. Although he'd called from the lobby to wake her up, she was dressed and waiting by the time he knocked five minutes later. When she opened the door he blinked. "I'm impressed."

"Why, thank you, Mr. Webster. They're nothing really—the slacks and sweater were just something I pulled off the sales rack." At Saks Fifth Avenue during her last trip to New York.

"I wasn't talking about the clothes."

She grinned wickedly. "Oh, you mean how quickly I dressed. I can do a lot of things fast... want to see me?"

"I wouldn't touch that one with a ten-foot pole."

"Chicken."

He stepped inside, and as he did so he produced a small waxy white flower and handed it to her with a flourish. "Speaking of chickens," he said conspiratorially. "Did you know they've finally discovered why so many people have trouble raising them?"

She knew she was being suckered, but bit, anyway. "No. But I'm sure you're going to tell me."

He grinned. "It seems they've been burying the eggs too deep."

Caroline groaned, smiling despite herself.

"If you like that one, I have a hundred more."

She took the stephanotis from his outstretched hand. "Is this how you control your women? By threatening them? And before breakfast yet!"

He flashed her a hopeful look. "Would it work with you?"

"Not a chance. I'm made of sterner stuff."

"Oh, yeah? What do you call a boomerang that doesn't come back?"

She thought for a minute, desperately wishing she had the answer.

Mike grabbed her hand and started for the door. "Give up?"

She nodded.

"A stick!"

She buried her face in the sleeve of his tweed jacket. "Uncle," she moaned. "Uncle, uncle, uncle."

"Stern stuff, indeed," Mike grumbled.

FOR BREAKFAST he took her to a tiny Mexican restaurant where he was known by name. They weren't offered menus; food just began to appear. The first item was thick, frothy chocolate, hot and spicy, prepared, she learned, the traditional Mexican way. Next came a plate of *huevos con papas y chorizo*—eggs cooked with diced potatoes and crumbled chorizo sausage. Caroline was skeptical, but out of politeness to the young waiter who hovered expectantly near she took a forkful into her mouth. It was delicious.

When at last she pushed her plate away, swearing she couldn't eat another thing, a platter of *sopaipillas* was placed between them. Mike urged her to try one of the puffy pieces of fried bread, usually served as dessert. "I couldn't," she said. "There isn't room left."

Opening his own and drizzling honey inside, he offered her the first bite. Again out of politeness, she accepted. She had barely swallowed what he'd given her when, with a sheepish grin, she reached for a *sopaipilla* of her own.

They left the restaurant, Caroline holding her stomach and moaning about the sins of gluttony, Mike promising to do his best to put ten pounds on her. Suddenly she straightened and pulled her hand from his. "My flower!" she cried. "I left it on the table."

Before Mike had a chance to react she was gone. He met her back at the door, noting her triumphant smile. The rescued flower now rested in the center of her palm. "Did you happen to notice?" she said. "I haven't asked you where you *found* this."

He took the stephanotis from her. Tucking it securely into the short curls over her ear, he turned her so that she could see her reflection in the restaurant window. The person she saw staring back at her was not the Caroline Travers she knew. The sophisticated veneer she had worked so hard to construct had cracked, letting some of the innocent girl she had thought long gone show through. It was a startling revelation. She would have stood there longer if Mike hadn't grasped her hand and led her away.

When they were in the car she turned to him. "What now?"

"Some friends of mine, Cory and Ann Peters, have invited us to dinner this evening. I have tickets for a rodeo this afternoon." He started the car. "Ever been to a rodeo?"

"Are you kidding? Remember I grew up in the west."

"Boy, am I glad to hear you say that. I was afraid I'd have to spend the day trying to explain the differences between bull riding and bronc busting."

She sent him a sidelong glance, her eyes wide. "What's a bronc?"

He sighed forlornly. "Maybe we should go to the zoo instead."

"Do they have broncs there?"

"No, but they do have a holding pen for perverse reporters."

"Is it big enough for company?"

A smile worked on the corners of his mouth, making his mustache twitch, a dead giveaway. "It could be—depending on the activity you had in mind."

"Dancing?"

"Only if it was to something slow."

"Dining?"

"As long as it wasn't a seven-course meal."

"Delectatious dawdling?"

Mike laughed heartily. "I thought I'd heard every expression ever used for that particular pleasure." He eyed her. "Is 'delectatious' a real word? It doesn't count if it isn't."

She feigned an expression of horror. "How can you even imply that I was being provocative? I was merely asking about dessert."

He pulled up to a stop sign, turned and looked at her, a wicked gleam in his eyes for the second time that morning. "You take care of the meal, sweetheart," he said in a terrible imitation of Bogey. "Leave the dessert to me."

Caroline suddenly felt very warm inside. "We could skip the steak and potatoes altogether," she said, her voice a seductive whisper.

He became serious. "I'm afraid if we do, we'll soon grow weary of the results. Richness is best when taken in small portions. It should be savored, like an ocean sunset."

Caroline met his gaze. "I've never known anyone like you," she said slowly, meaning every word.

He brought her hand to his lips and pressed a quick kiss against the back. "I'm assuming that's a compliment, so I'll say thank you." A horn honked behind them.

Caroline placed her tingling left hand in her lap, holding on to it and rubbing the spot he'd kissed. She glanced out the window. "Let's see—if I remember correctly, a bronc is a horse," she said softly.

THEY HAD TO LEAVE the rodeo early in order to get
to Friendswood, a little town southeast of Houston, on time. The Peterses' home was a rambling
brick ranch style nestled on several acres of heavily wooded land. They had added on to the house
several times over the past two decades, making it
look peculiarly unbalanced. Mike saw the puzzled
look on Caroline's face as she surveyed the house.
"They bought it for the horse barns," he explained, "not the aesthetics. Cory and Ann's
oldest daughter is a champion barrel rider. They
wanted someplace for her to practice that
wouldn't take her away from home all the time.
They've also built a basketball court for their
twelve-year-old son, who's already made plans to
play for UCLA in a couple of years."

"Didn't you say there were three children?"

Mike smiled warmly. "There's also a pre-
cocious three-and-a-half-year-old named Mindy.
So far the only thing she's expressed a fanatical interest in is teddy bears."

"So she's the friend you've been abusing the
bear for."

Mike parked the car in the wide circle driveway.
Before he had a chance to come around to get
Caroline, the front door burst open and a raven-
haired little girl with bright brown eyes, dressed in
pink pants and a white knit top, came bounding
down the stairs. "You're late," she accused, running up to Mike. She stopped her forward motion
the instant she saw Caroline emerge from the car,
and her exuberance immediately turned to shy-

ness. Quickly Mindy glanced around. Discovering none of her family had followed her down the stairs, she rushed to Mike's side, wrapping her arms possessively around his leg, peering at Caroline from behind his thigh.

Gently Mike coaxed her out in the open, picked her up and held her in the crook of his arm. "Mindy," he said, "I want you to meet a very special friend of mine. Her name is Caroline Travers. Caroline. . . this is my godchild, Malinda Peters."

Caroline was surprised when social graces overcame shyness and Mindy twisted around to extend her hand in formal greeting. "I'm pleased to meet you, Mindy," Caroline said, taking the child's small hand in her own.

Introductions over, Mindy burrowed back against Mike, tucking her head under his chin. "Are you the television lady?" she asked softly.

Fleetingly Caroline wondered how much Mike had told his friends about her. Anticipating Mindy's next question, she said, "I work on television a long way from here. You can't see me on the one you have in your house." Just then a man and woman came out from the back of the house. Caroline recognized Cory Peters, one of the astronauts on the upcoming shuttle flight. She had seen him at a press conference she'd been assigned to cover in Los Angeles almost a month earlier, a conference she had grudgingly attended because of her reluctance to run into Mike. She remembered coming away feeling oddly disappointed when he hadn't been there.

Cory was of medium height and build with hair that must have been carrot colored at one time. His facial freckles had faded, but the ones on his arms where he had rolled back his sleeves were still prominent and plentiful.

His wife was stunning. She had her daughter's dark hair and expressive brown eyes and was obviously pleased to see her guests.

Mike moved over to stand beside Caroline. Casually, comfortably he slipped his arm around her shoulders, offering her the kind of emotional shelter he'd given Mindy. Inwardly Caroline smiled at the gesture. Very few people in her life had thought she needed or would even allow such treatment—Mike hadn't bothered to ask.

He gave her shoulder a light squeeze. "Caroline. . . Ann and Cory Peters."

Ann's handshake was firm and welcoming; Cory skipped taking her hand, hugging her instead.

Mike, Mindy and Cory followed the two women into a large living room. Once all were seated, Mindy on Mike's lap, Caroline on the couch beside them, Ann and Cory on chairs opposite, Mike turned his attention to Mindy. Gently he asked her about her bear.

Immediately her eyes filled with tears, which she swiped at with the backs of her hands. Pulling her against his chest to comfort her, Mike softly said, "I have a terrible problem, Mindy. . . ." He patiently waited for her reply.

"What?" she asked at last, curiosity winning out.

"While I was searching for your bear I found another one who was lost. He was all alone, the saddest looking bear I've ever seen."

"What happened to him?"

"Well...I'm not sure. The only thing I do know is that he's all alone. I told him about you and how unhappy you've been since you lost your own bear. I didn't make him any promises...but I did tell him that, maybe, if you liked him enough, you might let him stay here until your bear comes home."

Mindy pushed against Mike's chest, sitting up to see him better. "Where is he?" There was a deeply suspicious thread running through her simple question.

"Out in my car."

For long seconds she stared at him. "I don't want another bear," she insisted. "I want my bear."

"If you don't want him to stay here, that's all right. I'll just have to see if I can find someone else to give him a home for a while."

Caroline closely watched the interchange between Mike and Mindy. She had never seen anyone without children of their own relate so easily to a child. He was going to make a wonderful father. The thought created a deep sense of unease. Mike should be going with someone who would eventually give him the chance to be a husband and father. With her he was traveling down a dead-end road.

While Mindy nestled back against Mike's chest

to mull over what he'd told her, Ann asked if anyone would care for a drink. Caroline asked for coffee; Cory and Mike each opted for a beer. Ann had gone to the kitchen by the time Mindy relented enough to investigate the new bear.

The front door closed softly behind her and Mike. Cory turned to Caroline. "Has Mike told you what happened to Mindy's bear?"

"No...he's been rather mysterious about the whole thing, actually."

Cory laughed. "That's typical of him. There's no mystery involved. It's just that you've caught him in the middle of doing one of his selfless things for another person, and it embarrasses him." He bent toward her, resting his elbows on his knees. "Ann had to go to Dallas a few weeks back. She took Mindy and the bear with her...the bear never made it home. Mindy's been impossible to live with ever since."

Caroline's smile was commiserating. "I not only had a bear I couldn't live without when I was Mindy's age, I also had a blanket. I can't imagine what I would have done if I'd ever lost either of them."

Cory nodded. "With me it was an old ratty elephant that used to belong to my brother."

Ann returned carrying a tray just as Mike and Mindy came back into the room. Mindy was holding the bear, but not lovingly the way she would have cuddled her own. This new bear she had stuck noncommittally under her arm. She let go of Mike's hand and walked over to her mother. Her whisper was unintentionally loud. "He's ugly, momma," and she held out the bear for inspection. Mike's pounding had aged the stuffed animal considerably.

Ann fought to keep a smile off her face. "Oh, I don't know, Mindy. He's certainly not as good-looking as your bear, but I don't think he's all that bad. Maybe if he had a bath and a new ribbon."

Mindy looked at the bear again, then back at her mother as if to say she doubted her sanity. Ann reached out to prop up one of the bear's lop-sided ears. "Why don't you take him into your room and see if he likes it there?"

Caroline noticed Ann glance over at Cory while surreptitiously crossing her fingers.

Mindy stared at the bear a few minutes longer, turned and left the room. Once she'd gone Ann gave Mike a look of deep gratitude. "I had no idea what it would be, but I knew you'd come up with something."

"It hasn't worked yet. There's still a chance I could wind up the owner of one slightly abused bear—"

Cory interrupted. "I think you're wrong, Mike. I saw the look in her eye when she left just now. Your bear has found a—"

Somewhere in the back of the house a door slammed. "Uncle Mike, Uncle Mike!" Tandem shouts were followed by loud footfalls.

"We're in the living room!" Cory called out.

A girl in her early teens with thick auburn hair swinging freely to her waist came bounding into the room, on her heels a boy with Mindy's coloring and slight frame. The boy tumbled into Mike's arms; the girl stopped in the middle of the room the instant she spotted Caroline. The unguarded look she sent, first to Caroline and then to Mike, was filled with pain. It was obvious the girl had a crush on Mike. Caroline felt instant compassion for her—to someone that age, love was an all-consuming thing.

Cory made the introductions, presenting his daughter Rebecca and his son, Kevin, with obvious pride. After all was calm again, with Mike questioning Kevin about his basketball, Caroline watched Ann go over to stand quietly beside her daughter.

Evidently she was aware of Rebecca's feelings. Mother and daughter exchanged a telling look that made Caroline's heart skip a beat. How often she had wished for a relationship like that with her own mother. Would they have had one if their world hadn't fallen apart? At moments like this she felt terribly cheated.

As she watched the two of them, Caroline suddenly understood what was happening. Mike had probably never brought a woman with him to the Peterses' house before. That would not only explain Rebecca's startled reaction, it implied something that made Caroline exceedingly uncomfortable. Mike hadn't listened to her when she had told him her career came before anything...or anyone. Bringing her here was tantamount to taking her "home to the folks" for approval.

Mike turned to her then and said, "Do you mind?" She realized she had been drifting with her disturbing thoughts. She hadn't the vaguest idea what he was talking about.

"No...not at all."

"We'll make it a short game."

"Take your time," she offered magnanimously. Her approval cleared the room of everyone except her and Ann.

The older woman came over to sit beside Caroline. "At least once a day I thank the powers that be that Rebecca isn't the klutz her mother has always been when it comes to sports. She plays basketball as well as Kevin, with an ease that infuriates him."

Basketball. That was the game they had left to play. Caroline slipped off her shoes and tucked her feet beneath her, snuggling deeper into the plump cushions of the old couch. "I wasn't permitted to play competitive sports in school," she said. "It wasn't considered ladylike. Since then I've never had the time or, to be truthful about it, the inclination to get involved in anything more strenuous than splashing around in someone's backyard pool or an occasional trip down the bunny slope."

"I would have thought, as young as you are, that you would have missed out on all that nonsense."

"Some ideas take longer to germinate in small-town soil than in big-city earth. Where I come from, it's still frowned on for a woman to work on a career, as opposed to having a job 'just to help out.'" Caroline picked a piece of lint from her pants. "But that's the material I use when speaking from my soapbox, hardly suitable conversation for a quiet Saturday afternoon. If you don't mind, what I would really like to talk about is you."

Ann slipped off her shoes, too, and drew her feet up. She turned to face Caroline, tucking her toes between the cushions. "Is this the reporter in you asking, or is this strictly woman to woman?"

Caroline thought a moment. "Probably a bit of both. I've been a reporter for so many years I think that in one way or another it overshadows everything I do." She smiled softly. "Whether I hear about a hermit on the Salmon River or a hurricane in the Solomon Islands, there's a part of my brain that shifts into gear, trying to figure how I would turn the information into a story. But that doesn't answer your question, does it? The main reason I'd like to know more about you is because you're Mike's friend. The secondary reason is simple—I'm curious about what it's like to be married to an astronaut."

Ann nodded in agreement. "Curiosity I can understand; when I get going on something I'm insatiable. I want to know everything about that subject that there is to know." She propped her chin in her hand. "Being married to an astronaut is an ulcer-producing mixture of heaven and hell. It's lonely. It's frustrating. It's a job that requires a woman to have an unshakable feeling of self-worth in order to survive with her own identity anywhere near intact.''

She stopped a moment. ''The pride you have in your husband's accomplishments is constantly tempered by the realization that to others he is essentially a disposable commodity. If something should happen to him, there are thousands lined up who would eagerly take his place—and more than a dozen who easily could. He is a publicity tool, used as cavalierly and purposely by NASA as a fashion model by a designer, both before and after a flight. And yet...because what he's doing is still unique, there are times that it's exciting beyond words. He belongs to an elite group, special people who have the 'right stuff.' These few men and women have pursued and are now living a dream I'm convinced is as old as man. I can picture the more adventuresome cavemen looking toward the heavens and trying to figure out a way to visit the stars.'' She smiled quickly, embarrassed. ''I didn't mean to wax poetic on you.''

''Don't worry about it.'' Caroline returned the smile. ''I have the same tendency to expound when I get wound up about something.'' She readjusted her legs. ''Where do you fit into all this?''

Absently Ann ran her fingers through her hair. ''You have to remember that I carry a double millstone. Not only am I an astronaut's wife, I'm a housewife. Neither job is designed to be particularly ego building.'' She hesitated, her eyes reflecting inner conflict, as if she was unsure of how much she should reveal. ''My struggle with

stereotyping, with being someone whose supposed
primary identity was that of an appendage to her
husband, damn near destroyed my marriage. It
took years of soul-searching before I realized I
was blaming Cory for things he had no control
over.'' She shrugged. ''We've been through some
tough times, even a separation that lasted almost a
year. All along I was so sure I was trying my
damndest to patch things up. I finally discovered
that the glue I kept trying to use was water
soluble—everything came apart again in the
weakest storm. Finally it took a terrific neighbor,
another astronaut's wife who had gone through
what I was experiencing, to help me realize my
own self-image was the core of Cory's and my
problems.''

Ann's revelations were more than Caroline had
bargained for. She had thought to make casual
conversation; Ann had bared her soul.

''The only reason I've told you all this,'' Ann
added, ''is because Mike and Cory are so much
alike. I thought some insight into the kind of men
they are might help you.''

Caroline considered what Ann had said. She ran
her hand along the back of the sofa, letting the
ribbing ride between her fingers. ''I must have
missed something, Ann. I don't understand the
connection.''

''Through all the years it took me to discover
who I was, and the subsequent upheaval those
years brought, Cory stood by. When he couldn't
understand my feelings, when what I was going

through was so uniquely female that there was no way he could empathize, he gave me the time and space I needed to work my problems out on my own. Cory is special—so is Mike. But they have a weakness. They are both vulnerable when it comes to someone they love."

Now Caroline understood. Ann was trying to protect Mike from the uncertainty, the reserve she had detected in Caroline.

"Mike has never brought a woman to our house before," Ann went on slowly. "I knew he wouldn't until he found that special someone he kept insisting he was going to meet someday. He's been looking a long time. . .I hope you realize how he feels about you."

Caroline stared at a crisp pleat in her light wool slacks. She was conscious of breathing, of forcing her chest to move against the band of panic constricting her. "It must be wonderful to have a friend like you," she murmured at last.

"I'm only one of many. Mike is an uncommon man." There was a long pause. "He's the only person besides Cory that I would have considered sharing my life with."

"And you're obviously afraid I'm going to hurt him."

"Only because you could do it so easily—" Ann's voice was gentle, her words pleading "—not because I think you want to." Again a door slammed and footsteps headed their way.

Cory, beaming, came across the room to give Ann a quick kiss. "Rebecca and I just trounced

Kevin and Mike.'' His face flushed from the exercise and the cool air, his eyes shining with unabashed love as he looked at Ann—he was far more handsome than Caroline had first thought. She looked up to see a similar loving expression in Mike's eyes.

She had to leave, to make her way to the door and run as fast and as far away as she could—to run until she dropped. But to physically remove herself from what was bothering her would not be to escape the panic that held her.

Kevin nudged past Mike. ''Winning by two points isn't 'trouncing' someone,'' he said, his irritation evident in his words and the disgusted way he threw himself into the nearest chair.

Mike ruffled the boy's hair as he walked by, his limp more pronounced from the strenuous game. ''You shouldn't have taught Rebecca that hook shot. She's gotten us with it every time we've played.'' He sat on the arm of the sofa, slipping his arm around Caroline's shoulders.

Her smile was tentative. How she wished she could ask him if they could leave. If there were only some way she could relay to him that spending the next few hours surrounded by his warmhearted friends was equivalent to torture for her. But she didn't know how to tell him about the panic...or the despair. He had brought her here to show her the kind of life he wanted them to share. Why hadn't he believed her when she'd told him she couldn't?

A terrible sadness overcame her. To destroy

that feeling, to right herself on a storm-tossed sea, she searched for a reason to be angry. It came easily. He had had no right to do this to her. She had told him from the very beginning that her career came first. She had never given him any reason to believe they could have what the Peterses had. Why had he done this to her, anyway?

"Caroline?" Concern was evident in the quiet, intimate way Mike spoke her name. "Is something wrong?"

She closed her eyes for a second, trying to erase the turmoil she knew he could see there. When she opened her eyes she forced a smile. "It's nothing. I, uh, I had a cramp in my foot."

Mike let her have her lie, sensing it would be a mistake to question further the look on her face while others were around. Reluctantly he admitted that he didn't want to know the reason behind what he had seen in her eyes. He wasn't ready to acknowledge that bringing her here had been a horrible mistake.

AFTER DINNER Kevin and Rebecca left to spend their Saturday evening with friends. Ann asked Caroline if she would like to keep her company while she got Mindy ready for bed. Her daughter, a combination of sweetness and perversity, had easily captured Caroline's heart. Since she had no friends or relatives with small children, the Peterses' youngest was a fascination to a hard-nosed reporter who thought herself immune to youngsters. For an instant she found herself regretting that she would never know the joy of having a child of her own. Caroline was stunned by the depths of her sorrow—remaining childless was something she thought she'd come to accept long ago.

Caroline almost sighed with relief when it was finally time to tell the freshly-scrubbed Mindy good-night. Ann bent to accept her daughter's hug and kiss while Caroline waited in the doorway.

"Be right back," Mindy said, escaping from her mother's arms. She bounded past Caroline and ran down the hall.

"She's probably just remembered that Mike's here," Ann said. "Usually she insists I send him in with her dad."

"Maybe it's her fancy new nightgown she wants to show off," Caroline suggested.

Ann smiled. "Of course."

Several minutes later Mindy came back down the hall, but instead of going to her bed she stopped in front of Caroline. In the manner of self-assured three-and-a-half-year-olds, she opened her arms for a hug. Caroline was momentarily taken aback but quickly recovered, bent down and embraced Mindy. There was nothing subtle or genteel about the kiss Mindy bestowed on her new friend—it was square on the lips, accompanied by a hard squeeze around the neck. "Night, Miz Caroline," she said, releasing her neck.

"Good night, Mindy," Caroline said, frantically fighting the tempest of emotions the child had so innocently stirred up. Where Mindy's arms had lain around Caroline's neck, there was now a feeling of loss. The lingering smell of soap and "little girl" made her dizzy. Again she knew a poignant sense of missing something she would never have.

Ann finished tucking Mindy in beside her new bear. She switched off the light, exchanged a final good-night, and the two women left.

"You must enjoy being a mother," Caroline said, groping for conversation, trying to hide the emotions that still swarmed through her like a hive of disturbed bees.

"It has its moments." Ann glanced at Caroline. "It's not all this idyllic, you know. There are times when I get so frustrated I wish I could throw my hands up in defeat and just walk away. I'm not one of those people who think motherhood is next to sainthood. It's a tough, mostly thankless job that, despite feminist rhetoric, has become unfashionable with the push for women to find themselves in more rewarding careers." She stopped and leaned against the hall linen closet, folding her arms across her chest.

"I have a degree in physics and a real passion for math. I don't try to fool myself that when I'm finished with this job I'll be able to step into the one I've been trained to do, at least not easily. Staying home was a choice I made when Cory was accepted into the astronaut program. It was a hard decision, and when things get bad around here I sometimes quietly regret it. But those times are like labor pains, miserable when you're going through them, forgotten afterward."

She reached out to touch Caroline's arm. "I'm telling you all this because I have a feeling you're under a great deal of pressure. I've thought about what I said to you earlier today, and I want you to know I'm sorry if I've added to that pressure."

Caroline started to speak, but Ann stopped her.

"Let me finish my little speech, and then I'll get off the podium. I believe what Cory and I have now is everything a marriage should be. I love that guy more than I could possibly express in words. Without hesitation, I would give my life for him. I know that sounds melodramatic, but every word comes from my heart.

"I guess what I'm trying to tell you is that I know there are less troublesome roads to travel—I wouldn't blame you if you chose one of them." Her hand closed around Caroline's arm. "The only thing I would ask of you is that if you believe your choice will exclude Mike, make it soon." Ann's eyes held a silent plea to be forgiven for intruding on something so private.

Caroline couldn't summon the anger she would have normally felt toward anyone who presumed to offer her such intimate advice. "I've already told myself essentially the same thing."

"I'm sorry if I came on heavy-handed today, Caroline. I didn't think I had the time to be a better friend before I said these things." Slipping her arm through Caroline's, she said, "Now let's move on to other things. There's coffee in the kitchen and men in the living room. What say we have some of one and join the other?"

Caroline tried to return the smile. She failed. "Normally I would be able to give you a great comeback for that."

"I think we're both a little wrung out."

When they had their coffee they joined Mike and Cory who were so involved in their discussion that they failed to notice the women's arrival.

"The arm has been giving us trouble again for the past week. Simon is beginning to think that whatever it is, it could go wrong during the flight also, that it's not just a fluke with the mock-up."

Ann sat down beside Cory. "Is this problem you two are hashing over something you'll be able to solve tonight?"

They both looked at her. Reluctantly Cory admitted it wasn't.

"Good. Caroline tells me she plays a mean game of pinochle. I'm not about to let her get out of the house without a demonstration. It's been ages since we've played four-handed."

SEVERAL HOURS LATER when it was time to leave, Ann took Caroline aside. "However this turns out," she told her softly, "I want you to know I like you very much. I just wish we lived closer and could become friends on our own if it doesn't work out with you and Mike."

Caroline's nerves were strung so tightly that Ann's simple statement brought an embarrassing well of tears to her eyes; immediately she tried to blink them away. "Thank you, Ann," she said, barely loud enough to be heard.

Ann put her arms around her new friend and held her close.

After the comforting hug, Ann held Caroline away from her to look into her eyes. "I'm truly sorry—" there was sadness in her eyes "—for both of you."

Mike and Cory came to stand beside them. They said their final goodbyes, waving one last time as Mike's Porsche pulled out of the driveway.

CHAPTER TEN

CAROLINE STARED INTO THE TUNNEL created by the
Porsche's headlights. "They're nice people," she
said, breaking the silence that had grown between
them since leaving the Peterses'.

"They like you, too."

"How long have you known them?"

"The three of us go all the way back to high
school."

"Did you realize Rebecca has a crush on
you?"

"I suspected as much." He reached for her
hand. "I consider it a terrific compliment. She's
an outstanding girl."

Suddenly unable to bear the familiarity, Caroline pulled her hand from his. Why couldn't he be
like everyone else? Most men would have been embarrassed to have a teenager mooning over them,
no matter who it was. "Where are you going?"

"I thought that after the few hours' sleep you
had last night, you might want to get to bed at a
decent hour tonight. So. . . I was headed for the
hotel."

"Do I have any choice in the matter?"

"Of course. . . ."

"I would like to see your apartment." It was almost a command.

"All right," he said, carefully trying to keep the surprise he felt from his voice.

MIKE'S APARTMENT was as Caroline had imagined, and yet somehow different. The living room was done in earth tones, shades of brown, gold and rust. None of the furniture matched, but everything blended harmoniously. While Mike fixed coffee in the kitchen she wandered around the rest of the apartment. Not even in the den, furnished with an oversize desk and shelves of books evenly divided between fiction and nonfiction, was there a solitary memento of his years of flying or his training in the astronaut program. After looking at the bedroom, also decorated in soft earth tones, Caroline drifted back to the kitchen. She stopped at the doorway just as Mike was sweeping spilled coffee grounds into the sink. "I like your apartment," she said. "It has a homey feel about it. There isn't any of the temporary quality that mine seems to have."

He looked up from his chore and flashed her a smile. "I'm glad you like it."

"Why?" she immediately shot back.

In the car he had decided he wasn't going to let her start the argument he'd seen brewing. "Because having you like my apartment is infinitely better than having you come in here, look around and say 'Yuck,'" he answered more easily than he felt.

"What would you have done if I had?"

"I probably would have told you that you had very bad manners."

"What would you say if I told you I had a miserable time at the Peterses' tonight?"

Mike turned on the water and washed the last of the grounds down the sink. He grabbed a towel and dried his hands. Flipping the towel back onto the rack, he turned to her. "I'm sorry. I sincerely thought you would like them."

"Whether or not I liked them has nothing to do with the way I felt the entire time I was there."

"And that was?"

"Maneuvered—manipulated."

"You're going to have to lay it out for me better than that."

"Why did you take me there?"

He shrugged lightly. "There was nothing mysterious or sinister intended. We were invited. I thought it would be a good way for you to meet my two oldest friends."

"If there was nothing going on, why did I feel like I was being inspected?"

"My best guess would be that you probably were. But there's nothing overly complex about that, either. Put yourself in their places. Wouldn't you be curious?"

Caroline ran her hand through her hair. "It was more than simple curiosity."

Mike's expression became guarded. "Did something happen at Ann and Cory's that I'm not aware of?"

"No. . . ." She sighed deeply. "Neither Ann nor Cory could have been more gracious hosts."

"Then what bothered you?"

She fought for the words. "It was the whole setup. Husband, wife, kids, house, horse, dog, cat—everything."

"That's how they happen to live, Caroline."

"Well, it's not how I want to live." There it was. Out in the open. She saw the jolt of pain her words had caused before he could lower his eyes to the floor. When he looked up again, the pain was gone.

"And that's what you meant by maneuvered? You thought the reason I took you there was to try to coerce you into the same life-style?" Although his words were spoken in self-righteous anger, deep inside he couldn't deny there was a grain of truth in what she had said.

"Am I wrong?"

"You're more wrong than right," he answered softly, wearily. "Ann and Cory knew I'd met someone I considered special—they wanted to meet you."

Caroline's vision started to blur with unshed tears of frustration, hurt and anger. She had vowed not to let Mike into her life, yet here he stood, capable of hurting her with terrifying ease. She felt like a tree that had grown twisted and gnarled by constantly buffeting winds, leaving it too few branches for protection. She couldn't let him disrupt her life. If it was this painful now to tell him she wouldn't see him again, what would it be like a week, a month, a year from now? "Mike. . . ." She looked at him, and suddenly realized she had been so deep in thought that she didn't know whether she'd spoken his name aloud.

"Don't say anything more, Caroline. Too much has happened this weekend already. We need some time."

"I have to—"

His fingers touched her lips, silencing her. "There is not a 'have to' in the world more important than the real reason we came here this evening. I want to forget the words between us for now and make lingering, wonderful, passion-filled love to you."

The bud of sensual warmth that had burst inside her earlier blossomed fully now. Her resolve, the goodbye she had been prepared to say, the knowing how wrong it would be to make love with him again, all were released like pollen in a windstorm—gone, impossible to recapture.

Mike drew her to him, his motions unhurried, his touch tender. When he bent his head to meet her upturned lips, she felt the sweetness of his breath caressing her mouth. His hands stroked her curving hip. They spanned her waist, then slipped beneath her sweater to brush the smooth skin of her back.

Vaguely she could smell the coffee perking. Every other sense was focused on Mike—the sight, the feel, the taste, the sound of him. His touch, whether on her waist, her arm or her hip, sent desire eddying through her.

Mike wanted to make love to Caroline more than he had ever wanted to make love to a woman. But as much as he ached for her, he knew just holding her would have satisfied the deeper craving in him. Disjointed images of her sharing his life, his apartment, his day-to-day existence, flashed before him, creating a need so strong it became a physical pain. *Caroline,* he silently pleaded, *let yourself love me. I have so much to give you—our need for each other is so great.*

He reached up to touch her face. His fingertips stroked the line of her jaw, the hollow behind her ear, the whisper-soft arch of her brow—touching, memorizing the feel of her. He cupped the back of her neck, and with a light pressure urged her to come to him.

When she kissed him a soft moan sounded in the back of her throat. It was wrong to make love to him. To do so tonight was to imply that they would have a tomorrow. Yet she couldn't tell him no. The lonely days would necessarily come, too devastating not to have this last night with him.

She opened her mouth, yielding to his entreating tongue. He coaxed her with loving words and caresses until the last of her reserve fell away and she allowed herself to be pulled along freely on the sensual ride.

Mike led her into the bedroom, where he slowly undressed her. When he pulled her sweater from her shoulders, he kissed the hollow at the base of her throat and the sensitive flesh above her bra. When he slipped her slacks from her hips, his lips pressed against her belly, his tongue making a moist circle around her navel. She dropped onto the bed, partially dressed, while he stripped off his own clothing. Sliding himself down beside her, he pulled her into his arms and held her.

Slowly he continued making love to her. He kissed her mouth, catching her lip between his own lips, touching her teeth, her tongue with exploring strokes. He kissed her eyes, the tip of her nose, the base of her throat. Gently he nipped her ear, letting his breath warm the moistness his tongue left.

Where her heart beat in the hollow of her throat, he pressed his lips, letting her excitement flow into him. Moving across her shoulder, he traced kisses along her collarbone, first in one direction and then the other. Easing her bra straps down, he followed their imaginary line to the softly mounded flesh above the beige lace. As he nudged the lace away with lingering kisses he heard her catch her breath. Then he moved lower still. Caroline's held breath became a sigh as he took her nipple into his mouth to tease the hardened bud with his tongue.

"Mike...." Her hands grasped the back of his head; they only held him, not pressing him forward, not pushing him away. "Mike," she gasped again, his name caught in her swift intake of breath.

"What is it that you'd like me to do?" he asked, wanting her to accept the feelings that tore through her by openly telling him how to please her.

She hesitated. "I want you. . .to touch me."

"Where?" he softly asked.

Again she hesitated. "Where you touched me before," she whispered.

Caroline couldn't see the smile her words provoked, but she heard Mike's sigh of pleasure as he slipped his hand beneath the wide band of lace at the top of her bikini pants and pulled them down. Tossing them toward the other discarded clothing, he slipped between her legs and lowered himself, pressing his lips to her inner thigh just above her knee. When he went higher, his kisses growing bolder, more impassioned, she tried to pull away from him in alarm.

"I didn't mean—"

He held her tightly. "Caroline, it's all right. I'm not going to do anything more than what you did to me."

"I know." She tried to shift away. "Mike, I can't—" His hand stole to the place she tried to keep from him. He touched her; she trembled with her need for more. After a while, when his mouth replaced his hand, Caroline learned that she could allow herself even this pleasure.

In the hour of making love that followed, she let him teach her still more ways to give and to receive pleasure. At last they lay quietly together in satiation, Mike holding Caroline in his arms. He kissed her temple. "Every hour we're together makes the time we're apart harder to get through. This next week is going to seem like a month." His words were spoken quietly, a simple statement of fact.

Caroline tilted her head back on his arm so that she could look into his face. "I can't see you next weekend," she told him, dreading what was sure to follow but unable to stifle her words.

"Oh?"

"I have other plans."

"Then I guess it will have to be the weekend after next."

"I can't see you that weekend, either."

"You've made plans for then, too?"

She nodded.

"And the following weekend? Is it also booked solid?" he asked tonelessly.

Caroline sat up, holding the down comforter tightly in front of her. She had changed her mind, deciding it was possible to go on seeing Mike, but only if he would agree to do so according to the original guidelines. "If you recall, when we first started seeing each other, I told you it was on a no-strings-attached basis. Nothing has changed."

He sat up beside her. "The hell it hasn't! It just so happens that I've fallen in love with you since then."

"For now...."

"What's that supposed to mean?"

"It means I have a right to protect myself against the day when you discover you no longer love me."

"And just when, may I ask, does this day occur?" The look she gave him made him realize she wasn't simply exhibiting a stubborn streak of independence; she was deadly serious.

"If I knew that I'd set up a tent and earn my living reading tea leaves." Angrily she tossed her head.

"All right, then, how can you possibly think you can predict my feelings at some future date?"

"Because you're human, aren't you? Since when are humans known for their fidelity?"

Mike raked a hand through his hair. She couldn't be basing her feelings on anything she knew about him. He had to be the victim of a prejudice she had formed long before meeting him. "I think it's about time you told me what happened to your marriage."

"My marriage has nothing to do with this."

"I believe that like I believe you're frigid."

Caroline turned away from him. She had known he wouldn't accept the lie. But to voice the circumstances of her failed marriage was to live through the pain, the mortification again.

"Tell me what happened, Caroline," he urged, his tone gentle now, pleading.

A long silence followed. Maybe he would understand. "I met Tom at the University of Nebraska," she finally began, purposely keeping her voice steady. "He was everything I had ever hoped to find in a husband—bright, ambitious, loving, romantic, attentive—the daydream of every young woman come true. We were married while we were still in college; it was a financial struggle but we survived, knowing the good times were just around the corner." Her fingers absently played with a feather working its way out of the comforter.

"When I was offered the weather job in Houston, I didn't want to go because it meant leaving Tom behind in Kansas City. We had moved there right after college so Tom could work for his uncle while he studied for the bar. His uncle had promised him a partnership as soon as he passed, so you can see why he had to stay in Kansas City. Anyway, Tom insisted I take the job. He said he didn't want to hold me back and that it would be 'sensually provocative' to have a commuter marriage."

Mike stiffened, sensing how Caroline's story was going to end.

"From Houston I went to Cleveland and then to Salt Lake City. It was exciting to be promoted so fast. I was completely caught up in my work. The marriage seemed better than ever. Tom passed his bar exam; the whole world seemed to be laid out at our feet." A frown suddenly creased her forehead, but she forced herself to go on.

"We had worked out a system: every other weekend I would go to Kansas City, in between Tom would come to wherever I was. One weekend, when it was my turn to go to him, I was given an assignment that made it impossible for me to leave. Because Tom was working on an important case, he couldn't come to Salt Lake City. But at the last minute I found I could get away, after all. . . . " Her voice had faded to a whisper.

"There wasn't time to call to let him know I was coming—" She shrugged lightly. Her fingers tugged harder on the feather; she almost had it worked through the cloth. "I thought it would be a wonderful surprise to just show up at the apartment...so I didn't call to have him pick me up. I took a taxi from the airport...." The feather came free.

Mike had to strain to hear her words. He fought an overwhelming urge to take her in his arms.

"I was so excited...I had received word earlier that day that a station in Seattle wanted me to anchor their evening news. I failed to see the strange car in the driveway. I didn't even notice that all the lights in the house were turned off except for those in the bedroom—"

"Caroline," Mike said gently, "you don't have to go on—I can guess the rest."

She did have to go on. She had to finish. She continued as if he hadn't offered her an escape. Once again she was that naive young woman, so filled with happiness and excitement to share that she ran up the stairs to the bedroom without pausing to announce she was home. "I found Tom in bed...making love to another woman...not just any woman, mind you...." Her self-deprecatory laugh caught on a sob. "But the woman I had considered my best friend for over five years."

She turned to Mike, her cheeks wet with tears. "Do you know what I did? I told him I had insisted the station give me the weekend off because I had to go home to tell my husband I wanted a divorce." Caroline fought to control her breathing. "The saddest thing of all was that he believed me."

Mike stopped trying to resist holding her. She came to him willingly, burying her face in his shoulder. When her breathing had calmed he said, "Caroline, you can't possibly think I'm like Tom." Yet he knew she did. "Just because one man—"

"If it were just one man or one woman or one isolated incident...don't you think I've tried...I didn't want to feel like this. I purposely paid attention to other people's marriages. Good people—people I like, some that I even love, like my mother and father." She couldn't bring herself to tell him that her mother had been betrayed by her father. Caroline still loved him because he was who he was, but it was a love laced with pain. "The odds are all against happily ever after, Mike.

"People hurt each other with the best of intentions." She was pleading with him to understand. "I refuse to let that happen to me again. I can't. If I get close to you, the time we would spend together and the distractions you would bring would keep me from pursuing my career the way I should. And then what happens to me one or even two years down the road? What do I have to show for the time and energy I've given you? Nothing but pain and loneliness. If I put into my job what you want me to put into a relationship, I will be one or two steps closer to achieving my goal. I know I won't have nights like this one, but then neither will I know the devastation that parting with someone always brings."

"How can you be so sure that what we have

isn't the exception to the rule? How can you toss it aside so easily?''

''Because for my entire life, whenever it came to relationships, my glass always seemed half-empty. When I've given myself to my work, the glass has been half-full. There are no exceptions for me.''

Mike felt as if he'd just lost a battle he'd never stood a chance of winning. He couldn't even be angry with her for deceiving him—from the beginning she had been completely honest about how far she would commit herself. ''I can't do it your way, Caroline,'' he said, unable to keep the despair from his voice. ''I can't be a casual sometime man in your life. I love you.'' He caressed the side of her face. ''You were right—without fully knowing why I was doing it at the time, I arranged this weekend to show you what I wanted for us. I was wrong not to have listened to what you were telling me all along; that would have saved both of us a lot of heartache.''

She didn't want to believe it was over. ''Mike, we could still see each other . . . we could at least be friends.''

''Now it's you who isn't listening, Caroline. When I told you I loved you, it wasn't just something to say. In an improbably short amount of time you have become the very air I breathe. I can't pretend it will be easier for me if we part now, but I do know that the longer we're together the harder it will be for me to walk away. You're only the second woman I ever seriously considered sharing the rest of my life with. I wanted us to have children.... I...I even went so far as to imagine how they would look. In the rush of thinking about what I wanted and how I felt, I completely ignored your feelings. It seems I owe you an apology.'' He released her and started to get out of bed. ''I'll sleep in the other room tonight. In the morning we'll see if we can't get you an earlier flight back to Los Angeles.''

She reached for him. ''Mike, are you sure? Is there no way we could—''

''You can't have it both ways, Caroline.'' He took her hand from his arm. ''As much as I love you and want to be with you, I won't agree to being anyone's stud service.''

She caught her breath. ''That's a terrible thing to say.''

''It's a terrible way to feel. Think about what you're asking of me—really think about it. When you're through, let me know if you come up with a more palatable conclusion.'' He went to the closet and removed an emerald-green robe. ''I'll see you in the morning.''

THE NIGHT was not an easy one for Caroline. By the time the sky had started to change from black to a deep purple, she still hadn't slept. If only Mike would bend a little. If only he would try to understand her position. What she wanted for them wasn't so unusual—it was the epitome of a thoroughly modern arrangement between two people who lived a thousand miles apart.

His comment about being a stud service had been a cheap shot, one she hadn't deserved.

Weary from lack of sleep and from trying to sleep, Caroline abandoned the effort and climbed out of bed. She went to the closet to see if Mike had another robe. He didn't. Going over to the chair where they had abandoned their clothes the night before, she picked through the pile until she found Mike's shirt and, shivering, slipped it on.

Carefully twisting the doorknob to produce as little noise as possible, Caroline stepped into the hallway on her way to the bathroom. When she passed the living room she was startled to see Mike standing at the window. He turned and caught her staring.

He had often dreamed of seeing her as she was now, her hair in disarray from sleep, wearing nothing save his shirt. The scene implied intimacy, familiarity, as if they were longtime lovers. Her standing in the hallway, more erotic in his oversize clothing than she would have been wearing nothing, created an image he knew he would never forget. It would haunt him on lonely nights, an unwelcome companion during long days.

"I was looking for the bathroom," she said, nonplussed by the intensity of his look.

"There's one just off the bedroom—the door next to the closet."

"Have you been awake all night?"

"There are some things I wanted to think about."

"Me too."

"Oh?"

"I was trying to find a way to make you understand how I feel."

"It isn't that I don't understand, Caroline. I just can't live the way you want me to. Love was a long time coming for me. For some unfathomable reason, it never occurred to me that when it finally did, it would be one-sided." He shoved his hands in his pockets. "I've discovered I like the way I feel when I'm in love—more than like, I've become addicted to it. Somewhere there has to be someone who's going to return my feelings. I've decided it's time I found out who she is." How easily he spoke the lie, as if he hadn't spent the night trying to accept the idea that he would probably live the rest of his life alone. Settling for second best had no appeal for him.

Caroline swallowed. "I'm truly sorry it wasn't me. Perhaps if we had met before...." She believed what she was saying. Didn't she? Because it was so hard to speak the words only meant that Mike was more special than all the others. It had never hurt like this to tell any other man goodbye, not since Tom. Instead of telling her she might be making a mistake, the pain served as a confirmation of her only choice. Breaking up would only hurt more later.

"Do you need anything from the hotel? I could drive over and get it for you." His seeming composure was rapidly disappearing. If she stayed in the same room with him, dressed as she was, he was afraid he would cross over to her, take her in his arms and forget all that had passed between them.

"No... I can change when we get there." How she wished she could go to him, ignoring if only for an hour the problems that kept them apart.

"Do you want some breakfast?"

"I'm not hungry."

"Coffee?"

She shook her head.

"Then why don't you go ahead and get ready. It seems pointless to prolong this."

"You're right," she said, desperately trying to think of something to say that might alter the course of their relationship.

When she didn't leave Mike raised his eyebrows in question. "Was there something else you wanted to tell me?"

Yes! she wanted to shout. But she couldn't express what it was. "No, I guess not." She turned and walked back down the hall to the bedroom.

Mike watched her go, aching to follow, unable to move. He sank into the chair that had been his bed that night. A voice pounded on his senses, echoing the question that had come to him in the blackest part of the night. *Would things have been different if I hadn't pushed her so hard?* It was his bane that he would never know.

THE FLIGHT BACK to Los Angeles seemed twice as long as the flight out. Caroline spent the hours staring through the window, lost in her own world, tallying over and over again the arguments that justified her actions. She left the plane convinced that her decision had been the right one.

She drove home by a circuitous route to delay arrival at her apartment, knowing it would seem more empty than when she'd left. She wasn't ready to face the desolation. Stopping at a seafood restaurant for a dinner she only half ate postponed her arrival even more. When she ran out of places to go, she headed for home.

Leaving her overnight bag in the hallway, she walked through the apartment to the bedroom without turning on the lights. She stripped off her clothing, dropping her expensive suit in a heap on the floor before crawling into bed. Grabbing the extra pillow, she wrapped her arms around it and drew it close. Long minutes passed. Her eyes grew accustomed to the dark. Her lip, where she had drawn it between her teeth to keep from futilely crying out her loneliness, had begun to bleed.

Tossing the pillow aside, Caroline swung her legs out from under the covers, stood up and headed for the bathroom. She shielded her eyes from the light glaring off the stark white walls while she groped for the shower faucets. As soon as the water warmed she stepped inside the enclosure. Her back to the spray, she reached up to cover her face with her hands, trying to muffle the sobs. She turned, letting the water strike her face, washing away tears she refused to acknowledge.

CHAPTER ELEVEN

A WEEK AND A HALF had passed since Caroline's return from Houston. Ten days in which she had risen each morning determined to get on with her life, and had gone to bed each night exhausted from the effort. John Wakefield had called in the middle of the first week to apologize for his stuffy behavior and to ask her to a premiere he had to cover the next night. She had politely refused, spending the evening watching an old movie on television, eating the only dinner she could find the ingredients to prepare—popcorn.

She was thankful that Randy had been tied up with other reporters since her return and was too busy to notice the undercurrent of despair she managed to hide from everyone else. With any luck she would be herself again before he noticed anything was wrong.

Entering the newsroom that day, she immediately headed for the daily-assignment board. Skipping across the line of reporters' names, she came to her own. Written in the first square below was "Dogfight Promoters," and below that, "Class on How To Flirt." Cindy Hamelin was her camera operator for the day. It would be the first time they had worked together.

Caroline would read the data she'd gathered on both stories on the way to the locations. Walking past the room where the cameras were kept, she spotted Cindy and stopped to give her a hand carrying her equipment. Fully outfitted camera operators carried almost seventy pounds, some of it around the waist, the rest either balanced on or slung over a shoulder. It was immediately obvious to anyone who attempted the job why it was important to keep physically fit. Cindy told Caroline she not only jogged regularly, but she also went to a gym to lift weights three times a week.

A few hours after they'd left the station, they finished a discouraging interview with two men who promoted illegal dogfights and the animal-control officers who tried to stop them. They had more than an hour to wait before their flirting assignment, so they stopped to eat at a health-food restaurant Cindy frequented.

"Believe it or not," Cindy said after ordering a meatless hamburger for each of them, "I've even talked Randy into forsaking red meat."

"Meat maybe. . . but what about French fries?"

She laughed. "You know him pretty well, don't you? I admit I haven't completely weaned him from all junk food, but I'm gaining ground." She folded her hands on the table and leaned slightly closer to Caroline. "I even managed to get him to own up to the fact that he had never jogged before he met me, doesn't have a grandmother within two thousand miles, let alone one he takes out every week, and has never been on a racing bike in his life.''

"My God—" Caroline choked on her herb tea "—how did you do that?"

"I told him either he played straight, or not at all. He said you had warned him to mend his ways, but that he'd ignored the advice until he was up to his knees in the stories he had flung around and didn't know how to free himself."

"Obviously I was the wrong person to tell him, that's all."

"Once he cut out all the garbage he'd been using on other women, we started getting along a lot better." Cindy smiled. "Actually, he's not such a bad guy to have around."

"You can tell all that after less than a month?" Caroline thought she was simply holding up her end of the conversation. Not until Cindy answered did she realize how dangerously close she was to paralleling her relationship to Mike with Cindy and Randy's.

"It takes a lot less than a month to find out whether two people have anything going for them. After that it's just a matter of discovering who squeezes the toothpaste in the middle and who rolls it up at the end. Frankly, I'd be surprised if Randy and I lasted a year. . . ." Again she smiled. "But I can tell you, it's going to be a memorable year."

"How can you possibly enter into a relationship with someone thinking it's not going to last?"

Cindy stared at Caroline as if she'd asked the question in a foreign language. "There isn't one thing about living that's offered with a guarantee. It's immaterial whether Randy and I last ten weeks or ten years. While we're together we're going to have a great time."

Caroline had never met anyone like Cindy. She was unsure whether to credit her naive attitude to her youth or inexperience. "Obviously the high divorce rate in this country doesn't bother you."

"If you're asking me if I think unhappy people should stay together for the sake of statistics or even the kids, I've got to say no. There comes a time when you have to cut your losses and get on with living. Too many people try to hang on to something that's gone sour. They only wind up making themselves bitter and miserable in the process."

"It's easier to maintain that philosophy when you haven't been through a divorce," Caroline said softly.

Cindy leaned back in her chair to give the waitress more room to serve the food. "What makes you think I haven't?"

"Your age, for one."

"Twenty-nine isn't old enough?"

Caroline's mouth dropped open. "I can't believe you're twenty-nine. You're older than I am." Cindy hardly looked voting age.

"I'll be thirty in four months. I have two sons, five and seven, who live one week with me, the next week with their dad. They think Randy is top drawer because he can outscore them on all the video games.''

"But doesn't it bother you that they might become too attached to him? You said you didn't think the two of you would last a year—I don't understand how you could do that to your kids.''

"My children are a big part of my life. I'm not about to shove them off to a sitter's every time I go out with someone. Sure they like Randy, but they also understand that friendships don't always work out or necessarily last as long as you might want them to. I wouldn't dream of denying them the good times they have with Randy and me just because someday, maybe, he might not be there. I said I didn't expect what we have to last a year. . . I might be pleasantly surprised. Once you get past all the macho garbage, he's one hell of a guy.''

Caroline was at a loss for words. Cindy's philosophy sounded wonderful, but it was far too simplistic to fit into the real world of jealousies and hatreds—if a person failed to fit into her scenario, did she never feel bitter and rejected? "You were lucky your ex-husband felt the same way you did.''

Cindy laughed. "The only thing he and I have in common anymore is a love for the children we created together. It was my 'free thinking,' as he called it, that drove us apart.'' She shrugged. "We had some good years, years I wouldn't trade for anything. Thank God we had sense enough not to prolong the bad ones.'' Cindy glanced at her watch. "It looks like old motormouth has done it again. I've been talking so long that we're going to be late if we don't hurry up and eat." She batted her eyelashes comically. "I would hate to miss out on something. Flirting has never been my forte."

Caroline sincerely doubted that Cindy had ever had to resort to anything more than simply walking into a room to be noticed. She picked up her pseudo hamburger and took a bite. Chewing thoughtfully, tasting the flavor and noting the texture, she swallowed. If she had learned nothing else from Cindy today, she had learned that the next time they worked together, *she* would pick the restaurant.

THE CLASS ON FLIRTING turned out to be more fun to cover than either of them had anticipated. A predominantly male audience that had started out coolly soon warmed up after lighthearted prodding by the teacher. In a private interview with the instructor, conducted at the break, Caroline learned that the three-hour class, offered twice a month, was not only filled for the following six sessions, but had a waiting list.

Later, on their way back to the station Cindy and Caroline tried to analyze the enthusiasm for something seemingly from another century.

"I think the most telling thing is the percentage of men who attend," Cindy remarked. "Didn't the instructor say it had never been less than sixty percent and that most of the time it was more?"

Caroline nodded.

"Of course, I'm not sure why it's telling or what it means." Cindy laughed.

"I'd say it means there are a lot of lonely people out there." Caroline's tone was thoughtful.

"Did you happen to notice that most of the women arrived in pairs, but the men came in by themselves?"

Caroline glanced over at Cindy, who was maneuvering the van through the congested streets of Los Angeles with the aplomb of a taxi driver. "And what's your conclusion as to the social significance of that observation?"

"Guys lead more lonely lives than women do. We aren't afraid to share our innermost thoughts, or to ask a friend to do something really dumb with us." She shifted in her seat. "Anytime you can unload your problems on someone, you feel better for it. Boy, I know I do. I have this super friend I went to high school with that I would crawl over hot coals to see. I can call her up at the end of an absolutely horrible day, and she'll have me laughing within fifteen minutes."

Caroline thought of all the friends she had made during her odyssey around the country, from station to station, and her purposeful decision not to keep in touch with them because of the unlikelihood that their paths would ever cross again. No...that wasn't completely true, she used to keep in touch...before her divorce. It wasn't until afterward— She decided to change the subject to something less hazardous to her peace of mind. "How long have you been a camera operator?"

Cindy gave her a puzzled look at the abrupt change of topic. "Almost four years now," she said slowly, her confusion evident in her voice.

"Where did you get your training?"

"I went to UCLA for two years, then transferred to SCRU."

Caroline smiled at the instant image of the SCRU float Cindy's words had evoked. Her smile quickly faded as other memories intruded. To banish the man she saw standing on that float from her mind's eye, she blurted out, "What are your plans for the future?"

This time the look Cindy gave her was more than puzzled; it was incredulous. "It just so happens that after spending all that time studying, I think of the job I have now in terms of a career."

Propping her arm on the window ledge, Caroline leaned her head on her knuckles. "I'm sorry. That was a dumb thing for me to say."

"I suppose it's reasonable that someone might think a woman would have a shorter tenure in this field than a man—I certainly have to work harder to keep strong enough to carry the equipment than a man ever would. And there are extra burdens on lots of women in predominantly male fields. Look at you, for instance. When was the last time you heard of a man being fired because his hair was turning gray or wrinkles had started showing through the pancake makeup?"

"That particular double standard can make people do outrageous things," Caroline agreed. "I knew an anchorwoman in Denver who refused to smile off camera for fear of deepening her laugh lines."

"Do you ever worry about your future?"

"Of course. Fear of being unemployable because I've lost the first flush of womanhood can give me a stronger boot in the rear and get me moving faster than just about anything else. The way I have it figured, I only have so many years to make it to the upper network level; after that I could knock on those doors until my knuckles were bloody and no one would answer. But from all I can determine, once you're there the powers that be will let you age a little. Personally, I don't think they'll ever hire a woman who's already past forty unless she has something on someone." Caroline recrossed her legs, nudging aside an empty paper cup someone had left on the floor. "If I don't make it within the next few years I won't make it at all."

"That seems so damn unfair."

"It's an attitude that's a long way from changing. No matter how many female reporters sue and eventually win their cases, they're not going to convince the populace that age can be as distinguished and as attractive on a woman as it can on a man. Especially when sponsors and ad agencies are using twelve- and thirteen-year-old girls to model sexy clothing."

Cindy broke the silence that followed with a hearty laugh. "Ms Travers—you're my kind of woman."

"I like you, too, Ms Hamelin."

A half hour later they drove into the back parking lot at KMTV. As was her habit, Caroline swung by the assignment board on her way to her desk. The next day hadn't been filled in yet. She glanced over to the long-range board and noticed the middle two weeks of February had been blacked out under her name. She stepped closer to read Sid Minkner's scrawling script. When she had put enough of the words together, she caught her breath in agonized surprise.

She was being sent to Houston and then to Florida to do a story on the shuttle launch. This had to be someone's idea of a joke. But whose? No one at the station knew she and Mike were no longer seeing each other. That was it. Someone was putting her on, thinking she would welcome the opportunity to be with Mike. That had to be it.

Looking away from the board, she noticed Sid at his desk. With forced casualness she walked over to him. "What's this thing about Houston?" Her mouth was so dry she could hardly speak.

"It was Mr. Paulson's idea. Seems NASA's putting on a special show for this launch because they're going to be repairing particularly complex satellites with free-orbiting astronauts. As I understand the scenario, none of the maneuvers are new, it's just the first time they've combined so many complex chores for one flight. They've invited press from all over, and since you've become our space expert, you got the assignment. Kavanaugh is going with you. All the other arrangements—food, lodging, transportation after you arrive—are being taken care of by NASA."

Frantically Caroline sought a reason to turn down the assignment. She couldn't return to Houston. Not yet. "I feel a little selfish about getting this job after the plum pieces you sent my way last fall. I don't want any hard feelings among the other reporters.... Wouldn't you like to offer it to one of them first?"

Sid looked up from the newspaper he'd been perusing for story possibilities. His eyes narrowed suspiciously. "Are you refusing the assignment?"

Declining an assignment, complaining about it or trying to switch with another reporter because the job seemed unpleasant was tantamount to journalistic suicide. "No...." She collapsed into the chair beside Sid's desk. "I'm trying to worm my way out of it by pretending I have altruistic motives." *Dammit!* She could feel her eyes starting to burn with tears.

Sid's voice dropped to a concerned whisper. "Hey, kid...what's the matter?"

"I have private reasons for not wanting to go to Houston right now."

The lines creasing Sid's wide forehead slowly faded as understanding dawned. "The big handsome fella who picked Paulson's roses and sent you the pizza?"

"You knew about the roses?"

"I simply put two and two together when I found the old man out there measuring footprints the next morning." He touched her arm. "I can get you out of this, if you want me to. But I can't do it without anyone noticing. It was Paulson himself who said you were to be given the assignment at our weekly strategy meeting."

"How long has this been on the boards?"

"We received the letter from Houston over a month ago. We decided to go with it because of the favorable response the station received on the last piece you did." He squeezed her arm. "See—if you weren't so damn good, you wouldn't get yourself into these predicaments."

She chewed on her lip while she considered his offer. "Let me sleep on it."

"Take two nights, a week, if you want. Like I said before, there's no way we can pull this off without everyone knowing something's amiss. I filled in the blocks under your name right after you left today. Everyone's seen it except the early-morning crew." His expression was regretful. "I'm sorry, kid...I wish I could do something more."

"Thanks, Sid." She stood up to leave. "I'll get back to you first thing tomorrow."

THAT EVENING as she was padding around her apartment in robe and slippers, searching through empty cupboards for something to eat, she received a phone call. Her answering "Hello" reflected the tumultuous day she'd had.

"Is this Caroline Travers?"

"Yes...?"

"Ms Travers, this is Albert Morrison." There

was a pause to give Caroline time to recognize the name. She didn't need it. Anyone with any ambition in the field of network journalism recognized the name of the man who did the hiring.

"Yes, Mr. Morrison. What can I do for you?" She wiped her hand, suddenly moist, on her robe.

"First of all, let me apologize for my unorthodox timing, but I thought it better to try to reach you at home rather than at the station." He didn't wait for a reply. "I'll be in Los Angeles the last week in February. I'd like to make arrangements to get together with you to discuss your future, if you're interested, that is."

With a coolness she didn't come close to feeling, she replied, "I am indeed interested. Any morning would be fine."

"Wonderful. I'll have my secretary call you within the next few days to set up the time and place. I look forward to meeting you, Ms Travers."

"As I do you, Mr. Morrison." Slowly she replaced the receiver. For long minutes she stood perfectly still, trying to absorb the knowledge that she had just answered the call she'd been waiting more than five years to receive. She felt none of the emotions she had anticipated, only numbness. The call had come earlier than she had ever dared dream it would—earlier by years.

A week later she got another unexpected call. Ann Peters would be in Southern California for several days and wondered if they could get together. They made arrangements to meet the next

day, a Saturday, at Ann's sister's house in Newport Beach.

Caroline had mixed feelings about the meeting.
She was delighted at the prospect of seeing Ann
again, but unsure how to tell her she didn't want
to talk about Mike Webster. She decided the best
approach was honesty. As soon as Ann mentioned
anything about Mike, she would tell her it was
over between them and that any further discussion
was useless. Period.

HAVING BEEN IN SOUTHERN CALIFORNIA almost a
year, Caroline knew that anyone who could only
afford a $125,000 home in Newport Beach was
considered near poverty level. But she was unprepared for the flagrant displays of wealth she
passed on her way to meet Ann. The money the
locals spent on cars and yachts alone was enough
to keep an average-size city running for several
years.

Caroline had to drive through a guarded gate,
where her name was checked against a list of approved visitors before she could get to Ann's
sister's house. She discovered, to her surprise, that
it wasn't as large as the residences on Orange
Grove Boulevard. But there was one large, multi-
million-dollar difference: this house sat on ocean-
front property.

Ann opened the front door before Caroline was
out of the car. She met her on the walkway, giving
her friend a hug of welcome. "This is quite a
place," Caroline said.

"Yes, isn't it? Agnes and Len haven't lived here very long, but they seem to like it." Ann took Caroline's arm and walked with her back into the house.

Caroline looked around at the obviously professionally decorated living room. "I can't see anything *not* to like."

"Oh, it's a nice place to visit, but I can't imagine living here." A laugh accompanied the impish twinkle in her eyes. "Come out to the patio with me—it's lovely."

And indeed it was. The flagstone terrace, surrounded by eight-foot walls of glass, put there to keep the ocean breezes from chilling the guests, was as large as Caroline's entire apartment. Taking the chair next to Ann's, she asked, "Do you come here often?"

"As little as possible. I'm always afraid I might break something. There are objets d'art sitting around this place that cost more than Cory earns in a year." Ann chuckled. "That's an exaggeration—though not by much."

"Speaking of Cory—"

"He's fine, as are the kids. Oh, but maybe that wasn't what you were asking."

"I was just wondering where he was."

"In Houston. Where else? He's attached to that place with a very short cord until they're through debriefing him after the flight. I'm spending a few days here with my sister when she brings her new baby daughter home from the hospital."

"Is that where Len—you did say his name was Len—is now?"

"Oh, my, no. Leave the dealership on a Saturday? While most people buy their luxury cars on weekdays, there is that percentage who drift in on Saturday. I don't want to make him out to be the personification of greed, just the next best thing."

Their conversation flowed as easily as if they were long-standing friends. When Caroline agreed that, yes, she was hungry and could eat some lunch, they went into the kitchen. Taking their sandwiches and soft drinks back to the patio, Caroline realized with a start that she was anxiously awaiting news of Mike. But Ann hadn't even mentioned his name.

When it was time to leave Ann walked her guest to the car. Caroline was halfway down the driveway when she stopped the car, got out and approached her friend. "Ann. . . how is Mike?"

Ann's smile faded. "I didn't think you would want to talk about him, so I purposely didn't say anything."

"I know. . . I thought the same thing."

"But?"

"I would like to know how he's getting along."

"First tell me how you're doing, Caroline."

"Me? I'm doing fine," she answered too quickly. "Well, maybe not fine. But things are looking pretty good for me. . . ." She was about to tell Ann about the phone call from Albert Morrison, then thought better of it.

Ann folded her arms across her chest. "We haven't seen too much of Mike lately. His job gets pretty frantic whenever a launch date approaches. I understand it's going to be even tougher on him this time because of all the press people who've been invited.''

Caroline should have known better than to question Ann about Mike. The woman protected him as she would her own family, and Caroline was the outsider who had hurt him. Besides, what difference would any other answer have made? It was better not to know. "Did I mention I'm one of those press people who's coming to Houston?"

Ann stiffened. "Is Mike aware of this?"

"I don't know whether he is or not." She started to get back into the car. "I tried to get out of going. . . ."

"I'll tell him you're coming—at least that way it won't be such a surprise."

"Maybe you and I could get together one afternoon while I'm there."

The other woman nodded, forcing a smile. "Call me."

Caroline waved as she drove away, trying not to dwell on Ann's change of mood.

That night was the worst she had spent since coming back from Houston. Only the appointment with Albert Morrison brought her any comfort. Knowing she was so close to her dream was like a confirmation that she had been right to break off her relationship with Mike. That knowledge did little to ease the ache she carried deep inside.

CHAPTER TWELVE

MIKE WAS WALKING up to his front door when the telephone started to ring. By the time he was inside it had rung five times. "Hello," he said, fully expecting to hear the hum of a dead line.

"Mike, this is Ann."

The tone of her voice, usually so filled with bubbling good cheer, sent a chill down his back. "What's wrong?"

"I was going to wait until I got back to call you, but I decided it might be better to give you a little warning. I saw Caroline today...she told me she's one of the reporters coming to Houston." There was a pause. "She said she tried to get out of going but couldn't."

Wearily he rubbed his eyes. "I saw her name on the list of confirmations, Ann. I've known since Wednesday."

"Are you all right?"

He smiled at the concern in her voice, his lip still feeling strangely naked without the mustache. Maybe he would try growing one again someday, a day in the distant future when looking at his own reflection in the mirror didn't remind him of Caroline. "Yes, sweet Ann, I'm okay." He forced more enthusiasm into his words than he felt. "I'm just tired, that's all."

"You and Cory are going to be basket cases before this launch is over."

"How did she look?" he asked softly, ignoring Ann's attempt to change the subject.

"Who?"

"Ann...."

There was a resigned sigh at the other end of the line. "She looked tired, and thin. Her clothes just kind of hung on her."

"That's how she buys them."

"Two sizes too big?"

"She thinks it hides her chest."

"A gunnysack wouldn't hide her figure."

"I once told her as much, but she didn't believe me."

"Mike?"

"Huh?"

"I don't think we should be doing this. Talking about Caroline isn't going to help you to forget her."

As if not talking about her would. "You're probably right. How's Agnes and her new baby?"

"Beautiful—both of them. You wouldn't believe me if I told you just how beautiful that little girl is." She laughed lightly. "Agnes keeps saying they must have made a mistake in the nursery."

"The new baby probably just takes after her aunt."

"If I weren't already married I'd give you one helluva chase, fella." Ann's words were a long-standing joke between them, usually said in reply to a compliment.

"And what makes you think I'd run?"

"Because you have brains underneath all your own beauty."

Mike smiled. "Take care, Ann. Don't let Newport Beach get the best of you."

"Don't worry, I won't. I'm leaving here and heading back to the real world as soon as I can."

They exchanged goodbyes and hung up. Mike stood for several minutes, his hand resting on the receiver, too tired to start the motions necessary to prepare his dinner, too tired to care whether he ate. He would have liked to think Caroline was feeling his loss, that perhaps somewhere deep inside she mourned the passing of what might have been—but he was too much of a realist to think she was losing any sleep over what had basically been her choice.

Usually a realist, he qualified. His tendency to blame their parting on Caroline's stubbornness brought a twinge of guilt now, as it had on several occasions in the past two weeks. No matter how hard he tried, he couldn't shake the feeling that his "all or nothing" attitude could have been less forcefully applied, and perhaps the result would have been different. He should have had sense enough to realize she was someone who couldn't be pushed that hard.

Disgusted with the futile direction his thoughts were taking, Mike left the room. He flicked the light on in the kitchen and began rummaging through the refrigerator. With each day that passed since he and Caroline had said their final goodbyes, the ache grew progressively worse.

Dammit! He shook his head as if trying to clear it. It didn't matter whether or not he'd come on too strong. A change of tactics would have meant absolutely nothing in the long run. Caroline had decided the direction she wanted her life to take, and nothing he did or said now or then would have made any difference. If he'd been more tactful he might have postponed the inevitable, nothing more.

Mike let the refrigerator door swing closed, flipped the kitchen light off and went to bed.

SEVERAL DAYS LATER Caroline was on a plane headed for Houston. As she settled down beside Randy, she gave her airline carryon bag one final shove with her foot to secure it beneath the seat in front of her. Taking one deep breath and then another, she tried to calm her nerves; lately she was turning into a blithering idiot.

If she was in this bad shape before the plane had even left Los Angeles, what was she going to do when she actually saw Mike? She could get sick, phone and tell Sid he had to send someone to take her place. *Get* sick? She *was* sick. Her stomach felt like the site for a range war between two rival flocks of birds.

Randy elbowed her. "Fasten your seat belt."

"Huh?" She stared at him blankly.

"Your seat belt?" he repeated slowly.

"Oh. . .yeah." Caroline clicked the buckle, pulling the tail so that the nylon strap rested snugly across her hips.

"Do me a favor, will you?" Randy said, pushing the button on her armrest to bring her seat all the way forward, as they had been instructed to do several minutes earlier.

"Sure. . . ."

"When the stewardess asks you if you want something to drink, say no. The way you're going, you'd have it spilled all over me two seconds after she gave it to you."

"You're imagining things. There's absolutely nothing wrong with me."

He took her hand and held it out in front of her, then let go. "You're trembling worse than a summer leaf that's just been told about autumn."

She dropped her hand back in her lap, intertwining her fingers, making a large fist. "I am not."

"Hey, boss lady," he said softly. "You don't have to pretend with me."

"I'm just a little wrung out, that's all."

"If that's the way you want it, then that's the way it is." He leaned back in his seat. "Poke me when we get to Texas."

"You're going to sleep?"

He turned his head and peered at her through his one open eye. "You have some objection?"

She had counted on his company to distract her from thinking about Mike. "How's Cindy?" she blurted out. "I haven't seen her in days."

Like a cat investigating a mousey squeak, he pounced. "Bingo!" He chuckled. "Hang on for another two or three minutes, and I'll tell you more than you ever wanted to know about the fair-haired Cindy." He glanced out the window, raptly watching as they made their final turn onto the runway. "You'll have to excuse me. I haven't done this often enough to be blasé about it. I still get a big kick out of takeoffs and landings."

Listening to Randy, she realized with a start that easily admitting to little-boy wonder over an ordinary flight was something Mike might have done. That was one of the things she had liked about him. One of many.

When they were airborne Randy turned back to Caroline. "Cindy told me you two have worked together several times in the past few weeks. She likes you a lot and is worried that you're eating a hole in your stomach with whatever's bothering you."

"How would she know about ulcers? I can't imagine Cindy ever letting anything upset her."

Randy laughed. "She told me she once had an ulcer so big it put her in the hospital. Maybe that's why she can recognize the symptoms in you."

"When did all of this happen?"

"Just before her divorce. She swore it would never happen to her again—says that in a way she's thankful she went through what she did, though, because it made her the easygoing person she is today."

"Things are still going well for you two, I take it?"

"So well that I'm seriously thinking about asking her to marry me."

The gasp of surprise came too quickly for Caroline to hide.

"I know," Randy said. "You're going to tell me we've only known each other a little over a month...she's older than I am by five important years...there are her two kids to take into consideration...." He was counting the points off on his fingers. "I'm immature...and why get married when we could just live together. Have I missed anything?"

Caroline forced a smile she didn't feel. "I don't think you're any more immature than any other twenty-four-year-old bachelor."

"That's it? That's your strongest vote of confidence?"

She met his hope-filled gaze, catching her lip between her teeth. "You're not sincerely asking my advice, are you?"

"Maybe not your advice—but I wouldn't object to listening to an opinion."

"That's tantamount to a convention of radicals inviting a conservative to be their keynote speaker."

"Sometimes it helps to get another viewpoint, no matter from which direction it happens to come."

He wasn't going to let her back off gracefully. She looked down at her clasped hands while she considered her answer. "I think getting married this soon after meeting each other would be a terrible mistake." He waited for her to go on. "You should know each other better, discover your likes and dislikes. It takes more time than you've given it to build a solid foundation."

"Does a solid foundation assure a longer or better marriage?"

"Of course it does." She thought then of the supposedly solid marriages she knew about that had collapsed after twenty years or even thirty years. "At least it should." When he only sat and stared at her, she finally admitted, "I don't know whether it does or not." She glanced up to see two stewardesses pushing a beverage cart, working their way down the aisle toward her and Randy. "But if you waited a while longer and discovered after the first blast of excitement had worn off that you weren't as enamored as you thought, breaking up would be far less complicated."

"Maybe what I want is for it to be complicated. That way we would try harder to make our relationship work out."

"You've already made up your mind, haven't you?"

"All I know for sure is a gut feeling that tells me if I don't go for this, I'll regret it as long as I live." He leaned his head against the seat. "When I was a little kid—the whole time I was growing up, actually—my mom would drag all of us to these huge family reunions every summer. There were people at those things even she didn't know. To entertain myself, I used to walk around and listen to the tales my relatives told one another.

"After the first couple of hours, when the bragging about how good they were all doing died down, what I called the 'almost' stories would begin. There were more of those than anything else. Fortunes almost made but for the investment money kept in the bank, moves almost made but for the comfort of staying in the same spot.... When the evening settled in a little deeper and the beer flowed more freely, these voices would grow hushed, and they would start to talk about loves almost won but for a moment's hesitation. I swore to myself that I would never grow old dreaming about 'what ifs' and 'maybes.' I vowed I would live my life taking the less-traveled fork in the road, and I'd never let the woman who caught my eye escape without a try."

"If you feel this way, why in the world would you ask someone like me to advise you?"

"I never meant to say I wouldn't look twice before I dove into strange waters, only that I wouldn't let the fact that they were unfamiliar keep me out."

"Where have you been keeping this sage side of you buried?"

"Why, beneath an exterior of devastating charm, where else?"

Caroline groaned. When she glanced back at him, a long-absent smile curved her mouth.

"Hold that!" he said dramatically. "I haven't seen you smile for over two weeks. Not since—"

"You've hardly seen me at all, let alone with a smile," she rushed to answer. His knowing look told her she hadn't fooled him.

Suddenly the stewardess was beside them offering drinks, effectively interrupting their conversation, to Caroline's profound, silent thanks. When the cart had passed Caroline lifted her glass in toast to Randy. "I know this is a radical thing for a conservative to say, but here it is...go for it!" They touched plastic cups, then took a drink of their colas, his regular, hers diet. No sooner had they swallowed than Caroline put her hand on Randy's arm and gave him an apologetic look. "I'll choke if I don't add...wait at least a few more weeks first."

Randy laughed aloud. "I think I could manage that." He took another swallow. "Now let's talk about you."

"Let's not."

"Remember the sage fellow you have for a traveling companion? He might be able to help."

"Trust me on this, Randy. There's nothing you can do."

He leaned over and quickly kissed her on the cheek. "Well, don't forget I'm here if you want me."

Caroline was embarrassed by her own feeling of surprise. How could she have forgotten how wonderful it felt to have friends who sincerely cared?

THANKS TO RANDY'S CONTINUING BANTER, the trip to Houston passed more smoothly than Caroline had anticipated. When the plane touched ground, however, not even his reassuring smile kept her heart from beating wildly in her chest. Nor did telling herself she wouldn't see Mike until that evening. He was scheduled to give the welcoming speech.

In her room at the hotel, while she dressed for dinner, she tried to analyze her strange behavior. She and Mike hadn't parted enemies, so she couldn't be nervous about any possible confrontation. True enough, what had happened between them had been her decision. Why then, even if she wasn't looking forward to being with him again, couldn't she at least feel neutral? Perhaps she was afraid to see any lingering hurt in his eyes. . . or afraid to face the uncomfortable possibility that he might try to renew their relationship. What would she say if he were to ask to see her again. . . on her terms this time?

Rather than dwell on the answer, Caroline left her room to search for Randy.

THE BRIEF ORIENTATION MEETING, to be held in the hotel's conference room, was set for nine o'clock that evening, giving reporters coming in from all over the country time to check in and get settled. Caroline purposely arrived as close to nine as she could, hoping to slip unobtrusively into the room with other latecomers. But there was no one around; they were all inside. She stared at the assembled crowd through the crack in the partially open side door, seeking familiar faces, seeing several she recognized. A strange reluctance to enter gripped her.

"Looking for anyone in particular?" an achingly familiar voice asked.

Caroline froze. Desperately she fought to regain the composure she had had only moments earlier. Unable to turn, she answered while facing the door. "I was supposed to meet Randy Kavanaugh here, but apparently we missed each other." She took a deep breath. "Shouldn't you be inside?"

Although Mike had spotted Caroline the instant he stepped out of the elevator, he had hesitated before going up to her, taking a moment to watch her odd behavior while trying to calm himself down. Ann had been right; she did look thinner. But to his hungry eyes, the sight of her was an incredible feast. For what had to be the hundredth time since they'd parted, he said a silent prayer of thanks that they weren't living in the same city. The proximity would have been unbearable. "How have you been, Caroline?" he asked, unable to keep an intimate tone from his voice.

"Fine. And you?" How cold she sounded.

Mike stiffened. "The same," he answered as coolly. He reached for the door, his arm accidently brushing hers; she jumped and pulled her arm against her body. A profound feeling of sadness washed over him. She couldn't even stand to be touched by him. "Wouldn't you rather wait inside?" he asked, pulling the door all the way open.

"No." She stepped aside, giving him far more room to pass than necessary. "I'm sure I'll be able to hear everything from here."

He glanced at her a final time before turning and walking to the podium.

The look on his face stunned her. She wasn't

sure what she had expected, but that he would treat her with indifference had never occurred to her. But wasn't that exactly what she wanted?

Caroline felt empty, confused, defenseless...as if she had been walking beside a calm sea until suddenly a great wave struck, forcefully washing the sand from beneath her feet. She struggled for balance.

After all they had shared, how could he look at her as if he hadn't really seen her? Yet, she ruthlessly reminded herself, that was exactly what she wanted. Mike's amplified voice brought her crashing back to her surroundings.

"Good evening, ladies and gentlemen. For the few of you I haven't had the privilege of meeting, I'd like to introduce myself. I'm Mike Webster, the NASA spokesman for the shuttle program—" Applause interrupted his words. "I'm going to make this as brief as possible so that you may retire early." He grinned, then added, "Whether it is to the bar or to your bed, I leave to your discretion—" This time laughter interrupted him. "First, let me say that NASA sincerely appreciates the additional media coverage your attendance indicates we'll be getting for this flight.

"Now for a brief rundown of the week. During your three days here at the Johnson Space Center, we'll be covering not only the standard tour, but several areas rarely open to the public. Late Thursday we'll fly to the Kennedy Space Center, and Saturday morning we'll watch the launch from VIP seats. My staff—whom I will introduce to you tomorrow morning—and I will be available at all times for questions. Now if there are no questions this evening, I'll say good night and meet you all at the buses tomorrow morning.''

A short man with a graying crew cut stood up. ''When will we get the press kits?''

''They'll be passed out on the buses tomorrow. But if you'd like one tonight, you can stop by my suite later.'' He looked around the room. ''Anyone else?''

Caroline closed the door, turned and slowly walked away. *He had shaved off his mustache.* A tightness started behind her eyes that changed into a tingling. She blinked and looked up at the ceiling. *Stop it!* She blinked again and yet again. Why should she care that he'd shaved it off? He had only grown it as a crazy, impulsive lark in the first place.

A door burst open behind her, and she heard the sounds of the meeting breaking up. Her eyes were misty with unshed tears, making it more difficult to search for an escape route. Seeing a door with a lighted exit sign overhead, she hurried over to it and discovered a stairwell. Caroline slumped down on one of the steps, her forehead on her knees.

She turned in surprise moments later when the door opened, revealing her hiding place to Randy. He looked concerned.

''Want to tell me what you're doing in....'' His voice faded as he stepped closer and noticed the thin trails of moisture on her cheeks. Awkwardly he folded his arms across his chest and mumbled something incoherent, then unfolded his arms and jammed his hands into his pockets. Finally he swore softly and reached for her.

Grateful for the shelter, she collapsed into his embrace.

"What's up, boss lady?" he tenderly asked.

"You...wouldn't...understand," she said, attempting to talk and fight a new flood of tears at the same time.

"Try me."

"*I* don't understand."

"Oh, I see."

She wiped her cheeks with the back of her hand. "What do you see?"

"Running into Webster again obviously wasn't as easy to handle as you thought it was going to be."

"What could you possibly know about Mike and me?" She couldn't keep the testy note from her voice. "I haven't said anything to anyone."

Randy reached into his back pocket, pulled out a folded handkerchief and handed it to her. "I can see the results. I don't need to know details."

"That's good—" her defensive answer was automatic "—because you're not going to hear any from me." Inwardly she recoiled at her stand-offish behavior; outwardly she gave no indication that she hadn't meant every word.

"Caroline...do you have so many friends that you can't use any more? Is that why you hold everyone who tries to get close to you at arm's length?"

"I...I...." She couldn't answer him. A lump was firmly lodged in her throat. She gestured helplessly with her hands, finally settling on a ragged shrug. "No," she whispered, desperate not to lose the easygoing camaraderie they had developed.

Randy stared at her a moment longer before he dropped his arm across her shoulders and guided her up the stairs. "This is the plan: we're going to your room. When we get there we're going to order a bottle of tequila, a couple of limes and a shaker of salt. After they arrive we're going to sit and consume said room-service items until I ask you to tell me all about Mike Webster, and you look at me and say, 'Who?'"

Caroline turned her head into his shoulder. "Do you suppose we could get some popcorn, too?"

"I'll sneak down to the bar and see what I can make off with. If by chance they don't have any there, we'll send someone to the nearest theater. One way or another, we'll get you some popcorn."

"I've never seen this side of you before." She looked up at him. "Where did you leave your white charger?"

They had reached the landing. "He's double parked in front of Cindy's house."

"I hope she knows how lucky she is."

"If you don't mind—" Randy laughed "—I'd like to get that on tape sometime before we leave Houston."

When they reached Caroline's room he contacted room service and placed the order, then hung up and turned to Caroline. "The tequila will be up shortly. While we're waiting I'm going across the street myself for the popcorn. If we send someone we might wait all night."

"You don't have to do that. I can do without."

He struck a dramatic pose. "Oh, yes I must. The thought has been planted—dire things may happen if it is ignored. Remember, I have a newly established reputation to uphold."

While she waited for both room service and Randy's return, Caroline wandered over to the window. Her view of the street below faded to soft focus as she struggled with the thoughts and emotions swirling through her. She was terribly confused about her reaction to Mike. She had anticipated an awkward scene because of his possible insistence on seeing her again. She should have been delighted that he'd made things so easy for her, acting as if they'd never been more than casual friends. Again Caroline felt the sting of tears.

A terrible pain in her chest made her catch her breath. God, what was happening to her? Every aspect of her behavior was inconsistent with her usual attitude. Why hadn't she told Randy she was simply tired and needed sleep? What was she doing letting him into her life? Friends were costly investments in time and emotion. To think she was contemplating an evening with Randy, an evening that was sure to turn maudlin after a couple of drinks. Surely she didn't need human contact so desperately.

Yes, you do, a voice within her argued. She was lonely and exhausted from the effort of trying to "go it alone." She needed Randy...she needed the warmth, the understanding, the tolerance his friendship promised.

THE NEXT MORNING, however, what Caroline needed most of all was aspirin. For the second time in her life she was suffering the agonies of overindulgence in alcohol. She thoroughly checked the side pockets in her purse and luggage on the off chance that she'd packed aspirin. The best estimate she could get from room service, since the staff was busy serving breakfast, was relief "within the hour," so she told them to forget it, gingerly dressed, ran a comb through her hair and headed for the lobby gift-and-sundries shop.

She was standing at the elevator, aspirin in hand, foolishly congratulating herself on making it back to her room without being spotted by anyone she knew, when Mike came up to her.

"Having trouble?" he asked, indicating her attempt to press the corners of the aspirin tin with enough force to pop it open.

"It's only a life-or-death struggle." She smiled weakly.

"Perhaps I can help." He held out his hand.

Either she let him open the tin or she would have to resort to using her teeth once she got back to her room. Caroline decided against risking the thousands of dollars her parents had invested in orthodontics and handed him the tin.

He opened it with infuriating ease and gave it back to her. "You don't look well."

"I'm not." Where was the elevator?

"Is there anything I can do?" He could have been talking to any one of the dozens of reporters staying at the hotel.

"You could send someone from the temperance league up to my room later."

"Oh...I see," he said softly. "I should have recognized the symptoms."

Caroline swallowed. A warmth penetrated her midsection as she remembered the only other morning of her life when she had faced a hangover—and that morning's conclusion. Where was that damn elevator? She glanced up from the spot she'd been studying on the carpet to see him looking at her with an amused smile. "You shaved your mustache," she said unthinkingly.

His hand went to his lip. "Yes...I did."

She almost asked, "Why?" but caught herself. "I guess I'd grown accustomed to seeing you with one...." She saw the look in his eyes, and her heart leaped. He answered her, but the quiet words were lost in the rush of people exiting from the elevator.

For long seconds they stood and stared at each other. Then Mike's arm came forward; for a breathless instant she thought he was going to touch her. But he only reached out to catch the door before it slid closed again. She forced a smile of thanks and stepped into the waiting elevator. Pressing her floor number, she watched Mike turn to join a group of men walking across the lobby. His back was to her as the door closed.

THIS TIME the aspirins-and-shower routine failed to work magic on Caroline's throbbing head and queasy stomach. When the buses returned from the Johnson Space Center early that evening, all she could think about was crawling into bed. A sympathetic but perfectly fit Randy brought her a large cup of soup, asked if he could be of any further service, then took off with a group of cameramen who were determined to discover for themselves the best bars in Houston.

The day had been agonizing for Caroline. She had fought what she considered stupid, insane, illogical fits of jealousy when Mike had even stood next to another woman. The first half of the day she had blamed her feelings on her physical condition; the second half, she had decided her condition was due to the tight lid she was forced to keep on her temper.

Somewhere down the line she was going to have to spend some time examining her ridiculous behavior. She refused to accept the answer Randy had so blithely insisted on the night before. She was *not* in love with Mike Webster. Perhaps if she had never been in love and so couldn't recognize the symptoms, she might have bought Randy's conclusion. But she knew what it felt like to take that particular ride. Gingerly she rolled over in bed, careful not to make any quick, jarring movements.

Even after she had become adroit at licking the salt and lime from the back of her hand, then washing it down with a swallow of straight tequila, she had been too embarrassed to answer Randy truthfully when he had casually asked if sex between her and Mike had been a problem. Somewhere, somehow, she had missed out on her generation's ability to discuss sex as informally as one would the next day's weather. So instead of telling him Mike's lovemaking had opened previously locked doors to a new and sensual world, one she had thought she would never enter, she had simply told him, "It was all right."

That was it! That was what was wrong with her. It wasn't love she felt for Mike, it was lust. The thought humiliated her, yet she hung on to it as if it were the lighted path through a twisting maze. Whenever her mind wandered or she began to question how lust could account for the pleasure she had felt just being in his company, she snapped her thoughts back to the comfort of her answer. She needed a solution she could control, even though it might be shaded by half truths.

A knock on her door sharpened the throbbing in her temples. Before she could get out of bed and slip on her robe there was another knock, only this time she heard "Caroline."

Mike had waited almost an hour after Randy told him Caroline was still not feeling well before deciding to check on her himself. It wasn't until he could convince himself he would do the same for any of the other reporters that he'd taken the elevator to her floor. Seeing her again yesterday had been harder than he had even imagined it would be. Made harder still by his uncontrollable tendency to interpret her every look, inflection and gesture as having more than the obvious meaning.

During the weeks apart, he had harbored a marvelous fantasy about what would happen when they saw each other again. Caroline would come to him; she would put her arms around him. The way she would hold him would reveal how she had ached with loneliness since they'd been apart. She would tell him she loved him and trusted him to love her in return.... But their meeting hadn't evolved the way he'd dreamed. The fantasy had died a cruel and immediate death the night before with her clipped words of greeting.

He could hear sounds from the room, and then her voice. "What is it, Mike?"

"I'd like to see you."

"Could it wait until tomorrow?"

"Caroline...it will only take a minute." If she demurred again, he would go. He heard the sounds of the locks being turned. The door opened. "My, God—you look awful."

She stared at him. "You don't look so hot yourself," she grumbled. But he did. He looked wonderful. She didn't want him there. He made her life complicated. She needed time to think, impossible for her to do rationally when he was anywhere near.

Mike reached out and pressed his hand against

her forehead. "You've got a fever," he announced.

"Does that mean I win?" she snapped.

His frown suggested he was as worried about her mental state as her physical state. "What's that supposed to mean?"

She sighed. "Nothing...." She swayed against the door. Whatever was wrong with her, she knew she couldn't handle it and Mike at the same time. "What do you want, Mike? I don't feel very good and would like to get back to bed, so if you'll—"

"Can I come in?" Not waiting for her reply, he stepped into the room.

Purposely, angrily, she continued to stare out into the hallway. Gesturing to the emptiness, she said, "I don't think that's such a great idea. You see, I'm not feeling real swell, and I would like to get some sleep." Mike's hand appeared over her head. The door eased out of her grasp and swung closed with a soft thud.

Bending, Mike picked her up in his arms as easily and presumptuously as if she were a wayward child up for a glass of water for the tenth time in the middle of the night. He carried her back to the bed. "I've been thinking about this stupid situation we've created for ourselves, and I've reached the conclusion that it would be nice if we could set all the nonsense aside and try to be friends."

He repeated the rehearsed words in a rush, the only evidence of the nervousness that controlled his every word and action. "I'm going crazy trying to pretend you're no different from any of the other reporters here. Don't you think it would be a lot easier if we could dispense with this awkwardness between us and get on with the jobs we have to do?'' When he had tucked her robe around her legs and pulled her slippers from her feet, he shoved his hands into his pockets to keep them from straying. ''That's my speech. What do you think?''

Caroline looked up at him. Was he serious? He wanted to be friends? *Fine!* she felt like shouting at him. *But there's just one minor problem. . . one doesn't usually lust after one's friends, and I can't think of anything else when you're around.* She sat up, pulling her legs to her chest. ''It's worth a try, I suppose. I'm not crazy about what's been happening, either.''

His smile was hesitant. ''Now that that's behind us, I'll go on to the real reason I came. What's the matter with you?''

''I'm not sure. This morning I thought it was a hangover.''

''And now?''

''I don't know.'' She propped her chin on her knees. ''Can alcohol cause a fever?''

''In a few people, under certain conditions, it's been known to do some strange things.''

''What about to me in a hotel room in Houston?'' She reached up to rub her temples.

Mike tensed at her innocently seductive answer. ''I was teasing, Caroline.''

''Oh. . . .''

Urgently needing to change the direction of their conversation, he picked up the cup Randy had left. "What's this?"

"Soup...I think."

"Chicken noodle, by any chance?"

She shrugged.

Mike pried open the lid. Bringing the cup to his nose, he sniffed. "Clam chowder."

Caroline clapped her hand to her mouth.

"Not your all-time favorite, I take it?"

"I think it just slipped even farther down the list," she mumbled through her fingers.

Mike replaced the lid. "All right, it's obviously not the clam chowder, so what *have* you had to eat today?" The way he asked the question, it was plain he felt he already knew the answer.

Caroline caught her lip between her teeth while she thought. "Coffee...."

"That's it?"

"I used cream," she said defensively.

He stood up and started for the door.

"Where are you going?" she asked, suddenly caring very much that he was leaving when only a moment before she had wished him gone.

"To get you something to eat."

Her stomach rumbled. "I don't think that's such a terrific—"

"Hunger is probably half your problem."

"Food is your answer to everything!" she seethed. "If my diet was left up to you, I'd weigh three hundred pounds."

"I don't think one meal a day is going to do you all that much harm."

"Mike. . . I really—"

"What?"

She sighed her defeat. "You might as well take the key." The words were barely out of her mouth when she realized the implication of what she'd said. For a painful moment they stared at each other, the poignant memory of another time, another place as tangible as the room surrounding them. Just being friends was never going to work for them, she realized. "Mike, maybe we should forget this—" The force of his look stopped her from saying more.

He glanced at the dresser, spotted the hotel key and went over to pick it up. "I'll be right back."

Caroline watched the door close. Panic gripped her. What they were trying to do was intelligent, even admirable, but was it wise? It was easy to proclaim friendship, but saying the words didn't neutralize the feelings, feelings that had no place in a platonic relationship.

Dammit! She couldn't be around Mike for five minutes without her pulse rate increasing. She should never have left Pasadena. She should have begged off the assignment and accepted the consequences. Anything would have been better than the torture she had gone through since boarding the plane in Los Angeles.

Rummaging through her overnight bag, Caroline pulled out a brush and vigorously forced it through her thick hair. She looked at herself in the mirror. Every day she eyed her reflection the same thought surfaced, in one form or another. In the not-too-distant future her face would become her enemy. The importance of crow's-feet, frown lines and laugh lines would be so blown out of proportion that each new one would precipitate a crisis. For someone who tried to ignore the way she looked, who had always been embarrassed by anyone else's mentioning her appearance, the idea of concentrating on the supposedly negative side of aging was repugnant. She hated the superficial aspect of her job more than any other. Yet she knew if she weren't very careful with her appearance, she would be benignly retired and on the outside by the time she was forty.

Caroline reached for her lipstick, but before the color touched her lips she stopped, realizing how wrong it would be to give Mike the impression that she had tried to make herself look better for him. They already had enough problems without her sending false signals.

Mike returned twenty minutes later, tapping lightly before he used the key. After propping pillows at her back, he set a tray on her lap and pulled a chair over so that he could sit beside her while she ate. With conscious effort he kept himself from reaching out to touch her, from resting his hand on her leg or brushing the curl from her forehead.

Caroline unwrapped her tea bag, placed it in the ceramic pot filled with hot water, waited a few minutes, then poured the tea into the cup. "Where did you ever find this?" she asked, inhaling the fragrant steam. "I haven't had chamomile tea since I was a child."

"It comes from knowing the right people," he said casually.

Fleetingly she wondered how far he had had to search to find the especially soothing blend. The thought was disquieting. She sipped the tea, then set it aside to reach for the silver dome covering the "main dish." Her mouth dropped open when she discovered a plate piled with slivers of dry toast.

In reply to the questioning look she sent him, Mike answered, "There's a bowl of hot chicken soup under that other lid."

She wrinkled her nose.

"Just the thing for a queasy stomach, sure to cure whatever ails you."

"Says who?"

"Says me. Now eat."

She did and was amazed at how good the simple meal felt in her hollow stomach. When the last spoonful had been consumed, Mike took the tray so that she could lie down again. He eyed her critically as she adjusted the blankets around her. "You're not going to sleep in that robe, are you?"

"No."

"Do you want some help—" But even the thought was too much for him to handle, let alone the words or the deed.

"I can take care of it," Caroline said quickly, her thoughts running along parallel lines.

"Then I'll be leaving."

"Mike?"

"Yeah?"

"Thanks."

"No problem. . . what are friends for?"

"Mike?"

"Huh?"

"You don't have to leave," she said hastily. "We could visit for a while." *What was she saying?*

"I can't. . . there's someone I, uh, someone I have to meet in a few minutes." As desperately as he wished it wasn't so, he knew there was no way he could stay with her and not ruin everything they had gained that evening. The ache he felt in his arms to hold her, the longing he felt for her to hold him were just too powerful.

"I'm sorry—you should have said something sooner. You didn't have to stay as long as you did."

He went to the door. "I'll see you in the morning, Caroline. If you need me for anything tonight, call me. I'm in room 611."

"I will. . ." she said, but they both knew she never would.

Once Mike had gone Caroline stared at the closed door for a long time. With a weary sigh she swung her legs over the edge of the bed and sat up. Her eyes immediately went to the red numerals on the digital clock. It was 10:25 P.M. Who could

Mike possibly be meeting so late at night? The question rankled. But it was the answer that caused the burning pain in her chest...she had absolutely no right to know.

CHAPTER THIRTEEN

THE NEXT MORNING when Caroline awoke feeling only a ravenous hunger, she decided her "illness" had been nothing more than a reaction to tension and fatigue—her body's rebellion against the mental strain she'd been under. After a shower she felt better than she had in weeks. Impulsively she reached for the phone and started to call room 611 to ask Mike to join her for breakfast. She changed her mind before the call could be completed. Last night had changed nothing between them.

Grabbing her purse, she headed for the hotel coffee shop. Although it was early, a line had already formed in front of the gardenlike indoor restaurant. Caroline picked up a newspaper to read while she waited. Glancing up from the front-page article on the upcoming launch, she absently gazed at the people already seated. Instantly her stomach knotted when she saw Mike sitting with a pretty blond woman whom Caroline recognized as one of the reporters staying at the hotel.

She couldn't look away. Uninvited knowledge from her flirting assignment, information she had thought nonsensical at the time, intruded. She noted the easy, relaxed way Mike sat, the way his body leaned toward the blonde in unconscious invitation. The interaction between the two people she watched was classic in technique as well as intent.

And then Mike smiled. It wasn't a grin or something half-expressed. It was a full-blown smile. Unreasonable, blinding anger shot through Caroline. How dared he, after coming to her room last night, after treating her with such— My God, what was wrong with her? She had no right to care how or why he expressed his pleasure in being with someone else. She tried to remember the last time he had smiled as freely in her company. She couldn't.

Confused and mortified by her reactions, she turned, ready to run back to her room—anywhere away from Mike—and collided with Randy coming to join her in line.

He grabbed her arms to keep her from falling. "What's your hurry?" he asked, catching her purse strap and pulling it back onto her shoulder.

"I...I forgot something."

"I've been looking all over for you," he went on without taking in her reply. "It never occurred to me that you'd be here."

"Oh?" was the best she could manage.

"I wanted to see how you were feeling this morning." His gaze swept over her face. "All right, from the looks of you, I'd say." He nudged her back into line. "Let's eat. I'm starving."

"But I was just leaving—"

"Hey, Caroline," he said in a conspiratorial whisper, ignoring her comment, "Mike just spotted us, and he's headed in this direction."

She caught her lip between her teeth for an anxious moment. "Does he know you've seen him?" Maybe she could still get away.

"Yep."

She took several deep breaths. When she looked up he was smiling and waving goodbye to the blond reporter. He turned and came toward them. He and Randy exchanged greetings before he asked Caroline, "How are you feeling this morning?"

She steeled herself to meet his eyes. "I'm fine, thank you. It seems all I needed was a good night's rest."

His gaze searched her face, seeking confirmation. Satisfied he said, "You're going to need the stamina of a bass guitarist in a rock band to get through the day ahead—the list of things to do and places to go reads like a subway timetable."

When she couldn't think of an equally flip answer, Randy came to her rescue. "I understand we might have a chance to use the shuttle flight simulator today."

Their conversation continued for a few minutes more while Caroline struggled to remain outwardly calm. Finally, when Mike said he had to leave, she dutifully and properly responded to his cheerful goodbye, even managing to hold her half smile firmly in place until he could no longer see her.

"That was exciting," Randy quietly commented.

"What?" She was still staring at the elevator Mike had disappeared into.

"If I could have recorded what just happened, I'm certain you two would have been nominated for Oscars for your performances."

She turned to look at him. "What are you talking about?"

"Aw, come on, Caroline, remember who you're talking to here. I've given too many performances myself like the one I just witnessed not to recognize a show."

When she refused to acknowledge his accusation, he went on. "Last night you never came right out and said what's going on between you two, but if I were to hazard a guess, I'd say you've had a serious lovers' quarrel and if you don't do something to patch it up real soon, it's going to be too late."

"It's already too late." She surprised herself by voicing her thoughts aloud. It had been too late for them from the very beginning. Caroline glanced at the brunet next to her and realized the woman was eavesdropping. "We'll talk about it later," she told Randy.

He sent the woman a withering look. "Why don't we go somewhere private where we can discuss this now?"

"Not now, Randy...please. Maybe tonight."

"Okay, boss lady," he said, slipping his arm around her shoulders to give her a quick hug. "If that's the way you want it. Just remember I'm here whenever you need me.''

That night Caroline insisted Randy continue his bar-hopping odyssey, saying she wasn't in the mood for anything but sleep, anyway.

The next day they were on a plane for Florida.

MIKE LEFT HOUSTON on an earlier flight than the one the reporters took; he wanted to accompany Ann and make sure everything was ready for the media tour when the press arrived. Midway into the flight the normally talkative Ann continued to stare out the window at the carpet of blue, the Gulf of Mexico, beneath them. Mike took her hand. ''Nervous?''

She returned his gentle squeeze. ''I wish I knew what was wrong with me, Mike. No matter what I do, I can't seem to shake this awful feeling of unease. It's like a squad of malicious gremlins is stomping up and down on my spine, making sure I don't enjoy myself.''

''I don't think it's abnormal for you to feel on edge. Cory's going to be a long way from home. As much as all of us like to have the public think the shuttle flights have become routine, you're enough of an insider to know that's simply not true.''

''It's more than that.''

''How so?''

She stared down at their interlocked hands. ''Do you believe in premonitions?''

''You mean like the one you had before my

crash?'' he asked, suddenly wary of what she would say next. ''How could I possibly say no?''

''This one isn't like the other two I've had. There isn't the sharp sense of panic I've always felt before...just this general feeling of malaise. Maybe that's why I don't trust the feeling.'' She gave him a ragged smile. ''Please don't say anything to Cory. He'll think I've flipped out for sure. I've been playing such a Pollyanna role around him lately that even the kids have started to get suspicious.''

If Mike did have a chance to see his friend before the flight, Ann's anxiousness was the last thing he would mention. Cory had lived with her too long not to realize how chillingly accurate her premonitions sometimes were. Her unease wasn't something Cory needed to carry with him on a flight that held higher possibilities for failure than any that had gone before. ''I'm surprised he didn't catch on to your strange behavior.''

''Are you kidding? His head is already in orbit. Living with Cory for the past two weeks has been like living with an android.''

''There must be a side to that guy I never see that makes him worth all the hassle he puts you through,'' Mike teased, trying to lighten Ann's mood. He was stunned when his bantering caused her eyes to fill with tears.

''I don't know what I would do if something happened to him, Mike. After sixteen years, we've kind of merged into each other's personalities. Before now I've never seriously faced the idea that Cory wasn't invincible.''

They had known each other too long for him to offer her empty words of reassurance. ''If something happened to Cory—either in the shuttle or on his way to or from work—today, tomorrow or next year, you would go on, Ann. There are times in our lives when the price we have to pay for the joy of loving someone is the pain of losing them.''

She leaned her head on his shoulder. ''When did you start spouting philosophy?''

''I've done a lot of things lately I've never done before.''

''This isn't getting us anywhere. Why don't you take my mind off of my own troubles by telling me about yours.''

''What would you like to know?''

''How did it go between you and Caroline in Houston?''

''I did my best to provide the opportunity, but the magical moment I had hoped would happen never occurred.''

She shook her head sadly. ''I just don't understand you, Mike. You've spent half your life looking for someone, and when you find her she turns out to be possibly the one woman in the world who won't return your love.''

''You exaggerate my greatness, as usual, sweet Ann. Anyway, since when is falling in love supposed to make sense?''

''So what are you going to do now?''

"I'm playing this one day at a time. I figure if I make it through the weekend, I'll make it through anything."

"Caroline's coming to the Cape?"

"With the others."

"I like her, Mike," Ann said after a moment.

"I know you do."

"Would it bother you if I spent some time with her while she's here should we get the chance?"

"Of course not. Why should I mind?"

"I don't know...I've tried to imagine how I would feel if Cory and I were separated and you were friends to both of us."

"And?"

"I think I would want whatever had driven us apart to be so powerful that you would have to take sides. Maybe I just can't understand why two people I like so much can make each other so miserable."

"I'm afraid you've dramatized our roles somewhat, Ann. I'm the one who fell into this situation like the proverbial ton of bricks...not Caroline. I knew in the beginning that I had to convince her I was worth falling in love with. Only I behaved like an adolescent moose, charging and crashing and demanding things I had no right to demand."

"If you know all this, why don't you simply back up and start over?"

"That's about as possible as backing out of a pan of hot tar with clean feet."

"How do you know she wouldn't welcome the chance?"

"Ann...you haven't been listening. I fell in love; Caroline did not."

"I think you're wrong, Mike," she said slowly.

Foolishly his heart lurched. Had Caroline told Ann something? "What makes you think so?" It was an effort to keep his voice calm. So little restored his hope.

"I'm not sure she knows it herself. Or if she does, I think she's fighting admitting it. When she came to see me while I was at my sister's in Newport Beach, she was anything but casual about you. I decided not to mention you at all; if anything was to be said she would have to bring up your name. I fully expected she would. She should have been defensive about you. I know I would have been—especially if you were really as obnoxious as you claim you were.

"But she was halfway down the driveway on her way home before she broke down and asked about you. I wish I could tell you what all I saw in her eyes. It was a mixture of sadness and hurt and such terrible longing that I don't think I've ever felt so sorry for anyone in my life. I could be wrong, but I suspect whatever it is that's standing between you is something she's carrying around deep inside her."

"But the point is, it doesn't matter what's controlling her, only that it prevents her from allowing herself to fall in love again."

"No. Her reservations only prevent her from *admitting* she's fallen in love."

Mike leaned his head against the cushion. "I would give anything if I could believe that."

"What would you do?"

He thought about that. What would he do? What could he do? But then the possibility that Caroline cared for him wasn't worth getting excited about. To let small mounds of hope build to mountains of disappointment was a useless and damn foolish exercise. Besides, Ann was speaking hypothetically. "Why don't we talk about something else for a while? I can only run around in circles for so long before I have to change rides or go crazy."

"All right," she reluctantly agreed. "But remember, you asked for it.... I've been dying to talk to someone about the new school-bond issue." In the past few years Ann had become deeply involved in local politics and issues, and she was seriously considering running for civic office as soon as Mindy was in school.

"Lay it on me," Mike said, scrunching farther down in his seat.

"That's what I like best about you." Ann laughed. "You're never afraid to show your unbridled enthusiasm for any subject."

DESPITE THE NEAR FRANTIC ACTIVITY that enveloped Mike the moment they landed in Florida, he made a point of seeing Cory one last time before the launch. The two men found a quiet office to share a cup of coffee and express emotions too personal to be spoken of in front of others.

"You know I'd never be here if it weren't for you," Cory told Mike.

"How do you figure that?"

"I've never told you about this before because it never seemed appropriate. Somehow, today seems the right time." Cory stared at the cup cradled in his hands as he slowly swirled the black liquid. "One day when we were seniors in high school and I was especially ticked off about something, I told you that a quarterback was nothing without a good center and that I thought it was unfair that you got all the glory. Do you happen to remember what you said to me?"

Mike smiled. He could remember fights with Cory when they were kids but no one in particular. He shrugged. "I'm sure it was something profound. As I recall, when I was a senior I thought of myself as extremely clever."

"You said if I wanted the glory, I had to stop playing the grunt; I couldn't have it both ways. You made me realize that even though deep inside I wanted what you always went after, I invariably took the safer path. That way, when I fell on my face no one was looking. It was a lot easier to handle."

"I never told you I'd decided to sign up to be an astronaut. As I recall, we were stationed halfway around the world from each other at the time."

"You didn't have to tell me; I knew you'd signed up the minute I read they were opening the program to new applicants. It was a natural progression I knew you wouldn't let pass you by."

They slipped into an awkward silence. Cory glanced down at his feet; Mike, his hands. Cory cleared his throat. "I gotta tell you, Mike, it doesn't feel right going up without you."

Mike stared at his friend, whose eyes were moist. "I can't say that it feels all that wonderful to see you go, either," he said softly.

The two men embraced. For long seconds they held each other, trying to express what they couldn't say with words. "Keep an eye on Ann for me," Cory said, disentangling himself. "She's been acting kind of funny lately."

So much for Ann's Pollyanna subterfuge. "I'll do that," Mike said.

"And Mike...if anything should happen to me—"

"Hey, what is this?"

"Just be quiet for a minute and listen, will you?"

Mike realized his friend was deeply serious. His comments weren't merely those of a man leaving to do a job more dangerous than most; they were edged with the sureness that something wasn't quite right. "What is it?"

"Ann and the kids. If something should happen to me, they would need you to be around for a while—"

"Cory, I don't understand why you would even feel it necessary to ask me something like that."

"Okay. Another thing...."

"Yeah?"

"I've put a lot of thought into this thing between you and Caroline."

"A little last-minute advice to the lovelorn to go along with the prophecy of doom?" Growing increasingly disturbed by Cory's strange intensity, Mike tried to inject a teasing note into their conversation.

Cory ignored him. "If you honestly feel she's the woman you've been waiting for, don't let her go, Mike. My life would have been nothing without Ann. I'd hate to think of you never knowing what I've had all these years."

"For God's sake, Cory," Mike said, his fears taking root. "If anyone hears you talking like this they're going to have the flight aborted and send you in to get your head examined."

Cory shoved his hands into his pockets. "There's nothing wrong with me. I just had a couple of things I had to get off of my chest, that's all. You can give me a hard time about this when we get back."

"Don't think I won't." But they both knew he wouldn't. What had passed between them would probably never be mentioned again. Mike glanced at the wall clock. It was time to go. He walked with Cory to join the other astronauts. Holding the door for his friend to enter the isolation area, Mike gave Cory a quick salute, a motion filled with a hundred meanings. "I'll be watching tomorrow—so don't screw up," he said quietly.

"Not a chance." Cory returned the salute, then

entered the area where he and his fellow astronauts would remain until the next day's flight.

THE MORNING OF THE LAUNCH dawned damp and cool. The brilliant blue sky was cloudless, a blank canvas ready for the broad white brush stroke of a streaking rocket bound for space.

Randy had spent the previous day searching for just the right camera angle. He wanted something that would add a new dimension to the standard fare. Since KMTV would be using the live programming provided by the network for the local stations to pickup or not, as they chose, Randy and Caroline were given more freedom to experiment with their own coverage. Not participating in the live coverage also allowed her actually to watch the launch instead of having it happen over her shoulder while she faced the camera and kept track of everything on the monitor. As it turned out, her only job that morning was to make notes for later use.

Discovering she was free, Ann asked Caroline if she would like to join her in the guest seating area while they waited out the two and a half hours of final countdown. Caroline had readily agreed, not knowing at the time that Mike would be with them. Busy with last-minute details, he didn't join the two women until the launch was on twenty-five minutes and holding.

Ann visibly relaxed when Mike finally eased into the seat beside her and reached for her hand. "Everything is progressing well," he said reassuringly.

A low-flying jet shot past in front of them. Ann jumped. "Take it easy..." Mike said, his voice steady. "That's just the plane they use to test the landing conditions on the runway."

"Why would they be testing a runway now?" Caroline asked.

Mike's hesitation was infinitesimal but long enough to be noticed. "The shuttle would land there should an emergency arise after launch."

Caroline could have kicked herself. How stupid of her not to have figured something so obvious out for herself. The last thing Ann needed was to be repeatedly reminded of the dangers involved.

Quickly changing the subject, Mike went on, directing his comment to Caroline. "For the people on board, this is probably the most nerve-racking time of the entire flight. They're out there with their hearts in their throats, methodically going through every conceivable last-minute test, desperately hoping nothing shows up to delay the flight."

"What are the chances something will happen?" Ann said absently.

Mike was taken aback by the question until he realized that out of deference to Caroline, Ann was trying to keep up her end of the conversation. Not only had Ann been a peripheral part of every shuttle launch to date, she could repeat in minute detail all the glitches that had occurred. Whether it was a crack in a solder connection that knocked out an on-board computer, or a fire caused by the auxiliary power units, she knew the when, where and why. "So far, everything is textbook. Just before I came in I heard that the test director had finished polling the people at their consoles, and they've all given their go-aheads."

The minutes slipped away, marked with digital precision on the clock in front of them. When the numerals were at 9:00 they stopped. Ann's eyes were focused on the clock; Caroline cast Mike a questioning look. "It's normal procedure to put the countdown on hold somewhere along the line," he said. "Just a bit of a breathing period to make sure everyone and everything has been checked and reported on." His gaze went to Ann. "How are you doing?" he asked softly.

"I'll be so glad when it's over," she answered as quietly. She forced herself to stop staring at the clock. "Caroline has been great company. Her being here this morning was a godsend. She pushed all the right buttons, and I never stopped talking."

Caroline met Mike's glance. "I simply asked her how the kids were."

"And now she knows a whale of a lot more than she ever wanted to, including all about Kevin's vow not to play basketball until his dad's safely home again. And what it's like to have three kids down at the same time with chicken pox." Her hand went to her mouth; she began chewing on a nail. "I should have called them to make sure they got up in time to watch the launch on television." She gave Mike a half smile. "That's silly...Mary will be sure to get them up."

"I also heard all about Mindy's passion for her new bear," Caroline said.

A voice came out of the overhead speakers, interrupting Mike's answer. *"Ladies and gentlemen, we have a go to continue countdown. It is now eight minutes and fifty-two seconds and counting."*

Caroline saw Ann squeeze Mike's hand so hard her fingers dug into his lean flesh. She was confused by the degree of nervousness Ann was displaying this morning. It didn't make sense that after all Cory's years of training, Ann hadn't grown accustomed to the idea that he would one day fly. Everything seemed grossly out of kilter.

Mike caught Caroline studying the other woman. Had he known she would be with them that morning, he would have forewarned her that Ann was under an unusual amount of strain. Although in the beginning he had tried to deny it and then ignore it, some of her fear had seeped into him. Cory's peculiar behavior the previous evening certainly hadn't helped his peace of mind, either. His insistence on discussing what would happen to Ann and the kids "just in case" had kept Mike awake most of the night.

"It is now six minutes and thirty-six seconds and counting."

Caroline looked around at the invited dignitaries, politicians, friends of the astronauts and assorted people who were there because they happened to "know someone." Excitement permeated the air as people shifted in their seats, casting furtive glances at the clock and then the shuttle. Some strove to be blasé; others openly expressed their awe.

Her gaze swung to the shuttle standing patiently on its pad, its belly hugging a gigantic fuel tank half again as tall and twice as big around as the shuttle. Flanking the main fuel tank were twin solid-rocket boosters, their skin made of half-inch-thick steel. A tower, standing behind the shuttle, was so crude-looking in comparison to the sleek spaceship, that it seemed constructed from a child's erector set.

"Four minutes and twenty-one seconds and counting."

How calm the disembodied voice sounded, seemingly as unaffected by the drama of the moment as if the man were announcing a train schedule. Behind her Caroline heard someone explaining the purpose of the auxiliary power units that had been revved up several minutes earlier, how the small motors pointed the rockets in the right direction and that they had caught fire during the ascent of one of the previous shuttle flights. Surreptitiously Caroline glanced at Ann to see if she had also heard, but the woman seemed lost in a trance.

"Three minutes and forty seconds and counting."

Ann's hand went to her throat. Her lips moved in silent prayer.

"Two minutes and twenty-two seconds and counting."

The cranelike arm that had been resting over the nose of the main fuel tank lifted and gracefully swung away.

Ann took a deep breath.

Mike stared at the shuttle, willing it to fly.

Caroline held binoculars to her eyes now, watching raptly the last-minute, computerized ministrations around the gleaming-white spaceship, wondering what thoughts were in the minds of the men and the woman on board.

"We have one minute and counting. All systems are go."

Caroline felt a flutter in her stomach and a gripping envy in her heart. Suddenly, more than anything, she wished she was on the shuttle. The power of her unanticipated feelings stunned her. My God, if she was experiencing such emotions, what agony Mike must be going through.

"It is T minus thirty-eight seconds and counting. The orbiter computer has positioned vent doors for launch configuration."

Through the binoculars Caroline could see small columns of white steamlike material coming from the shuttle and dissipating beneath the launchpad.

"T minus twenty-eight seconds and counting. We are coming up to take over control by on-board computers. We have a go for auto-sequence start."

Again, as when she had first heard about the entire procedure, Caroline reviewed exactly what happened when the ground-launch sequence com-

puter, located in Florida, relinquished control of
the shuttle to the computer on board the spacecraft, and then what happened after the shuttle
had cleared the tower on take off and control
switched to the computers at the Johnson Space
Center in Houston. Once the bits and pieces and
chunks of research Caroline had absorbed before
leaving California had come together, once she
had realized the precision and perfection needed
for a flawless launch, she had been awestruck. The
potential for disaster was everywhere, the possibilities endless.

*"T minus twenty-three seconds and counting.
Orbiter computers are now in command of the
countdown."*

Caroline's heart began to beat heavily in her
chest.

*"T minus fifteen seconds, fourteen seconds,
thirteen seconds, twelve, eleven, ten...we have a
go for main-engine start."*

Ann leaned forward, silently mouthing the
words, "I love you, Cory."

*"T minus five seconds. We have main engine
start."*

There was a burst of flame. Instantly plumes of
white clouds erupted from beneath the shuttle,
then shot out the sides with explosive force.

"We have solid rocket ignition."

An incredible roaring sound struck the ears; a
deep vibration shook the viewers as more than two
million pounds of aluminum powder inside the
twin solid rockets ignited. Along with the gut-

wrenching excitement, a momentary shiver of worry crept down Caroline's spine. Once ignited, the solid rockets could not be shut down—making them impossible to control. No man had ever ridden one before the shuttle flights. But the risk had been deemed necessary, because without the power gained by the rocket's brief two-minute burn, the shuttle, weighing well over a million and a half pounds, wouldn't have been able to lift itself off the ground.

"We have lift-off."

Only at that moment did Mike realize he'd been holding his breath through the last stage of the countdown. Transfixed, he watched as the shuttle roared to life, its massive thrust straining against gravitational restraints. In his mind's eye, he was in the cockpit with Cory as they left the ground, as the roll maneuver to put the shuttle on its back commenced. He felt the crushing thrust of the powerful solid rockets as they hurled the shuttle thirty-one miles into space in two minutes. The roar and shaking were tremendous, unlike the experiences of any previous space explorers'. One hundred and twenty seconds from lift-off, there would be a bang and then a surge of power as exploding bolts blew the two solid rockets away. With those gone and the main fuel tanks rapidly emptying, the shuttle's speed would increase dramatically. Soon the astronauts would reach a point where the engines had to be throttled back, or they would risk damage to the winged craft.

Later, when they had attained the necessary

height, whereby the view from the cockpit window showed that the sky had turned from blue to black, the main engines would be shut down. The shuttle would separate from its main fuel tank, and the crew would watch as the giant cylinder spiraled back to earth to eventually land in the Indian Ocean. When the tank was safely away, the shuttle would fire its engines and move farther into space. Thirty-five minutes later they would be fired again to set the orbit. . . and at last, for Cory the reality, the tangibility of at least one other man's dreams would be his.

For those left behind, the ones who watched the shuttle's journey from earthbound positions, this was also a magical moment. Even after the puffy trail had been pushed and pulled by crosscurrents until it appeared to be the path of a somewhat tipsy traveler, the spectators continued to watch.

Caroline turned to the two people beside her, their attention focused on the faint glow in the sky. Ann's face expressed a joy that belied the tears glistening on her cheeks. Mike's look was enigmatic. Suddenly he dropped his gaze and caught Caroline staring at him. For an unguarded instant his eyes communicated the agony he felt at being left behind. But as quickly it was gone as the rising commotion of the people around them, readying to leave, intruded into their sphere.

Mike turned to Ann. He put his arm around her and hugged her close. "Do you feel better now?" he asked gently.

She leaned against him. "I was so scared, Mike."

"I know you were."

Again she looked up into the sky. "Hurry home, my love," she whispered.

Caroline shifted so that she was able to see Mike without being seen. He looked tired; the past week had been hard on him. Or was it the past month? She should leave; she had told Randy she would meet him right after the launch to finish their exterior shooting. Still she made no move to get out of her seat. Why was she lingering? Her gaze went to Ann, but she saw only Mike. Mentally she traded places with the woman beside her. Where Mike's arm rested on Ann's shoulders, she felt the warmth of his touch.

She was tired, too. No...not tired, weary. And confused. Ideas, plans, dreams, hopes—all had developed angles and curves where they had previously been as sharp and straight as the beam from a laser. She had been so sure of what she wanted. In knowing her direction, she had possessed purpose and commitment. Now she felt lost, her emotions caught up in the panic of free-fall. Despite denials, she could no longer ignore the fact that she was deeply, emotionally involved with the man beside her. Yet the panic was so gripping that it had become impossible to let go of her protective parachute, even though it had collapsed.

She must talk to Mike. Maybe if she could walk

away from him knowing that what had been between them was truly over, she could shake free of the ties she felt bound them together. Unless she could find a way to think of him as just another man, her world wouldn't right itself again.

Before Caroline had a chance to tell Mike she wanted to see him, he announced he was late for an appointment, said goodbye and left. She watched him move through the crowd, acknowledging greetings and shaking hands, stopping twice to accept enthusiastic hugs. He was magnificent in the way he dealt with people. His goodwill was genuine; the affection he received was eagerly and honestly given. She turned back to Ann. "I hate to do this to you, but I have to leave also."

"Don't worry about it and please don't apologize. I'm all right now." She grimaced. "At least I'm better than I was earlier. I don't think I'll really breathe easy until the middle of next week."

"If I don't see you before you leave...." Caroline couldn't find the right words. "I guess what I want to say is that I hope our friendship doesn't end here." Could this be her saying these things? What had happened to the stone that was going to roll so fast it gathered nothing along the way?

The twinkle that had been missing from Ann's eyes returned. "I understand mail delivery between Houston and Pasadena has finally been approved. Rumor even has it that phone service will be hooked up any day now."

"You mean all the carrier-pigeon stock I just bought isn't going to make me rich?"

"I can think of a few things it might make you, but rich is not one of them."

Caroline heard her name being called, turned and saw Randy standing on the other side of the seats, scowling. "I've got to go, Ann. I'll call you," she said, rushing down the stairs. "We'll work something out."

"You have one week. If I haven't heard from you by then, dire things will come your way."

LATER THAT AFTERNOON an exhausted Caroline paced the lobby of the Public Information Building at the Kennedy Space Center. She and Randy had crammed two days' shooting into six hours in order to leave Florida a day earlier than planned. Although Randy had suggested the killing pace, saying he was anxious to return to Pasadena and Cindy, Caroline had readily agreed, hoping to use the built-in time off to put her wayward emotions in order.

The first step of her plan was to clear the air with Mike. It was important that their last meeting be as amicable as possible if she was to forget what happened between them. If their relationship was cleanly severed, it could more easily be set aside... or so she kept telling herself.

Purposely she wandered over to the hallway that led to Mike's office. The door was still ajar; the light continued to burn.

"Caroline..." a woman's voice called. "What in the world are you doing here?"

She swung around. "Ann. . . I thought you flew back to Houston this morning."

"I decided to take the grand tour first. Cory is so familiar with this place that he constantly forgets I'm not. He rattles on and on about things I haven't the foggiest idea about, so I decided to familiarize myself with some of them while I had the chance. That takes care of why I'm here. What about you?"

"I, uh, I wanted to talk to Mike before I left for home."

As Caroline had feared she would, Ann immediately looked hopeful. "He's not here," she said. "He left for Houston right after the launch to get back to the control center. But I know the number there if you want to call him."

"Please don't, Ann," Caroline said, trying to let her friend down easily. "It's not what you think."

"Oh. . ." she said softly, obviously disappointed.

"I just wanted to. . . to say goodbye."

Ann gritted her teeth. After a few seconds she sighed heavily. "Do you have any idea how hard it is for me to stay out of what's going on between you and Mike? I find it incredible that any problem is so insurmountable that it can't be cut down to size with a little bit of compromising. Just what is it Mike is asking of you that's so damn impossible?"

Caroline was startled by the intensity of Ann's anger. She reached up to rub her aching temples, turned to walk away, then turned back. It was so tempting to unburden herself of the frustrations and uncertainties by sharing them with Ann. She stared into Ann's receptive face. *Well, why not?*

"Before I met Mike," she began, "my life was like a desk top filled with neatly stacked papers. I knew where everything was and where everything went. When Mike came along it was as if someone had thrown open a huge window and let in a great gust of wind that destroyed everything I had worked so hard to put together." She held her hands out, a plea for understanding. "Ever since then I've been frantically trying to recapture those pieces of paper, but they keep flying around me, just beyond my grasp." Her voice dropped to a choked whisper. "But the worst thing. . . the thing that is tearing me apart, is that I'm not sure I'll ever be able to put things back the way they were. Or if that's what I really want. *I'm so damn confused.*"

Ann grabbed Caroline's elbow and steered her to an out-of-the-way corner. "It seems to me there's at least one thing you know for sure, and that's how unhappy you are with your life now." She paused. "Am I right?"

Caroline nodded.

"All right, then, wouldn't the next logical step be to confront Mike to see if he feels the same way about his situation." Again she paused. "Are you with me so far?"

"Yes. . . ."

"Since delaying the confrontation gains nothing, I think you should fly back to Houston with me this afternoon.''

"I'm not sure I'm ready." Caroline sank into the chair beside Ann. "Before I flew to Houston last week I was absolutely convinced breaking up was the right thing for us." The words poured out in a rush, air escaping a balloon. "When I saw Mike I was prepared for him to try to get something going between us again. He didn't. He was warm and wonderful and fun to be around, and to him I was like one of those ducks that float by on a revolving wheel in a shooting gallery, indistinguishable from every other duck. I discovered something in myself I had never known existed—jealousy. It didn't seem to make the least bit of difference that I had told myself I didn't want Mike; all I knew was that I didn't want anyone else to have him." Caroline shook her head. "You can't imagine what it feels like to want to dump a platter of food on some poor woman just because the guy you've decided you didn't want for yourself happens to smile at her. My God, it's so demeaning.''

Ann laughed. "That's nothing compared to how it feels when you actually let loose and do something about it.''

Caroline's head snapped up. "You didn't.''

"An entire gin and tonic down the cleavage of a senator's wife who thought redheaded astronauts were 'just the cutest things.' ''

"At least you had a right to behave that way." She gave Ann a forlorn look. "I feel like a robot that's gone into sensory overload. I used to see the world through different eyes. My pessimism has abandoned me, yet I've been hurt too badly in the past to ever embrace optimism again. I feel lost.''

Ann sat down in the chair next to Caroline. "It seems to me that if you decided to go back to living your life the way you had been, you would probably never suffer seriously. But you're never going to know any of the moments that make the time we're here on earth worthwhile, either."

"I used to think the trade-off was fair."

"And now?"

Could she turn her back on the friends who had come into her life lately? Randy, Cindy, Ann, Cory... Mike. "The last thing in the world I want to do is go back to the way I was." But she was still so scared. The idea of allowing herself to become vulnerable again terrified her.

"After listening to you, I think you've already reached a decision, Caroline. You just haven't given it a voice."

"I still don't know how Mike feels."

"Why don't you ask him?" Ann said quietly.

CHAPTER FOURTEEN

As soon as Mike arrived at the Johnson Space Center he headed for mission control to check on the progress of the shuttle flight, already several hours old. He was pleased but not surprised to discover everything going according to plan. Still, despite the assurances, he couldn't shake the lingering unease planted by Cory and Ann. This was one flight he would be happy to see come to an end.

After talking to several of the specialists at the center and hearing the term "routine flight" repeated at least a dozen times, Mike headed for his office. When the priority calls awaiting him were out of the way, he checked on the members of the press who had remained at the center, made sure they were being taken care of and answered several questions before he was able to get away again. He was back at mission control several hours later, but by that time the earlier joviality had markedly diminished. At first Mike thought the staff was just settling into routine work after a particularly beautiful launch, but he soon began to sense an undercurrent that told him differently.

He made his way over to Lisa Malorey, the astronaut whose job as capcom made her responsible for relaying instructions and communicating with the shuttle astronauts. Five-feet-four-inches tall, with long blond hair and dark brown eyes, Lisa was a favorite with the media, who used phrases like "cheerleader" and "all-American" to describe her. Because of the tags she'd been given, she had deemed it wise to contain her bawdy sense of humor and normally salty language whenever reporters where anywhere near. The consequences were frequently hilarious to those who knew her well as she struggled for alternative ways to express herself. To the press, she only seemed refreshingly shy.

While Mike waited for Lisa to finish taking a report on the cargo-bay doors from one of the mission specialists on board, he surveyed the room, jammed with consoles. Here and there a flicker of a smile or a snatch of conversation made him think he was imagining there was anything wrong. But then he would see quickly exchanged glances or a somber face, and his anxiety crept a little closer to dread.

As soon as there was a break in the conversation Lisa turned to him. "What can I do for you, Mike?"

"Set my mind at ease. How is everything going?"

"Who's asking? You or the media rep?"

"I am."

"We've lost three of the six crew so far, with

one doubtful. Two are so bad they're having trouble functioning.''

"Damn—'' That one or two astronauts in each flight would suffer space-adaptation syndrome, or SAS, was expected, but to lose two-thirds of the crew was more than any mission could handle, especially one so laden with work. "Is Cory one of them?''

"He's the doubtful. His symptoms seem to be milder.'' She caught her knee between her hands. "How is he around his kids when they get sick? Is there a possibility he's suffering sympathy malaise?''

Mike shook his head. "After working his way through school as a hospital orderly, nothing fazes him.''

"Well...maybe he's coming down with a cold, then.''

"Maybe.... Thanks, Lisa.'' Over her shoulder Mike had spotted Fred Chippendale, one of the physicians who had been working with Cory's crew.

"You're welcome,'' she said, turning back to her board.

Making his way over to Fred Chippendale, Mike thought of all the times he and Cory had discussed the possibility that Cory would be one of the thirty to fifty percent of space voyagers who reacted to zero gravity by getting sick. Since NASA hadn't yet come up with a way to determine susceptibility, every flight carried a "wait and see" element. To a few, the lack of appetite, malaise, headache, nausea, fatigue and vomiting were debilitating; to others, only a minor inconvenience. "Fred..." he called out, trying to stop the doctor before he left the room.

The tall, angular man turned when he heard his name. "Mike...what can I do for you?"

"You can tell me what's going on up there."

"For the media?"

"Give it to me both ways."

"Mission specialists Barker, Elroy and Jenkins are suffering mild forms of SAS and have begun medication. They are currently taking pills that contain a combination of scopolamine, a drug that blunts sensation, and dextroamphetamine, which counteracts scopolamine's dulling effects. We anticipate their full recovery within the normal amount of time." He reached into his shirt pocket. "I'm a step ahead of you this time, Mike," he said, smiling as he handed him a piece of paper. "I've written everything down."

"I appreciate that, Fred." He looked at the list of medications and dosages before refolding the paper. "It makes it a lot easier to have everything in front of me during a press conference." The paper went into his jacket pocket. "And now, how about telling me just what in the hell is going on up there."

"Elroy is continuing to hold his own. Barker and Jenkins are down with extreme cases of nausea and vomiting." He began tugging his earlobe. "Peters is the one who has me stumped. According to his own account, he's going through a rather mild reaction to SAS, but for some reason his pulse rate has increased.''

''You think he has a fever?''

''That has to be the answer. I can't believe it's stress, not after all the times I've monitored him under pressure. Everyone who goes up expects SAS to hit them, so I can't buy Peters's story that having so many of them down is enough to cause him any undue distress.''

''Is there any kind of bug going around he might have caught before he left?''

The tall man snorted. ''There's always something going around.''

Mike frowned. Was it possible Cory could be coming down with chicken pox, despite his doctor's assurances to the contrary? He raked his fingers through his hair. ''Keep me posted on this, will you, Fred?''

''For any besides the usual reasons?''

''Cory Peters is an old friend of mine.''

''I wouldn't worry. It's probably nothing more than a cold.''

''Yeah...a cold.'' Mike thanked him and excused himself. He resisted using the air-to-ground private communication loop NASA maintained with the astronauts. As much as he would like to talk to Cory, Mike knew that doing something so out of the ordinary would be a sure way to lift more than one set of eyebrows. The last thing Cory needed right now was more probing questions from ground control. With more than half the crew sick, he had enough on his hands.

BECAUSE OF THE NUMBER OF PEOPLE returning home after attending the shuttle launch, Caroline was unable to get a reservation to fly back to Houston with Ann. She bade her friend goodbye, promising to call as soon as she knew when she would be arriving. After checking with several airlines and discovering the earliest flight she could arrange was at four o'clock the following afternoon, Caroline decided perhaps it was best that she have some time alone. She needed to sort out her feelings. There were so many things to think about. She called Sid Minkner, requested and was given the rest of the week off.

During the sleepless night she spent in a hotel room that for some reason seemed even more impersonal than most, she thought about her parents. She tried to understand what had happened between them by rerunning her mother's story of the marriage breakup, then her father's. It was only when Caroline placed herself in the scenario and began questioning her father that she realized she had never actually heard his angle of the divorce.

Caroline had fought taking sides; once she had even covered her ears and screamed at her mother that she had no right to talk about her father the way she did. Her mother had slapped her and burst into tears, saying that even her own daughter had turned against her. It was the last time Caroline had questioned her mother about her version.

An hour before the sun would mark the start of another day, she got out of bed and took a walk along the deserted beach. Stopping beside a half-submerged seashell, Caroline dug away the sand with her toe. She could feel her heart beating heavily in her chest, hear it thundering above the sounds of the ocean in her ears. During the hours she had already spent thinking, somewhere... sometime...despite her resolve not to, she had finally admitted to herself that she had fallen in love with Mike Webster.

As she stared at the horizon her eyes fixed on the spot where sky met water in ever increasing delineation as the earth turned to meet the sun. Her agony the night she had found Tom in bed with her best friend, Ruth, became as real to her as if she had been magically transported back to relive the moment. She felt herself again that innocent young woman, so excited about the surprise she had brought her husband—herself—that she ignored everything else. She could see herself carelessly dropping her purse and coat onto the Queen Anne chair by the door before bounding up the stairs.

At first her mind had refused to accept the message her eyes sent her. What she saw was not right. It was impossible. The people were misplaced. It was only when Ruth let out a tiny gasp as she pushed an elegantly manicured hand against Tom's bare shoulder, and he turned to see Caroline standing in the doorway, that she had accepted what she saw.

Even after all the years passed, she could still feel the stabbing pain, the struggle to breathe.

Deep inside she still choked on the tears she had refused to shed back then.

Suddenly great gulping sobs shook her body as she found the means to cry out her ancient hurt to the vastness of the empty sea. Why had the man she had loved and trusted betrayed her that way? Why had her friend, the woman she had cared for as she would a sister, been the one to join him? What had she done to them that they would do that to her?

Unable to stand any longer, she sank to her knees, covering her face with her hands. The tears, so long in coming, at last tore through the barriers she had constructed. The hurt, so long held inside, demanded full release.

When the torrent of emotion sweeping through had settled into an occasional hiccup, she thought of how, months ago, she had openly wondered how Tom and Ruth had survived that weekend. Only a few days later, she learned they had married and were expecting a child.

Caroline closed her eyes. An image of her mother appeared. Slowly that image changed until it was herself she saw. Was this the way she had survived? A bitter, reclusive woman, alone on a beach? Who had paid the price of the faithlessness?

Finally, after years of struggling with a hurt so deep it had become the controlling force in her life, Caroline understood something she never had before. Her only mistake, her only "crime" had been choosing the wrong people to trust. For that one mistake she had punished herself mercilessly. But now it wasn't only herself she was punishing; it was Mike, too.

The wind whipped her short curls against her forehead. Her hands lay folded in her lap as she stared at the sun reflecting off the point in the ocean where the swells became breakers. She took deep breaths of the salt-tinged air and grieved for the lonely, isolated woman she had become. The grief threw the doors of need wide open and allowed her to acknowledge her consuming ache to be with Mike—to have him hold her, love her, to be with her always.

MIKE DELIBERATELY ARRIVED at mission control the next morning before the work shifts changed. He wanted to question personally the men and women who had been in contact with the astronauts the previous night. He learned that Barker and Jenkins had been given additional medication, an antihistamine, and then yet another drug to help them sleep. He was grateful he didn't have to report the astronauts' medical problems to the media right away. To have it common knowledge that those aboard the shuttle were on medication—medication so strong they would have been grounded until all traces were out of their systems if they'd been military or commercial pilots—was not considered "good press."

Keeping the crew members' condition low-key had become fairly easy since the first shuttle flights. The astronauts themselves had begun to request that their medical problems not be made public knowledge during flights. Since that time all personal information had been communicated on the ground-to-air loop and only released as deemed absolutely necessary.

The report on Cory was apparently inconclusive. He was no worse or better than he had been the day before. He had slept—not well, but then adapting to weightlessness didn't happen the first night up. In space it was impossible to experience the sensation of lying down or resting one's head on a pillow.

Unlike an earlier shuttle crew, which had been stricken by severe SAS, this one didn't have the extra day in orbit that would allow them to wait for the worst symptoms to pass before they started work. Today, their second day in space, was critical to the entire mission. In a few hours they were to maneuver the shuttle within thirty-five feet of a crippled satellite, reach out with the manipulator arm and haul the satellite in. Next they would try to repair any obvious damage, and if successful, return the satellite to orbit. All going well, further experiments would follow.

Mission specialists Teresa Barker and Frank Jenkins were the two astronauts assigned to the arm. Each had spent over a thousand hours learning to operate the skinny mechanical appendage and were considered the best out of the ten who had been trained for the job. Outfitted with shoulder, elbow, wrist and grabber joints, the arm required an incredible amount of coordination to manipulate the double-hand controls and keep the complicated machinery from accidentally bashing a hole in the side of the spacecraft. The operation demanded sharp, quick reactions, not ones dulled by medication.

Mike watched the ground crews change shifts, noting how they engaged in muted conversations while exchanging concerned glances with those who caught their eye. Conferences were called. Fred Chippendale struggled with long-distance judgments on Jenkins's and Barker's reflexes. The rendezvous drew closer.

With almost no time left to make a decision, tempers were short. Everyone knew heads would roll for anything but the correct calls. But there was more to the problem than that. Should something go wrong in the satellite retrieval, should the shuttle be damaged, the lives of all the astronauts would be in jeopardy. Millions could be spent on research and computers and backup units, but no one could figure out a way to control the body's frantic struggle to cope with the absence of gravity and the disorientating shifts in positions caused by weightlessness.

FINALLY, AFTER THE SUCCESSFUL MEETING of shuttle and satellite in late afternoon, with Teresa Barker showing distinct signs of improvement, ground control decided the crew should make a few dry runs with the arm before attempting to capture the satellite and bring it on board. The silence, the tension in the mission-control room became almost palpable as Teresa calmly reported her progress in a voice that relayed none of the high drama of the moment. Given the go-ahead for the real thing, she acknowledged the order with a snappy "Yes, sir."

A short while later, both on earth and in a spaceship far above it, a collective, audible sigh of relief met Teresa's announced "Mission accomplished." While Barker and Elroy prepared to leave the shuttle's living quarters to go outside to the cargo hold and try to repair the satellite, Mike searched for Fred Chippendale. He found the weary-looking man pouring himself a cup of coffee.

"Any update on Peters?" Mike asked.

Fred gave his earlobe a thoughtful tug. "I haven't said anything to anyone, but I'm beginning to get a little concerned. As soon as it became obvious how sick Barker and Jenkins were, Peters started backing off on his own symptoms. Now he's trying to convince me he's never felt better—but his heart rate is still up. As a matter of fact, it's even higher than it was yesterday."

Mike wasn't surprised by what Fred told him. Minimizing his own discomfort was something Cory would do. "I take it that means he still has a fever?"

The doctor nodded.

"Is there a chance he could be coming down with chicken pox?"

The doctor almost choked on his coffee. "Chicken pox?" He wiped away the drops of brown liquid that had landed on his jacket. "I assume you've a reason for suspecting chicken pox above measles or mumps?"

"All three of his kids are currently at different stages of the disease."

"Has he had chicken pox before?"

"Yes, when he was eight."

"Then it's highly unlikely he's gotten it again... but it's worth remembering."

CAROLINE WAS IN THE BATHROOM packing the last of her toiletries in her overnight bag when the telephone rang. Randy frantically answered her "Hello."

"Thank God I caught you," he said, ignoring the preliminaries. "Is there any chance you wound up with one of my tapes?"

"From the shooting we did here in Florida?"

"Yes, I'm missing the launch. Only the most important one."

"If I didn't have it, which I don't, where would you suggest I look?"

Randy's despair manifested itself in a quiet groan. "I haven't the slightest idea. It could be anywhere."

"I'll retrace our steps here... you check with the airline."

"If it didn't mean my rear end, I wouldn't ask. I know you wanted some time—"

"That's okay. I owe you one."

There was a moment of silence. "You do?"

She owed him more than one. He had been a far better friend to her when she desperately needed one than she had been to anyone in a long time. "I'll tell you about it sometime. Now think hard... where did you go without me that day?"

They spent the next several minutes retracing their movements the morning of the launch. Caroline wrote the places down, carefully trying to account for every minute of the day until Randy had boarded the plane for Los Angeles. When they were confident they had thought of everything, they wished each other good luck and hung up.

Almost three hours later, she was at the airport sending the tape to Randy in Los Angeles. She had found it sitting on a shelf at one of the security gates, where it had been turned in the day before.

Because she had missed her late-afternoon flight while searching for the tape, she had to make new reservations. This time she managed to get an early-morning flight to Houston. Stuffing the ticket folder into her purse as she walked from the terminal, she vowed that nothing would make her miss another plane out of Florida. She would be on her way to Houston the next day if she had to hitchhike to the airport or rent a boat. Nothing, no one, was going to keep her from seeing Mike. The thought sent a shiver of anticipation up her spine. Since she had finally admitted she was in love with him, she had been bursting with the need to tell him. The words, repeated over and over, were ready to spill from her. She had thought she would get to say them that night—the wait would be torture.

MIKE REACHED UP to rub his eyes, weary from lack of sleep and from continuously staring at the consoles. When he had decided to stay at mission control the previous night, he had planned to catch a few hours' sleep in his office, only a short distance away. He had yet to leave the building.

"Mr. Webster...." A soft female voice coming from behind him caught his attention.

He turned to see the new receptionist who took care of the desk at the main entrance to mission control. Young and bright-eyed, she looked fresher than anyone he'd seen in hours. "Yes..." he said.

"There's a call for you." Her head tilted coquettishly to one side. "I can have it switched in here, if you like."

"Please."

"I'll send it in on line three." She looked around, then indicated an empty desk. "Over there."

"Thank you."

"You're welcome." The smile she gave him was hopeful, inviting. "Let me know if I can be of any other help to you. I'm just outside." She pointed back to the way she had come in.

"I'll remember."

"Well...goodbye." Her hand rose, her fingers fluttered.

Could he possibly be getting old? Mike smiled despite himself. Lately it seemed that the younger the women, the more direct their approach. He went over to the desk, waited for the button on line three to light, then picked up the phone. "Mike Webster speaking."

"Mike, this is Ann. Is Caroline with you?"

"Caroline? With me?" He couldn't conceive the reasoning behind her question. "No..." he answered her at last. "Why would you ask me something like that?"

"I was supposed to pick her up at the airport, but I got caught in traffic—there was a terrible accident tying up all but the fast lane—anyway, by the time I arrived she was gone. I've searched everywhere. I'm still at the airport."

"Have you tried paging her?" *What was Caroline doing in Houston?*

"Twice."

"Did you check home to see if she left a message for you there?"

Ann let out a frustrated sigh. "I can't get through. Ever since she's been quarantined, Rebecca has been living with the telephone stuck to her ear."

He knew he shouldn't ask; the answer would probably only add another brick to the wall between him and Caroline, but he had to know. "Ann...why is Caroline in Houston?"

There was a long pause before she answered. "I don't think I should be the one to tell you, Mike. That should be up to her."

What in the hell was that supposed to mean? A tightness gripped his throat. "Whatever you think best." His voice was a carefully controlled monotone.

"Mike—"

"I really have to go now, Ann."

"Wait...just one more question. How is Cory?"

Because he wasn't sure how much Ann had been told, he was in the difficult position of possibly frightening her by revealing too much, or making it seem he was hiding something by saying too little. He decided to be straightforward. "He says he's recovered from the minor SAS symptoms he was feeling yesterday, but he still has a slight fever."

"Fever? I didn't know anything about a fever. When did that start?"

Mike pressed his palm against his forehead, his eyes closed. "Only a couple of hours into the flight. I've talked to Fred Chippendale about it, and he said Cory's probably coming down with a cold."

"What do you think?" Her voice betrayed her sudden disquiet.

He answered her carefully. "I don't have any reason to doubt Fred."

"Mike...Cory never runs a fever. I've seen him through every kind of illness, and never once since I've known him has he run a temperature."

His thumb and index finger massaged his eyes, meeting at the bridge of his nose.

"I'll pass that on to Fred as soon as I see him."

"I'm leaving for home now. As soon as I arrive I'm going to disconnect Rebecca's phone so there won't be any reason you can't reach me. I want to know what's happening to Cory the minute after you find out." Fear changed the quality of her voice, making it crackle.

"As soon as I hear anything I'll call you."

"Call me even if you don't."

"I will." He waited for her to hang up.

"Mike?" she said loudly, as if to catch him.

"Yes?"

"I almost forgot...if Caroline should call, explain what happened, will you?"

Unreasoning anger shot through him. "Don't worry about Caroline, Ann. She can take care of herself. She's completely self-reliant."

Before Ann could answer a loud cheer sounded in the background.

"Mike?" she choked. "What was that noise?"

"I'm only guessing, but I'd say the repairs they attempted on the communications satellite were successful."

"Oh..." she said. "I'm so glad."

"I don't think you're the only one. You can bet Cory is sporting a grin from ear to ear."

"Well, that makes it one down and two to go. They'll be on their way home soon."

Mike chuckled. "Lest you forget, sweet Ann, there are a few experiments still scheduled before they retrieve the long-duration exposure-facility satellites."

"I've never felt like such a coward. If someone offered to wave a magic wand that would put me to sleep until this was over, I'd jump at the chance."

"Hang in there—it's only a few more days."

"Call me—"

"I promise." They said goodbye. Mike listened for the click of Ann's phone before he replaced the receiver.

He'd been doing all right before Ann's call. And then, with only the mention of Caroline's name, he had once again been thrust back into the world that awaited him outside mission control.

An unnatural quiet settled over the room, intruding on Mike's thoughts as effectively as an explosion. He turned to join the others, and the collective tension struck him like a physical force. Immediately he scanned the room, looking for the cause of the disquiet. Lisa Malorey met his questioning look with a worried frown. Mike focused on the clipped communication between shuttle and ground. It didn't take long to discover the problem that had cast a cloak of anxiety over even the most easygoing men and women in the room. The shuttle's mechanical arm wouldn't return to its resting place.

Mike grabbed a passing console operator. "What happened?"

"We don't know. Everything was textbook right up to release. The arm extended fine, but when it tried to let go of the satellite, the claw wouldn't open. Then when they tried to bring the arm back in, nothing worked.''

"Damn—'' Mike jammed his hands deep into his pockets. Again he scanned the room, this time looking for Fred Chippendale. He found the doctor talking to John Quincy, the astronaut scheduled to pilot the next shuttle flight. Walking up to the two men, he said, "As soon as you're through here, Fred, I'd like to talk to you.''

"Go ahead,'' Quincy said. "I have to get back to work, anyway.''

When he was gone Mike steered Fred to a quiet corner where he was sure they wouldn't be overheard. "This fever thing—''

"Yes, Peters still has it.''

"Well, it seems he's one of these types who never run fevers.''

The doctor's thick eyebrows drew together in a frown. "Then there must be other symptoms. He's not telling us everything.''

It was on the tip of his tongue to suggest the doctor query one of the other astronauts about Cory's condition, but the words wouldn't come. Creating a situation that would draw undue attention to his friend could easily jeopardize Cory's career. To fly future missions, he needed to return home from this one with a string of *well done*'s to his credit. Now, with the arm out of commission, the last thing he needed was a worried friend spotlighting his supposed physical problems.

If the crew couldn't get the mechanical arm working again, the mission would be considered a failure. They would return to earth to the *I told you so*'s of every politician who had ever spoken against the shuttle and wanted to get a mention in the press. Even if they could fix it, the repairs might take days. Time that had been scheduled for other work. But there wasn't any choice. As it was, the astronauts certainly couldn't bring the arm back to earth for repairs. Unless the appendage could be re-folded into the ship and the cargo-bay doors closed behind it, they wouldn't be coming home at all.

CHAPTER FIFTEEN

CAROLINE CALLED ANN as soon as her plane arrived in Houston the next morning. It took several minutes to wheedle out the information that all was not right with Cory. When Caroline suggested she would drop by the house before her talk with Mike, Ann said she wouldn't hear of it.

"But since I won't let you come here and expose yourself to chicken pox, I guess you need somewhere to go while you wait, don't you?" Ann said slyly. "It sure seems to me that the logical place to wait would be at Mike's apartment." When Caroline demurred, Ann added a convincing argument. "It would be a lot easier on him than finding the time to meet you somewhere else." Without pausing to listen to Caroline's objections, she rushed on. "He keeps a key with the lady who manages the complex. I'll call her and tell her to expect you. See how eager I am to help when the news is good?"

STRUGGLING WITH HER INTENSELY UNCOMFORTABLE FEELINGS of trespassing, Caroline let herself into Mike's apartment. Before leaving the airport she had called his office. Shyness had overcome her at the crucial moment, so that the message she had given his secretary had simply stated where she would meet him, not how eager she was for that meeting. The secretary had promised to relay the message when and if he checked in with her before he left for home.

As she had the first time she had walked into Mike's living room, Caroline felt she was coming home, in one sense. The overstuffed couch with its assortment of loose pillows invited snuggling; the chairs, grouped for conversation, hinted at a person interested in people. She set her suitcase down beside the door, mute, unintentional acknowledgment of a thread of doubt: would she be welcomed back into Mike's world? The possibility that he might not want to resume their relationship was too painful to consciously consider.

Because she couldn't shake the feeling of being an intruder, Caroline stayed in the living room, first reading the paper she had found on the porch and then watching the noon news on television. While she listened to the local and then the national on her old station, she felt like someone who had unsuccessfully tried to return home. So much had changed—the set, the tone, the style were not only radically different, there was only one reporter she recognized.

Finally, in late afternoon when her stomach began making obnoxious noises, she relented and left her self-imposed confinement to go into the kitchen for something to eat. Afternoon slipped into evening and more news. With longer coverage came more details of the shuttle. She learned of the malfunctioning arm.

Caroline started to call Ann, then stopped, not knowing whether her call would bring comfort or anxiety. A mental picture of Ann at the launch flashed through her mind. While she knew she could not provide the support Mike had, she could at least put forth the effort. She dialed Ann's number. Mindy answered, saying her mom would be right there.

"Caroline. . .is everything all right?" Ann was out of breath.

She was taken aback by the question. "That's what I called to ask you."

"Oh, you must have been watching the news." She chuckled. "And *that* must mean Mike hasn't come home yet."

"No, he hasn't." A warm flush bathed her cheeks. She went back to safer conversation. "I understand there's something wrong with the mechanical arm."

There was a scuffling sound in the background. "Excuse me a minute, Caroline." In a muffled voice Ann said, "Mindy and Kevin, I've told you twice already to get that dog and yourselves out of this room. Once more and the dog goes outside for the rest of the day." There was a pause several seconds long. "I'm sorry," she said, her voice again clear. "They were playing tag in front of my grandmother's china cabinet, and that demands immediate action."

Caroline smiled. "The confinement continues, I take it."

"For all of us. But I think I've found a way to survive. This morning I called a wonderful bed-and-breakfast place Cory and I stayed in a couple of years ago and made reservations for the first weekend he's free after he gets home. I'm using the promise of that weekend to keep me going. Kind of like the carrot dangling in front of the donkey."

"I'd better let you get back to what you were doing. I didn't mean to—"

"But I never answered you. No, I'm not overly concerned about the problems they're having up there. I feel bad that it isn't the perfect flight they had all hoped for, but I'm sure none of what's happened is the fault of anyone on board. So it shouldn't work against them. They still have several days to get the arm fixed, and they're bound to learn from the experience. Everything that happens out there teaches them something."

There were a dozen questions Caroline would have liked to ask, but the one important one had just been answered. Ann was holding up fine. "Let me know if—"

There was a loud crash in the background. "Gotta go, Caroline. I'll talk to you tomorrow. Be sure to give Mike my love."

"I will." Caroline's hand rested on the receiver long after she'd returned it to the cradle. She wondered if three cases of chicken pox could ever be called fortuitous. The distraction of having three nearly well, restless children confined to one medium-size house seemed to be a blessing in disguise for Ann.

Sorting through a stack of magazines, Caroline found one she hadn't read that afternoon. She considered looking through it while lying down on the couch, but hesitated. After two sleepless nights, she was afraid she would doze off. Instead she curled up in the corner, her feet tucked beneath her. In less than half an hour she had not only worked her way into a prone position, she had turned out the light and given up all effort to keep her eyes open.

CHAPTER SIXTEEN

TOO TIRED to take the extra five minutes to put the Porsche in the garage, Mike parked in the driveway, reasoning that he wouldn't be home long, anyway. He was only planning to take time for a shower and change of clothes. He had put off leaving mission control until the astronauts themselves had abandoned the broken mechanical arm in favor of sleep. Slipping his key into the lock, he tried to remember when he'd ever felt so strung out. He couldn't. There wasn't anything that quite compared with the sustained tension of the past two and a half days.

Except for that nagging question. Although he had tried to bury them beneath crisis-filled thoughts, Ann's words, "Is Caroline with you?" kept resurfacing.

Once inside Mike reached for the light switch, then changed his mind; undemanding darkness was easier on his tired eyes. With the sureness of someone who never rearranges furniture, he started across the living room on his way to the kitchen. Before he had gone two steps he collided with something on the floor, stumbled and twisted his leg. He caught his breath as pain shot up his leg, its tentacles reaching deep into his groin. The intensity of the spasms robbed him of breath. Only in his mind did he find the energy to say the profane words he had learned in his youth.

"Mike?"

His name, tentatively spoken, penetrated his orange world of agony. "Caroline?" he gasped.

"What's wrong?" Her voice held concern edged with panic.

His only answer was the rushing sound of his intake of air as he tried to move.

She reached for the table beside her, searching for the lamp. Finding the base, she followed the cool brass upward until she touched the knob. A quick turn, and the room filled with light. When she saw Mike her hand went to her mouth to stifle her cry of surprise. Bent over, grasping his bad leg as if it were broken, he turned his face to her. She untangled her own legs from the jacket she'd been using as a blanket. Rushing over to him, she saw her suitcase lying on its side and realized what must have happened. She reached out to touch him, then pulled back. She had never seen anyone in the throes of such terrible suffering. "Is there anything I can do?" she asked, a plea in her voice. "Should I call an ambulance?"

He tried to answer her, but finally just shook his head.

Unable to stand there and do nothing, she ran to the bathroom, wet a washcloth and brought it back to wipe the perspiration from his face. With light, loving strokes she caressed him, watching closely for a sign that the pain was lessening. "Do you have something to take, some medicine I can get for you?"

Slowly his breathing began to normalize. "No... nothing," he managed to say.

Caroline's fingertips replaced the washcloth. Lightly she touched his forehead, his jaw, his temple. "I'm so sorry," she whispered over and over again. "It was stupid of me to leave my suitcase there."

Another spasm of pain contorted his face as he straightened. "It's all right, Caroline," he breathed. "Stop apologizing." He tried to walk, but it was too soon, and he swayed off balance.

Reflexes dictating her action, Caroline stepped forward. Her arm went around his waist. "Lean on me."

Mike hesitated. To lean on anyone, for anything, was as alien to him as asking for help. He was mortified that Caroline was seeing him like this.

Suddenly Caroline understood what Mike was thinking. She looked at him, forcing him to meet her gaze. "Either you let me help you," she said, "or I'm leaving." The words, the tone of her voice, were deadly serious. "It works both ways, Michael Webster. If I'm to put my trust in you, then by God, you're going to put yours in me."

Mike's heart lurched. If she was going to put her trust in him? Just what did that mean? He shifted his weight until it rested lightly across her shoulders. Hope, joy, nudged at the lingering pain for room in his thoughts. For the first time in recent memory, he allowed himself the luxury of believing in dreams.

"Now where do you want to go?" she asked.

He indicated a nearby chair. "Over there is all right."

She thought a moment. "Are you sure you wouldn't rather lie down?"

"Caroline," he said softly, unable to contain himself any longer, "what are you doing here?"

"I'll tell you later."

His hand touched her chin, forcing her to look at him. "Tell me now." His heart thundered in his chest, his ears.

She hesitated. "If I do it will be all wrong. I'll forget half of what I wanted to say."

"Tell me, Caroline," he coaxed.

"I'm here because I finally admitted to myself that I love you," she whispered, the simple sentence saying it all.

He let out a shuddering sigh and tenderly drew her close, the pain momentarily forgotten in the all-encompassing elation that surged through him. He didn't care about any of the rest—the where or why or when—only that she loved him. Suddenly, with her words, his gray world had filled with color, his tomorrows now shone with wondrous promise.

Where Caroline's head rested against his chest she could hear his heartbeat. Loud and clear and strong, it spoke to her, telling her she had found a home where she would be loved and cherished. A home where her fears and doubts could be laid to rest. She felt his lips press softly against her hair. Tilting her head back, she met his mouth in an achingly tender kiss.

"I can't promise you we'll never disagree," he said.

"I know."

"Or that I'm always going to be as understanding as I should be about only seeing each other a total of one week out of every four."

"I know."

"But I can promise to love you more than you've ever been loved and to never give you reason to doubt me."

She smiled. "I know that, too," she said softly. She saw him involuntarily wince as another spasm of pain went through him. "Come on. Let's do whatever it takes to make you feel better. Then we'll talk." They headed for the hallway. "And I promise I won't leave things lying around from now on."

"This thing with my leg has been coming on since last night. Stumbling over your suitcase was just the final insult. Since the accident, whenever I stand on concrete two days running, I'm asking for trouble."

"I don't understand why you don't keep something around to help you with the pain."

They turned sideways to maneuver past a small chest in the hallway. "It goes back to when I was in the hospital. I learned how terrifyingly easy it is to become dependent on pain killers. Since then I've gone without.''

When they reached the bedroom, Caroline helped Mike lower himself until he was sitting on the edge of the bed. She bent to remove his shoes.

"I can do that," he protested, reaching out to stop her.

She gave him a frustrated look. "I know you can. But now you don't have to, do you?" With infinite care she slipped the shoe from his right foot. "I seem to remember another time when I undressed you and you didn't mind at all."

"Caroline...I...."

Suddenly she realized how insensitive she had been to try to parallel the two times, as if purposely comparing his physical prowess then and now. She looked at him. "I'm sorry...again. That was a stupid thing to say."

"No, it wasn't. It was wrong of me to have tried to hide what I am from you. I lied when I told you my leg created no lingering problems." The words were more difficult to say than he'd ever imagined. To express something aloud that he hadn't fully admitted to himself was to destroy all lingering illusions. "I have physical limitations that will affect us in many of the things we do together," he said quietly. "Limitations that will probably become more pronounced as I get older." He took her hand, holding it so that his thumb rubbed across her knuckles. "I will never be able to convince myself it doesn't matter that the accident grounded me for life, but it's something I've come to accept. I know whenever I see a launch there's always going to be a part of me that will ache to fly, too. And there's not a damn thing I can do about that."

Caroline had grown so self-centered in her own misery. If she had only taken the time to look at the tragedies endured by others, what she had experienced might have been put into proper perspective long ago. She shuddered when she thought of the isolated, lonely direction her life had been taking. What kind of a person would she have become if Mike and others hadn't bulldozed their way in?

She squeezed his hand. "I think in your way," she said softly, "you're trying to tell me there's something I should be concerned about. I can't believe you think the problems you have or don't have with your leg would make any difference to how I feel about you. It wasn't your beautiful body or even your devastating smile I fell in love with." She grinned. "Or your athletic prowess, for that matter. After all, when a thirteen-year-old girl half your size can beat you at basketball...." A shrug and shake of her head expressed her gentle teasing. "What can I say?"

"If it wasn't my looks or my talent, what's left?"

Her eyes narrowed speculatively. "I suppose it could have been the mustache."

Mike caught his breath as another cramp sent pain shooting up his leg. After the worst was over, he tried to smile. "Give me a few weeks on the mustache."

Her eyes had grown serious. He made it so easy for her to forget that he was hurting. "What can I do to help you?"

"Nothing really...I just have to wait it out. The worst is usually over in ten to twenty minutes. The rest gradually subsides over a day or so."

"And there's nothing you can do to make your leg feel better any sooner?"

"Sometimes if it's convenient I soak in a hot bath."

Caroline stood up.

"Where are you going?"

"To start the bath water."

He frowned. "Caroline—I can do that. I'm not totally helpless."

She planted her hands on her hips. "You may not be helpless, but you sure as hell are hard-headed."

"No, I'm not," he insisted, struggling with words never expressed. "It's just that I'm embarrassed for you to see me like this," he finally said.

Her heart went out to him. How much had it taken for him to admit that to her? "Well, you're going to have to get over it. I've already seen you without clothing," she gently chided, deliberately pretending she had misinterpreted his meaning. "Or have you forgotten?"

He shook his head, a smile playing at the corners of his mouth. "I can't believe any of this." He caught her hand. "Tell me again."

The warmth of his voice sent happiness bubbling through her. She came up beside him and bent to meet his upturned mouth with her own. As his lips touched hers, her senses cried out in celebration. "I love you," she said. Once more they kissed. "Do you want to hear it again?"

"And again...and again."

She straightened. "Not until you've had your bath."

This time he did smile. "Being married to you is going to—"

"Married?"

"Is there something wrong with that?"

"Are you asking me to marry you?"

"It seemed a logical progression."

Somehow she had missed thinking about marriage. After her agonizing decision to let herself love again, marriage seemed anticlimactic. "Wouldn't you like to get to know me a little bit better first?"

"No."

She ran her hand through her hair. "Well, that was short and to the point."

"Caroline Mary Travers—will you, or will you not, marry me?"

"You remembered my middle name."

He glared at her.

She answered him with an impish grin. "I guess so."

"*So much for romance!*" he shouted.

"One of us has to be down-to-earth and practical. We can't both go around stealing flowers."

"Who says?"

"Trust me on this one—I'm not the type to get away with it."

"You underestimate yourself. You're an oilman's dream of untapped riches. Somewhere beneath that crusty exterior is an adventuresome kid just begging to be set free."

She stared at him, thinking hard about what he'd said. "You're full of beans, Webster. What you see is what you get. Never will these hands be accused of purloining petunias, pansies, periwinkles or popdragons." She turned and walked into the bathroom.

"Popdragons?" he called after her.

"I couldn't think of another flower that started with *p*."

While the tub was filling she came back to help Mike take off his clothes. When he stood up his face was again contorted with pain; the easy bantering faded into a quiet time. The effort it took him to get into the bathroom and then into the tub made her wonder if the benefits could possibly be worth the struggle. As his leg slipped beneath the water she noticed the meanly knotted muscles.

After she'd rolled up a towel to cushion his neck and flipped the switch for the whirlpool, she sat on the side of the tub and waited for his breathing to settle into a normal rhythm that would indicate a lessening of the pain. "How often does this happen?" she asked.

"It depends on how hard I push myself. If I ignore the warning signals too long, as I've been doing lately, my leg will spasm more frequently and for longer periods." He reached for her hand. "But I'm tired of talking about me." He brought her hand to his lips. "Tell me what made you change your mind about us. I want to hear everything."

Caroline took a deep breath, held it for a moment, then released it as a heavy sigh. There were a hundred ways she could answer him—they all led back to one indisputable fact. "Despite everything I said or did or tried to force myself to feel, I fell in love with you. I managed to pretend it wasn't true for a while...but then one day I just couldn't pretend anymore. I did a lot of hard thinking the day and a half I was stuck in Florida, and I realized I was living my life for tomorrow, forgetting that tomorrow never comes. I discovered that a very important part of me wants what Ann and Cory have. And that despite my resolve to go it alone, I need friends like Randy. And I need you."

"And what about Tom?" he asked gently. "How does he fit into your new way of thinking?"

She tried to smile, but her feelings for Tom were still too ambivalent for anything so dismissive. "It took me some time, but I finally understand something. Tom was a jerk. He didn't deserve what I had to offer, but I was too blind to see anything but failure on my part. I couldn't put what happened into proper perspective until I met you and discovered what it really meant to love someone and to be loved by them in return. I knew all about giving, but I knew nothing about taking. The times you and I have made love, you actually cared more about my pleasure than your own. That's never happened to me before. I didn't know what to think, how to react. I doubted you—I suspected your motivations. I don't anymore."

"And trust?"

She slipped off the edge of the tub so that she was kneeling on the floor in front of him. Dipping her hands beneath the gurgling water, she began to gently knead his leg. "I've thought a lot about trust and what an important part it's going to have to play in our relationship. The conclusion I reached was that either you trust someone or you don't. There's no middle ground."

"And you trust me?"

Their gazes met. Communicating as much in the way she looked at him as in the words, she softly said, "Yes...in all things."

"I love you, Caroline." His voice was warm, like sunshine after rain.

She smiled. "Tell me again."

He reached for her. His hand held the back of her neck and drew her to him. "I love you..." he murmured against her lips, her closed eyelids, the tiny pulsating spot at her temple.

Licking flames of desire scorched her, making her skin flush, her breasts swell. "Mike...we shouldn't," she gasped.

He ignored her. "Caroline..." he sighed. "My beautiful, shy Caroline. Are you really here?" He placed his mouth firmly over hers in a kiss that trumpeted his own growing need. His hands went from her face to underneath her arms. He lifted her and slid her into the tub with him so that she was sitting on his lap, her feet hanging over the side.

"Your leg—" she said, ignoring her own fully clad body.

"Is fine," Again he kissed her.

Warm water churned around her, soaking her slacks, making her pale mauve blouse cling like a second skin. Mike's hand cupped her breast; his thumb passed over the nipple, stroking the hardened flesh. A cry came from the back of her throat as her passion mounted. Aggressively her tongue sought entry into his mouth. She had never known such sensuous heat, such desire. Each time they came together seemed merely a continuation of the last, with their need for each other honed.

Where he touched her she ached for more; where he did not she burned with need. His hand moved to the buttons of her blouse. Her heart thudded heavily in her chest, a coded message for him to hurry. At last the material was pulled aside, and all that lay between his questing hand and her skin was the delicate lace of her bra. Neither the deep dusky areolae surrounding her hardened nipples nor the creamy white of her breasts were hidden by the thin lacy covering. Nor was the small blue vein where he pressed his lips. He moved his head to touch the soft curve of flesh above the lace with the tip of his tongue, licking away the sparkling drops of moisture.

Unclasping the hook at the back of her bra, he slipped his hands beneath the material, supporting the fullness of her breasts before brushing the cloth aside. For long moments he stared at her, his passion-filled eyes caressing the perfection he'd uncovered. His gaze went to her face. "Your breasts are beautiful," he said simply. "I love touching them."

He bent his head, letting first his breath and then his lips touch the sensitive flesh everywhere but the dusky peaks. Soon she began to move against him, letting her body speak the words of longing she was still too shy to say aloud.

When at last he drew her nipple into his mouth, a moan sounded deep in her chest. His tongue flicked across the probing flesh, the strokes becoming firmer, more demanding. She caught his head between her hands and pressed him closer, crying out her need. "Mike...."

He looked up at her, his breath coming in short, quick sighs. He shook his head as if to clear it. After a moment a rakish grin curved his mouth. "This whole things smacks of incredibly poor planning."

Her mouth twitched in a return smile. She glanced down at her soaked clothing. "Not to mention a touch of insanity."

"Did I ruin anything?"

"Only my composure." She felt as if she'd been

caught in a violent updraft and that the wind had suddenly died.

He helped her back up to the side of the tub, pulled the towel from behind his head and handed it to her. Using his arms for strength and his left leg for support, he stood up.

Caroline eyed him, looking for signs of pain. All she saw was a magnificently built man in the prime of his life. A private smile lighted her eyes. She was especially pleased to see that his ardor hadn't cooled. Abruptly he bent, reaching over to turn off the Jacuzzi and drain the tub.

Thinking he'd lost his balance, Caroline cried out in alarm.

"I can see we have some work to do," he said, reaching for a towel of his own. After a quick swipe he casually wrapped it around his waist and moved over to help Caroline, still in the process of peeling her clinging blouse from her arms.

"I've not only learned to live with the inconvenience of my leg," he told her. "I've learned to adapt. You're going to have to let me be the judge of what I can and cannot do, my love. And," he added meaningfully, "you are also going to have to let me decide how much pain I'm willing to endure in the pursuit of pleasure." Tugging her bra down her arms, he tossed it into the sink to join her blouse, then reached for the button on her pants. "*This* is one of those times, by the way." With a long, sensual stroke he slid the zipper down its erotic path.

He lowered himself to the edge of the bathtub,

drawing her to stand between his knees. While he pulled her slacks over her hips and down her thighs, she leaned her hands on his wide shoulders for balance, then stepped from the soggy mess.

Lovingly Mike brought his hands up the outside of her legs, his thumbs coming to rest on the swell of her hip, his fingers curving over her buttocks. He pulled her to him, pressing his face against the flatness of her belly. Hooking his thumbs over the now nearly transparent nylon of her wet bikini pants, he slowly pulled them down, caressing the exposed skin with his mouth and then his tongue, in whisper-soft kisses.

When she stood naked Mike stroked her anew, learning the texture, the feel, the warmth of her belly, her thighs. Caroline called out his name as his hand gently separated her legs on an upward journey; she caught her breath as he touched the place of her greatest need. She moved against his hand, feeling the urgency inside her grow until the storm of passion had almost caught her totally.

"No...not yet," she said, her voice a choked whisper. "I want it to be with you this time."

Mike led her into the bedroom. He lay across the bed and then reached for her. She hesitated.

"Are you sure we should be doing this?"

"The only thing I'm absolutely sure of is what will happen to me if we don't."

Her breasts brushed against the mat of hair on his chest as she bent over to give him a kiss. "And that is?" she teased him.

"You don't want to know."

She caught his earlobe between her teeth. "What about the incredible fortitude of the male libido you once told me about?"

"It was a lie."

Her tongue slowly outlined the curve of his ear; her breath warmed the moist trail. "I'm shocked at you, Webster."

His hand slid smoothly from her waist to her stomach before dipping past the triangular mound to unerringly find its target. He smiled when she let out a tiny gasp of pleasure. "Still have doubts about whether or not we should be doing this?" he asked, his voice suddenly husky with passion.

She moved so that she could carefully straddle him, taking him into her with a soft moan of welcome.

Mike reveled in her unabashed aggressiveness, her concern, her eagerness to bring him fulfillment. His hands went to her waist and then to her ribs and then to her breasts, gently kneading their softness. Grasping the back of her head, he brought her to him and held her as he gave her a deep plundering kiss. An incredible swell of pleasure was rising inside him. More than anything he wanted Caroline to be with him on this journey. His hand slid between their bodies to intimately caress her, to put her on the crest of the wave he would soon be riding.

He listened to the sounds of her breathing, her caught sighs, the cry of anticipation. . .they rode together.

Afterward, as she lay snuggled against his side

she said, "If we combined both of our savings, how long do you suppose it would be before we had to go back to the real world?"

Mike kissed the top of her head. "However long it was, it would be too soon."

"It scares me to think we might never have gotten back together if I hadn't stopped being so stubborn."

"I don't think stubbornness had anything to do with it, Caroline. You were living under some long shadows. You just had to learn how to walk away from them and live in the sunshine again." He pulled her closer. "Besides, I wasn't through with you yet." He laughed lightly. "Neither were Cory and Ann."

She frowned, puzzled.

"They've been on my case since they found out we weren't seeing each other anymore."

"The more I hear about those two—" Caroline snuggled back into his side "—the more I like them."

The sharp ring of the telephone intruded on his answer. Caroline rolled over on her side and reached for the receiver, handing it to Mike.

"Yes?"

"Mike, this is Lisa Malorey. I'm at mission control. . . I think you'd better get over here as soon as you can."

"What's the matter?" Cold dread smacked up against him like a wall of ice, making him feel sick to his stomach.

"I'd rather not discuss it over the phone."

"I'll be right there." He handed the phone to Caroline.

"What is it?" He just sat there as if she hadn't spoken. "Mike," she said sharply, "what's happened?"

"I'm needed back at mission control."

"What's wrong?"

"I don't know . . . but I'm sure it's not good."

CHAPTER SEVENTEEN

FEAR OVERRODE THE LINGERING PAIN in Mike's leg as he sped through the blackness of night on his way to mission control. There were hundreds of possible reasons for the call he'd received, but it would be an exercise in futility to even consider them. He didn't have to be told; he knew. There was something terribly wrong with Cory.

As soon as he was back inside the windowless building that served as the remotely beating heart and never sleeping mind of the shuttle, he began a frantic search for Fred Chippendale. He ignored the instructions he'd received immediately upon entering the building. A hastily called meeting of crisis experts was underway, but he wasn't needed there. Conflicting opinions would merely be volleyed back and forth—which pieces of information should be released to the press, what was the official attitude going to be? Mike had little stomach for that scene. Far more important things preyed on his mind.

As he walked through the hallways he had to stop himself from grabbing the nearest person and demanding to know what had happened while he'd been gone. Whenever he felt himself giving in to the urge, a peculiar impulse held him back. He felt that by listening to possibly muddied details, his ability to help Cory would be impaired. He desperately needed to keep his mind free for the clearest, most precise answers he could get, to avoid hearsay, gossip or supposition.

Finally he halted a harried-looking young man with unfashionably long hair to ask him if he knew where Chippendale was.

"Dr. Chippendale left for home about an hour ago," the young man said. "They've put in a call to try to reach him, but as far as I know they haven't been able to. Dr. Schondel is filling in for him this evening." He stepped closer. Dropping his voice to a confidential tone, he added, "Frankly, I think I'd rather have her in my corner, anyway. She's the one who had sense enough to figure out what's been going on with Peters all along."

Mike's stomach knotted. Sensing a situation was worlds away from actually being faced with it. Despite all his forebodings that Cory was the emergency, a trace of hope had refused to die until that very moment. "Where is she now?"

The other man's hand went to his chin. Absently he rubbed a light stubble of beard. "The last time I saw her she was talking to the capcom."

"Thanks." Mike started to walk away.

"Say," the man called after him, "wasn't Peters a friend of yours?"

An explosion of crimson-colored fury slammed into Mike's mind. His hands curled into fists. "What in the hell is that supposed to mean?"

The man's eyes grew wide. He stepped backward. "Nothing...I just thought you two knew each other, that's all."

Mike began to tremble as fury grew to rage. He jammed his hands into his pockets. In a menacing voice he said, "Until Cory Peters has officially been proclaimed dead, which I'm assuming he has not, you will give him the courtesy of referring to him in the present tense." He took a step forward. "Have I made myself perfectly clear?"

"Yes, sir," the other man quickly answered, taking another step backward.

Mike gave him a withering look, turned and headed toward the capcom station, afraid that if he stayed another moment he would vent his unreasoning anger on the stunned man. Forcefully he controlled the speed of his steps, reluctant to bring attention to himself.

He quickly searched his memory to identify Erica Schondel. The name was familiar, but that didn't necessarily mean they'd ever met. Eventually, in one context or another, he came across the name of just about everyone at NASA who was directly involved with the shuttle.

The instant before he saw her, a mental image flashed into his mind. One word described her—short—in height, hair, temper. What she lacked in charm, however, she made up for in professionalism. He was glad she was the one taking care of Cory.

As Mike approached, Erica Schondel looked up from the papers in front of her, responding to his worried scowl with a curt nod. Closing the folder, she stood up and stepped forward to meet him, perfunctorily extending her hand. "What's kept you?"

"I had to go home for—"

"Please, spare me the details," she snapped. Moving past him, she said, "Follow me."

Inconsequentially he noted that the top of her graying head barely reached the middle of his chest. Somehow when in the process of ordering people around, she seemed far taller. He accompanied her into the empty director's office.

Tossing her folder onto the desk, she said, "Stop me when you want to write any of this down." She gave him a puzzled look. "Where's your notebook?"

Now he understood. She thought he'd come for a briefing before meeting with the press. "I don't need one," he answered, deciding it best not to correct her.

She shrugged. "I'm not going to pussyfoot around, Webster. I'm going to give it to you straight. After that, it's up to you and the others to decide what you feel you want the world to know." Hiking herself up to sit on the corner of the desk, she leaned forward, her hands resting on the edge. "Approximately fifty-eight hours ago, which works out to be a little over six hours into the flight, Cory Peters complained of symptoms that indicated he was suffering a mild case of space-adaptation syndrome. When it became evident that three other crew members were also down with SAS, two of them so severely they couldn't do their jobs, Peters informed ground control that his own symptoms were subsiding. Monitoring indicated Peters continued to have a slight increase in pulse rate, which meant a probable elevation in temperature, but it was deemed inconsequential in the absence of other symptoms.''

Mike reached up to rub the back of his neck, as much to hide his shaking hands as to massage his muscles. Never in his memory had he struggled so hard to remain outwardly calm.

''Because of the amount of attention focused on the other problems aboard the shuttle, Peters managed to keep his deteriorating physical condition hidden from ground control until a little less than an hour ago. At that time we were informed by mission specialist Frank Jenkins that Cory Peters had become incapacitated with pain.''

Mike lost the battle to control his rising panic. ''Would you get to the point?'' he shouted.

Erica Schondel's head snapped up. Her features drew into a disapproving frown and then into an expression of dawning understanding. ''You're not here to get answers for the press, are you?''

The silence between them was strained. ''Please...'' Mike finally said, the word softly, poignantly spoken.

Whereas she had seemed comfortable and sure of herself before, she now fidgeted and stalled for time. She started to answer, then stopped. She swallowed. ''His appendix has ruptured,'' she said at last in a low monotone.

Mike could feel the blood drain from his face, leaving it cold and tingling. "Bottom line—what does it mean?"

"Under the best of circumstances a ruptured appendix is still considered an emergency, but it's one that usually has a good prognosis." Erica Schondel sighed. "Without any treatment at all, death is likely. Peters is somewhere in between the two. As you know, there are antibiotics on board. We have begun treatment—"

"How long does he have?"

She scowled. "You know better than to ask a question like that."

"Goddammit, don't play games with me. Tell me what his chances are."

"The sooner we can get him back here, the better his odds will be. We need to get inside him and mop up as much of the poison as we can, then insert a drain for the rest before we put him on massive, continual doses of antibiotics." She looked down at her slowly swinging feet. Again her voice softened. "Every physician has a story he or she will tell you about a patient who walked around with a ruptured appendix for days before seeking treatment, and somehow lived to tell the tale. Perhaps Peters will be one of those."

"That's his only chance? To be one in a million? Someone so different from all the others that doctors remember him?"

"Not if they can get the mechanical arm fixed soon enough and get him back here."

"And just how soon does that have to be for Cory?"

She shook her head. "I don't know for sure."

It had finally happened. One of the predictable, life-threatening medical emergencies the people involved with space travel had feared since man first left earth. Something they had feared so much in the beginning that serious consideration had been given to removing the appendixes from all astronauts before allowing them to fly. After that idea had been discarded, discussions centered on teaching rudimentary surgery as part of the training program. That way, if an astronaut's appendix should rupture in space, someone on earth could "talk" one of the others through the operation. That idea had eventually been abandoned as impractical.

Shuttle specialists had been lulled into a false sense of confidence, because, unlike a lengthy trip to the moon, on a shuttle the astronauts were supposedly never more than two orbits or three hours away from landing. Plenty of time to take care of most emergencies, including a ruptured appendix. Plenty of time if the crew could only close the cargo-bay doors and return to earth without tearing the shuttle to pieces on reentry.

CAROLINE WANDERED AROUND MIKE'S APARTMENT, waiting for his call. She wore the glow from their earlier lovemaking like a thick down jacket, consciously protecting herself from the threatening chill of reality. It wasn't that she doubted any-thing that had happened between them, or re-gretted her decision to tell Mike she loved him. Yet years of believing the worst made her incapable of fully trusting such seemingly total happiness. She couldn't shake the feeling that somewhere, if only she looked hard enough, there was a fatal flaw that would nullify this wonderful new start.

She padded into the kitchen, looking for some-thing to eat. Standing in front of the open refrigera-tor, staring at but not seeing what was inside, she sighed. She wondered what idiot had proclaimed that pessimists had it easier in life because they were always pleasantly surprised when something good came along. Well, she wasn't pleasantly surprised; she was dubious and more than a little frightened. And it seemed the happier she felt, the more frantic she became.

Without having noted one item in the well-stocked refrigerator, Caroline slammed the door, groaned and headed back to the bedroom. Catch-ing her reflection in the hall mirror, she stopped and stared. *Smile,* she commanded her image. *At long last one of the wonders of the world is yours, and by God, you will be happy about it.*

Deciding her best course of action was to keep busy, she called home to pick up the messages on her answering machine. After she had listened to John Wakefield ask her out to a concert, Randy tell her how wonderful she was for finding his tape and a poll taker promise to call back later, a crisp-sounding woman with a definite East Coast accent announced she was Albert Morrison's secretary. She went on to say that Mr. Morrison would be in Los Angeles a week earlier than originally planned. Ms Travers's appointment to discuss possible employment with the network had been changed; the new time would be considered confirmed if Ms Travers hadn't called back by the next day.

Caroline felt as if she were standing on a platform, her luggage all around her, her ticket in her hand, helplessly watching the train she was supposed to be on slowly disappearing down the tracks. She had been rescheduled to meet the man who could make her employment dreams come true in exactly six hours and fifteen minutes—and he was half a continent away.

MIKE OPENED THE DOOR to the smoke-filled meeting room. Quickly he scanned the assembled group of men and women, noting their fatigued and worried faces, their tension-filled postures. Acknowledging several gestured greetings as he moved down the table to an empty chair, he concentrated on the angry words being exchanged between Fred Chippendale and Lisa Malorey. No longer under the restraint of her public image, Lisa blasted the ragged-looking doctor in language that echoed her deep-seated fears, accusing him of gross incompetence for the missed diagnosis.

Using Mike's entrance as a tool to bring the meeting back to a semblance of order, Robert O'Dell, chief of ground control, tapped his pipe against the table in a signal for quiet. "Let's get back to our main reason for being here, shall we?" He glanced at the man next to him. "Yockum, give Webster the rundown and status on the arm."

The balding engineer pushed his glasses higher on his nose with his index finger, then folded his hands on the table. "Astronauts Jenkins and Elroy are currently in the process of preparing to leave the shuttle to attempt one last repair maneuver on the arm. Should this attempt fail, they have been instructed to manually force the claw open in order to release the satellite. They will then try to fold the arm back into the cargo bay themselves."

Mike recoiled. Under the best of circumstances the work the astronauts would be doing on the arm was fraught with danger. He shuddered to think that the crippled ship might produce another casualty. "And if they fail?" Mike asked, his voice deceptively calm.

"The arm will be dismantled and left in space along with the satellite."

"How long do you anticipate all this will take?"

"We're in the process of working out a time projection. I'll get it to you as soon as it's ready."

O'Dell looked across the table to Fred Chippendale. "You're next."

Chippendale shifted uncomfortably in his chair. "I haven't had a chance to go over everything yet, but I think the story the agency should go with is the one that will bring us the most sympathy. Since we have the opportunity to take the spotlight off the mechanical problems by playing up the fact that we have an astronaut with a ruptured appendix who is near death, I feel we should go with that." He nervously licked his lips. "Besides, if we do it my way and Peters dies, we can't be accused of hiding anything. And if he lives, we can play up the superhuman measures that were taken to save his life. Either way the agency comes out on top."

Mike abruptly stood up, his chair skidding across the floor and crashing against the wall. Planting his hands on the table in front of him, he leaned threateningly toward the cowering doctor. *"Cory Peters will not be turned into a media event for NASA,"* he said, his tone ominous. Purposely his gaze swept the room before he strode to the door and turned to face the stunned assemblage. "Listen to what I'm about to say very carefully, because you're about to hear NASA's official version of what's going on." He spoke slowly, distinctly. "Astronaut Cory Peters is down with an undiagnosed illness, characterized by a general feeling of malaise and moderate to severe upperquadrant stomach pain."

A mocking smile momentarily curved his mouth. "Because the National Aeronautics and Space Administration has always been noted for putting its astronauts' welfare above all else, every effort is being channeled into the repair of the mechanical arm and the immediate return of the shuttle." He swung on Robert O'Dell. "If any of you have any questions, meet me in the press room in ten minutes. I'll call on you in turn." He left, not bothering to close the door behind him.

His long stride took him back to the office where he had met with Dr. Schondel. Once inside the starkly efficient room, he leaned heavily against the cool oak door. The moment had arrived. He couldn't put it off any longer. He had to make a phone call he would have given ten years of his life not to make. He knew Ann would still be asleep, and he hated to rob her of the last hours of rest she would probably have for days.

But he also knew she would never forgive him if he didn't. It seemed so heartless to tell her about Cory over the phone. Yet it was the phone or sending someone else to the house. His control over the information given the media would disappear the minute he left to go to her himself. Suddenly he thought of Caroline. He dialed his home number. A terrible sinking sensation struck him when she didn't answer. Shoving the feeling aside, he called Ann. She picked up the phone after the first ring.

"Hello," she said, her voice alert.

"Ann, it's Mike."

"I've been waiting for your call," she said with a sigh of resignation.

"Pack your overnight bag. There'll be someone at the house to pick you up in about an hour. I figured you'd want to be at Edwards when they landed."

"They're not coming down at the Cape?"

"The cloud cover is too dense."

"Mike?"

His heart went out to her. "Hang in there, babe. He's going to make it."

DESPITE HER FATIGUE, Caroline couldn't sleep on the plane. Dark doubts about successfully combining her career and marriage kept surfacing. The harder she tired to push them down, the more strongly they surged. She might as well have been trying to hold a dozen helium balloons underwater with only her hands.

How long would it take for Mike to grow impatient with their long-distance, weekend relationship? Yet when she tried to imagine herself telling Albert Morrison she didn't want the job, a voice deep inside her insisted it would eventually be as harmful to their marriage if she were to toss aside something she had worked so hard to attain.

Two hours later, when she arrived at the West Coast network headquarters, she still hadn't reached a decision. Albert Morrison met her at the door to the office he had borrowed for the interview. His warm smile and firm handshake immediately put her at ease.

"Ms Travers...I've been looking forward to meeting you," he said, leading her to a chair beside a table that held a silver coffee service. Impeccably dressed, his hair a premature burnished silver, his eyes a clear sparkling blue, Albert Morrison was the kind of man who made heads turn when he walked into a room.

"Certainly not as much as I've been looking forward to meeting you," she answered. "Frankly, I hadn't anticipated it would be this soon, however."

"Someone of your talent should have been brought to my attention long before this." He offered her a cup of coffee.

Afraid to trust her trembling hands with the fragile-looking bone china, she declined.

He settled back into the chair opposite her. After taking a sip of the aromatic brew, he looked at her over the rim of the cup. "Usually the first part of my interview consists of a half hour or more of carefully controlled casual conversation in which I try to get to know you." He smiled at the unintentional alliteration. "However, because I've seen you on tape and because I'm trying to fit four days' worth of work into three, I will get right to the point." He returned the cup and saucer to the table. "There is a network opening in the Washington bureau. I understand your work in the political field is limited, but I have every confidence you'll catch on to the intricacies of the position without untoward difficulty. The position can be whatever you want it to be, essentially, either an exceedingly rewarding job in itself or a stepping-stone to higher plateaus."

Caroline was speechless. Last night with Mike—and now this. She'd been given a magic lantern and two wishes out of three. Only the "happily ever after" had to be granted. But then maybe it wasn't possible to have the third if she insisted on keeping the first two. "I have to think about it, Mr. Morrison."

His eyes flashed his surprise. "How long did you have in mind?" he asked slowly.

"I don't know." She shook her head. "Last week I would have said yes before you had a chance to finish asking me. Now I just don't know."

"Does your decision involve some problem you would like to discuss?"

She was in agony. How could she hope he would understand something so alien to the male character? How often did a man have to struggle with the kind of decision she was being forced to make? It was only then that she realized she had already subconsciously thought about having to look for a new job, one closer to Mike. . . certainly not one farther away. "I'm going to be married—my husband's job would be half a continent away," she blurted out. "The marriage plans are still so new, I haven't had a chance to work out the possible ramifications of a long-distance arrangement."

"I see. . . ."

She could not give up this opportunity. She would never forgive herself if she did. "Perhaps we could reach a compromise," she said. "Instead of the standard three-year contract, I'd be willing to sign for just one and at a lower salary." She grinned. "*Slightly* lower salary. That way, if you were unhappy or if I were unhappy, we could amicably part ways at the end of twelve months instead of the usual thirty-six."

"You really do want the job, don't you?"

"There's only one thing in my life I've ever wanted more."

He smiled. "I won't ask you what that is."

"Well?" she asked, giving up the effort to appear nonchalant.

"I think your terms can be worked out without any problem. Something tells me you're going to be even more of an asset to our Washington bureau than I had first thought. I hope whatever it is you have to work out with that new husband of yours turns out to be to the benefit of all of us. May I ask the lucky man's name?"

"Michael Webster. He works for NASA."

Albert Morrison's eyes lighted with recognition and a hint of amusement. "Yes...we've met once or twice," he said. He took Caroline's arm as he walked her to the door. "My secretary will be getting in touch with you about the details of your contract and who will be working with you from our legal department. Since we'd like to have you in Washington as soon as possible, I'll have our lawyers get in touch with KMTV to see what it would take to get them to release you early."

They talked a few minutes longer before Caroline turned to leave. She was halfway through the outer office when she remembered something she had wanted to ask. "By the way, Mr. Morrison, how did you find out about me in the first place?"

"I received a tape of your work from a close mutual friend, along with a glowing recommendation."

Caroline was puzzled. She couldn't imagine a friend they would have in common. "Who?"

This time his eyes openly twinkled with merriment. "Michael Webster... he works for NASA."

A slow smile worked at the corners of Caroline's mouth. "Yes..." she said. "We've met once or twice. As a matter of fact, I'm going to be seeing him soon. Is there any message you would like me to pass along?"

"Please... tell him he was right. I owe him one."

MIKE PACED the tile-covered concrete floor of mission control, his limp growing more pronounced with each pass, his eyes constantly shifting from one monitoring console to the next, his ears tuning out everything but the clipped communication between Lisa Malorey and the astronauts who were outside the shuttle working on the mechanical arm. As Teresa Barker operated the control panel for the arm from inside the spaceship, she abruptly requested permission to try one last time to put the mechanical appendage through its normal routine before starting the alternative, time-consuming dismantling task.

Because they were using the open communication line, their conversation was kept rigidly formal and as low-key as possible. Long, anxious minutes passed as those on the ground watched and listened and waited. After an unusually extended period of time had passed without comment from Teresa Barker, the silence was broken by sharp laughter. Teresa explained. "Our illustrious pilot, Cory Peters, who is understandably anxious to get home, has just suggested that Elroy try a good swift kick.''

Mike saw Robert O'Dell exchange looks with the engineer next to him. After a hurried conversation O'Dell turned to Lisa Malorey. She listened intently for a few seconds, then broke into a broad smile. Speaking into the microphone she said, ''You have a go-ahead from ground control on astronaut Peters's suggested maneuver.''

Mike caught O'Dell's attention. In response to his silent question, the chief of ground control shrugged and responded with a look that said, What the hell, at this point anything's worth a try.

''The results appear to be negative, ground control,'' Teresa's voice announced.

''Tell them to try again,'' Lisa said, not waiting for official instructions. ''Only make sure they hit it harder this time.'' She turned to O'Dell. ''My father always told me that when your initial attempts with a fine-adjustment tool don't work, the next step is to go after a bigger hammer.''

Several anxious minutes passed, during which only the whirring of the cavernous room's operating equipment could be heard.

''Well, I'll be—'' came an indistinguishable static-altered voice.

Almost simultaneously words and gestures of surprise and elation swept through the men and women on the ground; the monitors registered movements from the mechanical arm. Mike closed his eyes and let out a deep, pent-up sigh.

After the celebration had quieted, Mike made

his way over to the station that operated the private communication loop between mission control and the astronauts. Once there, he sat rigidly in the gray padded chair, listening through headphones as Erica Schondel talked with mission specialist Mark Thompson about Cory's condition. At the first break in the conversation Mike turned to the doctor. "How is he doing?"

"All right, but he's terribly uncomfortable. I'm holding off on the pain medication until just before reentry; then I'm going to load him up for the trip home." Erica Schondel leaned back in her chair. "If he continues to respond to the antibiotics as well as he has been, I'm confident we're going to get him through all right."

They were the first words of encouragement Mike had heard her express. Now, for the first time, he allowed himself to hope. In response to the incredible euphoria sweeping through him, he grabbed the unsuspecting doctor by the shoulders and gave her a resounding kiss.

"Wait a minute!" she gasped. "He's not home yet, you know." Running her hand through her short-cropped hair, she surreptitiously glanced around. Suddenly she laughed, a low happy sound that released the tension. Catching his mood, she reached over and playfully punched Mike's arm. "Just remember who supplied you with that good news when the real celebrating starts."

He winked devilishly. "Damn—if I weren't about to be married...."

"Now that's certainly an original excuse."

He smiled. "It is for me."

"Well, that must mean congratulations are in order." Turning back to her work, she cast him one last lingering glance. "Why is it the ones worth having are all taken?"

AFTER CAROLINE LEFT THE INTERVIEW she stopped at the first public phone she could find and tried to reach Mike. He wasn't home, nor was he in his office. She tried calling again as soon as she arrived at her apartment, with the same results. When she still couldn't reach him an hour later, she dialed Ann's number. A strange woman answered. "Mrs. Peters isn't home."

Caroline was momentarily taken aback. Previously Ann had refused to leave the house even to get groceries while Cory was away. "Can you tell me when you expect her back?"

"I'm not sure. Would you like to leave a message?"

"No. . . I'll call again later."

"It might be better if you let Mrs. Peters return your call. Like I said, I'm not sure when she'll be home."

Caroline absently began twisting the telephone cord around her hand. Her reporter's instincts told her something was definitely wrong. "Can I expect to hear from her by this evening?" she prodded.

"Probably not. . . ."

"Then I'll just call back in a few days." She thanked the woman and hung up. First Mike and now Ann. What was happening in Houston? Again she picked up the phone and started to dial the station to see if the news services were carrying anything about the shuttle, but before she had pressed the final number, she stopped. She still had four more days off. There was no way she wanted anyone at the station to know she was in town.

ANXIOUS TO GET BACK to mission control to listen to the transmission of the shuttle's reentry, Mike tossed the remnants of his nondescript lunch into the garbage and left the cafeteria. He made a quick stop by a wall of public phones, trying once more to get in touch with Caroline. When she didn't answer at his apartment he tried hers, not really expecting to find her there but needing somewhere else to look. As soon as he realized he'd reached her recording he hung up, not bothering to leave a message.

Worry nagged at him. Could she possibly have panicked over his insistence that they be married? Her thinking had undergone a radical change. It wouldn't be too farfetched to assume she might want to step back and give their relationship some serious second thoughts.

The tasteless lunch he had partially consumed felt like a lead ball in the pit of his stomach.

Lost in his disquieting thoughts, he entered the tension-filled mission-control room with all the subtlety of a bear crashing through the woods. Several heads turned to watch him as he whipped by. Lisa Malorey, who was returning from a coffee break, was the first to penetrate his portable black cloud. "Hey, why the frown?" she asked. "We're in the home stretch; you should be smiling."

His head snapped up. "What?"

"Of all the people here, I expected you to be sporting the biggest grin."

He let out a sigh. Raking his hand through his hair, he said, "Has there been any word from Edwards? Do you know if Cory's wife arrived there all right?"

She nodded. "Almost two hours ago."

Before he could question her further, they were both drawn to the voice coming through the speakers. "Reaction control jets have been fired."

It was beginning. The announcement meant that the orbiter had just been turned around so that it was now flying backward, engines first. When the shuttle reached the Indian Ocean the main engines would fire for two minutes to slow the spaceship down slightly from orbiter speed—approximately twenty-five times that of sound. After the slow-down, the shuttle would begin to drop, its position changing so that the nose pointed straight up in preparation for the ship's hitting the atmosphere over the Midway Islands. Then the nose would begin to turn toward land.

THE THIRTY-FIVE MINUTES the shuttle took to go from the Indian Ocean to the Midway Islands passed in a rush of activity. Then as the ship hit the atmosphere, the trouble-plagued silicon-fiber tiles lining the orbiter's belly came into play. The heat-dissipating tiles were the ship's only protection against the incredible 2,500°F atmospheric friction produced upon reentry.

Mike wordlessly watched the consoles and monitors. Without effort he could follow the flight as if he were aboard. When at last the ship reached fifty miles up and began its landing bank, he breathed a little easier. He felt the sensation of the nose dropping until the shuttle was diving at ten times the angle of a commercial plane coming in for a landing. Then at approximately 1,800 feet, over California's Mojave desert, it was time to lift the dive gently, lower the landing gear and touch down.

The homecoming celebration at mission control was subdued as all staff waited for the ambulance to arrive and word to be sent about Cory Peters. Time that had passed so quickly before now dragged. Each minute without word added to the weight of the next, until the room was filled with a heavy, oppressive silence.

Abruptly the speakers crackled to life. "This is Edwards Air Force Base."

"Go ahead, Edwards," Robert O'Dell answered.

"I have a message for Michael Webster from shuttle pilot Cory Peters."

O'Dell glanced at Mike. Mike nodded. "Please relay the communication."

"Roger, Houston. The message follows. 'I can't say I haven't had more fun, but all things considered, it was a hell of a ride. Wish you'd been there.'"

Mike felt his throat tighten; his eyes filled with

tears. *Thank God.* He repeated the prayer over and over to himself in a litany of happiness. Slowly he turned and left the building and the boisterous celebration, walking from the artificial light into the bright afternoon sunshine.

By the time he reached his car, tears glistened on his cheeks. How good, how sweet, how wonderful was his life. *Caroline,* he silently pleaded, *make this day perfect. Be there when I get home—share this moment with me.*

But the minute he walked up to the front door, he knew she wasn't at his apartment. With a hand grown suddenly heavy with numbing fatigue and disappointment, he turned the handle. Once inside he tossed his keys on the chair by the door, his jacket across the chair back.

There wasn't a trace of her in the living room. It was as if she'd never been there—as if he'd dreamed everything. He went into the kitchen. Stuck to the refrigerator door was a large piece of lined paper.

My dearest, darling, magnificent Mike,
    I'll explain why I had to leave for Los Angeles in such a hurry when I call you tonight. Meantime, think of me and know that I'll be thinking of you. I love you.

                                                                Caroline
P.S. Do you know how to make an elephant fly?

Mike carefully folded the paper and put it in his pocket. His world was complete, after all.

CHAPTER EIGHTEEN

As SHE EMERGED from the Houston airport terminal, Caroline hailed the nearest cab. She gave the driver Mike's address and settled back against the seat for the long ride. A short nap on the plane had helped to keep her going, but she knew if she didn't find time for some uninterrupted sleep soon, she was going to collapse. Still, the three and a half days remaining of her minivacation seemed too precious to waste in unconscious activity. However...the thought of waking in the morning with Mike beside her, to reach for him and have him there, to have him reach for her and....

A private smile played at the corners of her mouth. Maybe she should give this bed thing a little more thought. When she did, she immediately felt a flush crawling up her neck. She had better find something else to think about, or she was going to be a basket case by the time she arrived at his apartment. Her smile became a tiny laugh of pleasure. Somehow she didn't think Mike would mind too much.

An overwhelming urge to be with him struck her with heart-thumping need. Since she had dismantled and discarded the barriers that kept her from admitting her love for him, she had been bursting with the need to be with him, to hold him, to tell him. And tell him yet again—now. Her body tingled to touch him, to feel him. Her mind overflowed with words of love. She had so much to give; there was precious lost time to be made up.

She had wanted to bring him a gift, nothing expensive or spectacular, just a token that said, "I've been thinking of you—I love you." But the airport shops had been filled with tourist things, not gifts for lovers. She knew he wouldn't care that she came empty-handed. Still she had wanted something that would light up his eyes as his crazy gifts of flowers had hers.

Flowers! That was it. She would bring him flowers. And not the easy way, from a florist. She leaned forward. "Are there any parks in Houston with flowers in bloom?"

The driver thought a moment. "About the only place that's got anything blooming around here would be the Hermann Park Garden Center."

"Take me there."

"You gotta be kidding, lady. That's at least an extra hour. Do you have any idea how much that's gonna cost you?"

"I don't care."

He shifted his hat farther back on his head. "It's your money."

Eventually they arrived at the park, and Caroline started to get out of the cab. "Hold on," the driver said. "If it's all the same to you, I'd appreciate it if you'd pay me first."

"But I'll be right back."

"Yeah, well, I've had stranger things happen to me, so if you don't mind, I'd like my money now."

She took the fare from her wallet and placed the bills in his hand. Before releasing her hold on the money, however, she said, "Now I want you to wait for me. I won't take more than a few minutes."

"I'll be right here. Take your time."

Caroline walked over to the beautifully laid-out formal garden. She was immediately attracted to the profusion of blooms on the camellia bushes, the dark waxy leaves making the pinks and reds of the flowers even more pronounced. Quickly she selected the largest and most perfect blooms, all the while fighting the part of her that insisted on rebelling against her behavior. She had fewer than a half dozen flowers when a deep male voice said, "And just what, may I ask, do you think you are doing?"

She turned around slowly, frantically seeking an explanation that would sound better than the truth. There wasn't any. She tried her most dazzling smile on the angry uniformed man. He just glared at her, his arms folded tightly across his chest, his feet planted in an unyielding stance.

She decided to try the direct approach. Her mouth painfully dry, she tried to swallow. "Is there anything at all that I could say that would get me out of this situation gracefully?"

"I sincerely doubt it. I've worked here for over ten years, and I've yet to hear someone come up with one good reason for destroying public property."

Destroying public property? "I hardly think picking a few flowers is grounds for that kind of accusation."

"And just how long do you think these gardens would be here if everyone had your attitude?"

Caroline could see it was time to try a little humility. "Would it help if I said I was sorry and promised never to do anything like this again?" So much for Mike's insistence that she "cut loose" occasionally. If she got out of this, she wouldn't even look at a flower in a park again.

"Not a bit."

Caroline's eyes widened. She had a sinking feeling she was in bigger trouble than she had first thought. "Listen...." She tried to sound reasonable. "Why don't I just pay for the flowers I've picked by making a donation to the arboretum."

"Don't try to bribe me. It only makes me madder."

"Bribe you?" she gasped. "I've done no such thing. I was simply looking for an equitable solution to this problem." She forced herself to lower her voice. "Since you don't care for my suggestion, what restitution did you have in mind?"

He drew himself up in a self-righteous pose. "I've already put in a call to the police. We'll let the courts decide what's to be done with you."

"The police?"

"They should be here any minute now."

"You can't be serious."

His eyes narrowed. "It is my job to protect this garden from people like you, and I take my work very seriously. I use every means at my disposal."

Out of the corner of her eye Caroline saw a police car pull up behind the taxi. The driver looked from the police to Caroline and back again. He shook his head, readjusted his hat, leaned forward and started the cab. Before Caroline could stop him the yellow car had pulled away from the curb. "Wait—" she called out, but it was too little, too late. She stared forlornly at the departing vehicle, feeling abandoned. But it wasn't until the two uniformed men were standing in front of her requesting her identification that she realized it wasn't desolation she should feel; it was panic. She had left her purse in the cab.

On the way to the police station the officers promised to do everything possible to help her retrieve her purse while once again, almost apologetically, explaining their position. They told her they felt bad about taking her in, but that she had committed a crime. Without some kind of identification how were they to know, if they issued her a citation, that she wouldn't give them a false name? They assured her that the minute someone arrived who could identify her, or her purse was found and she could identify herself, she would be released on her own recognizance.

Caroline felt embarrassed—no, embarrassed wasn't strong enough. Mortified was a more fitting word. The first time, the only time in her entire life that she had tried to pilfer anything, and she was going to jail. She pressed herself into the corner of the back seat, trying to hide from the occasional curious glance sent her way, even though she knew it was ridiculous to think anyone would recognize her.

The officer who was driving looked up into the rearview mirror. "Next time you want to take flowers to someone, you might consider a florist. Houston has quite a few good ones. I understand roses are kind of high sometimes, but you could get a bouquet of daisies or something like that pretty reasonably."

She met his gaze, noting the teasing twinkle. "Thanks...I'll be sure to remember that the next time I have the urge to become a notorious flower burglar. Especially since my clever MO is now permanently on file."

Both the officers chuckled. "If it were up to me," the driver said, "I'd let you go, what with you being from out of town and all. I think the parks are pretty safe, anyway, but the old goat insisted on signing a complaint. It was taken out of our hands."

Caroline sighed, sinking lower in the seat when she spotted a child pointing her out to his mother. "You don't have to explain," she mumbled. "I understand."

When they arrived at the station Caroline was taken to an office area that contained several desks. At one of the empty desks she was told she could use the telephone. Sitting with her hand resting on the receiver for several minutes, she searched for the easiest, least embarrassing way to ask Mike to pick her up at the local jail.

She needn't have worried about how to tell her future husband delicately that he was engaged to a criminal—he wasn't home. Nor was he at work. Caroline tried Ann's. The same woman answered who had been there earlier that morning, and with the same noncommittal reply.

A half hour later she tried again. And then a half hour after that. Still no answer. Caroline consumed cup after cup of coffee and watched as the faces of the officers who had begun to grow familiar to her changed into strangers as shifts traded. Evening arrived, then night. Still she called, and still there was no answer. Impatience and embarrassment slowly changed to worry and frustration, which gave way to cold dread when it finally occurred to her that Mike might have gone to California to surprise her. She could very well wind up spending the night in the holding cell if she wanted any sleep at all.

She glanced at the large clock over the sergeant's desk. It was almost ten. If she couldn't reach Mike by ten-thirty, she would swallow her pride and call the night manager at KMTV to identify her and cable her money. The thought made her cringe. What a wonderful topic of conversation her afternoon at the police station would make when the network brass called to get her out of her contract. And that it would be discussed she had no doubt. Humorous anecdotes were the staff of life to people in the news business.

When her self-appointed time arrived, she reached for the phone with a trembling hand. She listened to the ring—two-three-four-five. Just as she started to replace the receiver a groggy "Hello" sounded on the line.

"Mike? Oh, thank heavens!"

"Caroline..." he mumbled. "Where are you?"

She hesitated. There was just no easy way to say it. "At the police station."

"Where?"

She repeated the information, adding her location. "Don't ask any questions—just come and get me."

"I'll be there as soon as I can."

She replaced the receiver and heaved a shuddering sigh of relief. Swiveling in her chair, she noticed several of the officers had stopped their work and were staring at her. She gave them a weary smile and a thumbs-up signal. They broke into spontaneous applause.

"WHERE WERE YOU?" Caroline asked, following Mike out the station door after gaining her freedom. Before he had a chance to answer she went on, "I even tried Ann's...something funny is going on out there."

"You haven't heard what's been happening with Cory and the shuttle?"

She shook her head.

"Come on." He took her elbow. "I'll fill you in on the way home."

"You haven't told me where you were today," she said, trying to keep up with his long strides.

"I've been home all afternoon and evening... asleep."

"But I must have called a dozen times."

"When I'm really tired I can sleep through anything."

"I certainly have a lot to learn about you."

He gave her a broad grin. "Not nearly as much as I have to learn about you. How long do I have to wait before you tell me what's going on?"

She groaned. "This entire thing is all your fault. The closest I ever came to a jail before I met you was passing by one in a car. I've never even worked the crime desk or gone out to cover a trial."

He laughed at her plaintive sound. Stopping in the middle of the sidewalk, he pulled her into his arms. His kiss was warm and wonderful, filled with love and joy. He leaned against a nearby building, tugging her along, holding her in front of him, his hands resting on her waist. "Now tell me what happened. How is it that I've led you down the path to ruination?"

She stared at his chest. Absently she began tapping on the middle button of his shirt with her fingernail. "Do you remember telling me I had to learn to be less rigid—that every once in a while I should break loose and try something crazy... like purloining a flower?"

"Uh-huh...."

"Well, I followed your advice." She laid her forehead against his collar. "And look where it got me!" she wailed. After a few moments she tilted her head back to peer up at him. "It looks like you're going to have to take me as I am or put up with only seeing me on visiting days."

He ran his hands along the length of her back. "We'll just have to find less dangerous ways for you to show your exuberance."

"Like?" she asked suspiciously.

A low, exciting sound came from the back of his throat. "If I were to show you here, we would be arrested on the spot. What I had in mind is best done in the privacy of one's own home."

"Sounds interesting...."

"Wait—stop! The last thing in the world I need right now is for you to talk to me like this. I've been teetering on the edge of excitation every time I've thought about you for the past ten hours."

"Mmm...you say the nicest things."

She slid her arms around his neck. The kiss she gave him was explosive, leaving both of them trembling with their need for each other. "Let's get out of here..." she murmured.

Arm in arm they walked to the car. When they were on the freeway and headed for Mike's apartment, Caroline reached over and took his hand in hers. "I understand I have you to thank for the job offer I received today from the network." He glanced at her, a look of genuine surprise in his eyes. "I don't understand. What job offer?"

"Albert Morrison?" she prodded his memory. "The tape you sent him that your friend made of me?"

"Oh, that. So Morrison got in touch with you?"

"Yes. . . and he offered me a job with the Washington bureau."

"And you said?"

"I told him I would take it, but only on the condition that it be for twelve months instead of three years. I have to find out if marriage and politics are going to mix."

He squeezed her hand. "You're still afraid of the long-distance thing, aren't you?"

Reluctantly she admitted she was.

"What would you have told him if you had known I've been offered a promotion that means moving to Washington?"

"Is that true?" she breathed.

He smiled. "Yes, it's true. I've been postponing my answer because of us. I figured it was hard enough to court you with half a continent between us. I sure didn't need any more land separating me from you."

She leaned over and kissed his cheek. "It's going to work out all right for us, Webster," she said softly. "I can feel it in my bones. You just made me realize what makes us so special, so different from anything I've ever known. I like you every bit as much as I love you."

Mike let go of her hand and reached under the seat. Carefully he pulled out a single, perfectly formed camellia blossom. "This seems an appropriate time to give you this."

She stared at the bright red flower. "Where did you get that?" she asked, her tone deceptively calm, not betraying in the least the overwhelming urge she had to scream.

"On the way here I drove past a park. I figured you might need some cheering up, so I took a couple of minutes to get this for you."

"I suppose the park was one that had lovely formal gardens?"

He cast her a puzzled frown. "Yes...as a matter of fact, it was. I asked the caretaker if I could pick—"

"Was he a stern-looking man, around fifty, wearing a park uniform?"

"Yes. He said he lived nearby and spent a lot of his off time, as well, tending the gardens."

"And he let you pick a flower?"

"Yes..." he answered slowly, understanding dawning.

"I don't believe this," Caroline groaned.

Mike placed the flower on her lap, put his arm around her shoulders and hugged her tightly. "I guess you were right—some of us have it and some of us don't," he said. Laughing, he quickly kissed the top of her head.

"I'm not through with you yet, Webster." If she couldn't best him with flowers, she could still try to outcorn him. "Have you figured out how to make an elephant fly?"

"No...."

Triumph was hers. "Well...first you have to get this *gr-rreat* big zipper."

For the blink of an eye, Mike responded with stunned silence. Then a rumbling started deep in his chest, ending in a wondrously happy chuckle. "The years are going to be good to us, my love."

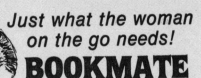
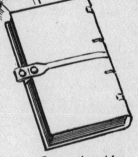

Begin a long love affair with

HARLEQUIN SUPERROMANCE.™

Accept LOVE BEYOND DESIRE **FREE.**

Complete and mail the coupon below today!

- -

FREE! Mail to: Harlequin Reader Service

In the U.S.
2504 West Southern Avenue
Tempe, AZ 85282

In Canada
P.O. Box 2800, Postal Station "A"
5170 Yonge St., Willowdale, Ont. M2N 5T5

YES, please send me FREE and without any obligation my
HARLEQUIN SUPERROMANCE novel, LOVE BEYOND DESIRE. If you do
not hear from me after I have examined my FREE book, please send me
the 4 new **HARLEQUIN SUPERROMANCE** books every month as soon
as they come off the press. I understand that I will be billed only $2.50 for
each book (total $10.00). There are no shipping and handling or any
other hidden charges. There is no minimum number of books that I have
to purchase. In fact, I may cancel this arrangement at any time.
LOVE BEYOND DESIRE is mine to keep as a FREE gift, even if I do not
buy any additional books.

NAME _____ (Please Print)

ADDRESS _____ APT. NO.

CITY _____

STATE/PROV. _____ ZIP/POSTAL CODE

SIGNATURE (If under 18, parent or guardian must sign.)

SUP-SUB-22

134-BPS-KAP3

Enter a uniquely exciting new world with

Harlequin American Romance™

Harlequin American Romances are the first romances to explore today's love relationships. These compelling novels reach into the hearts and minds of women across America... probing the most intimate moments of romance, love and desire.

You'll follow romantic heroines and irresistible men as they boldly face confusing choices. Career first, love later? Love without marriage? Long-distance relationships? All the experiences that make love real are captured in the tender, loving pages of **Harlequin American Romances**.

What makes American women so different when it comes to love? Find out with **Harlequin American Romance!**

Send for your introductory FREE book now!

Get this book FREE!

Mail to:

Harlequin Reader Service

In the U.S.	In Canada
2504 West Southern Ave.	P.O. Box 2800, Postal Station A
Tempe, AZ 85282	5170 Yonge St., Willowdale, Ont. M2N 5T5

YES! I want to be one of the first to discover

Harlequin American Romance. Send me FREE and without obligation *Twice in a Lifetime*. If you do not hear from me after I have examined my FREE book, please send me the 4 new **Harlequin American Romances** each month as soon as they come off the presses. I understand that I will be billed only $2.25 for each book (total $9.00). There are no shipping or handling charges. There is no minimum number of books that I have to purchase. In fact, I may cancel this arrangement at any time. *Twice in a Lifetime* is mine to keep as a FREE gift, even if I do not buy any additional books.

Name   (please print)

Address   Apt. no.

City   State/Prov.   Zip/Postal Code

Signature (If under 18, parent or guardian must sign.)